# THE MEDALLION

Copyright 2017-2022 by Priscilla B. Shuler
All rights reserved.

Fourth Edition.

ISBN-13: 9781974642939
Cover Design by Vic Shuler of Shuler Graphic Design
Layout by Rachel Newhouse for elfinpen designs, http://elfinpen.com

Gretchen's prayer taken from Psalm 139, KJV

For more information on the author's work, visit:
https://priscillabshulerartistauthor.com

Or contact the author via email:
mooandpoobear2932@gmail.com

CONTENTS

CHAPTER 1
*Introit | 1*

CHAPTER 2
*Gathering Hope | 17*

CHAPTER 3
*Sections 1 - 7 | 19*

CHAPTER 4
*The Strength of a Mother's Love | 35*

CHAPTER 5
*Acquisition | 39*

CHAPTER 6
*Precarious Homecoming | 41*

CHAPTER 7
*Help Arrives | 45*

CHAPTER 8
*Amazing Discovery/Recovery | 51*

CHAPTER 9
*Exposing Deception | 63*

CHAPTER 10
*Teresa's Inheritance | 71*

CHAPTER 11
*Night of Drama | 81*

CHAPTER 12
*Changes Made | 85*

CHAPTER 13
*Danger Nears | 89*

CHAPTER 14
*The Revelation | 91*

CHAPTER 15
*Righting a Wrong | 99*

CHAPTER 16
*Unstable Heart | 101*

CHAPTER 17
*Unwanted Change | 105*

CHAPTER 18
*Gone | 113*

CHAPTER 19
*The Vision | 115*

CHAPTER 20
*Deliberation | 123*

CHAPTER 21
*Working the Plan | 127*

CHAPTER 22
*The Extraordinary Madam | 133*

CHAPTER 23
*Rescue | 139*

CHAPTER 24
*Reunited | 143*

CHAPTER 25
*Back To Normal? | 145*

CHAPTER 26
*Phoenix Rising | 149*

CHAPTER 27
*Transformation | 157*

CHAPTER 28
*Debut Danger | 161*

CHAPTER 29
*Just Due for Two* / *169*

CHAPTER 30
*Deep Feelings Emerging* / *179*

CHAPTER 31
*Unexpected Lovers* / *183*

CHAPTER 32
*Another Wedding* / *193*

CHAPTER 33
*London Debut?* / *199*

CHAPTER 34
*Camouflaged Couple* / *207*

CHAPTER 35
*Another Rescue* / *215*

CHAPTER 36
*Contrition* / *219*

CHAPTER 37
*London's Shame* / *227*

CHAPTER 38
*New Beginning* / *233*

HOMES AND CHARACTERS | 243

# CHAPTER 1
# INTROIT

UPON A LARGE, low interior stone buttress in the vast kitchen, she sat. Alone. Her knees drawn up snug against her breast. A dark-gray, ragged skirt pulled tightly around her legs, covering all except her bare toes, she blinked and dozed off and on. One might consider the waif to be deformed and unsound of mind, until perchance one glimpsed a promising wisp of golden hair lifted by a warm draft from the ovens or noticed her eyes—a glint of intelligence to be seen cast off from the reflections of the fires.

This orphan waif, raised by a dark gypsy woman, was brought up to believe was her natural mother and never questioned their obvious differences. She had been given the name of Teresa Jane by the young girl who paid with her life at her birth. Teresa became the child of Gretchen (otherwise known locally as The Witch) by inheritance.

Wrapping her tired body in the permeating warmth being thrust out from the massive fireplace, she drew forth some little vestige of energy emerging from her soul. The child had finished her scullery duties and hung back as the kitchen became deserted. She hoped to pilfer a still-usable stub of a candle to take to her cell. Since all candle stubs were cast into a black iron cauldron and held until someone took the time to melt them to be recast with new wicks and readied for use by the downstairs servants, she was sure no one would note that a stub was missing.

Rousing, she found it difficult to propel her body into motion, and so continued to sit in contentment, mesmerized by the dancing shadows playing across the stone walls like pale yellow ghosts. She began to consider how her promotion to house service had been eagerly sought. Over the past years, she had watched and envied the bonneted and uniformed maids going about, their skirts swishing as they busied themselves with unknown chores. Dissatisfied with the daily filth she'd had to live with during her first years of service to this house, she lifted her head and shook it gently as if in answer to some question posed by the wavering ghosts milling about. And never mind the near-daily scuffles with Boyd as he attempted to smear her cheeks with a swipe of chicken shit he'd pulled from between his toes.

She smiled as she recalled their last encounter before her slight promotion. She simply had enough of his mischief and decided to go at him full strength. Tilting her head toward one of the ghosts, she grinned from the remembrance, almost relishing the feeling of her knuckles cracking against his chin, and the next mighty swing with her left fist smashing into his nose, to delight in seeing the blood sling out. She'd have hit him again as he went down, but someone pulled her by the scruff of her neck with the words: "Enough now, girl. Mustn't kill the poor lad." If nothing else, she was grateful her promotion had shed her of Boyd.

From the tender age of ten, she had been chasing chickens, wringing their necks, plucking feathers (carefully sorting them for stuffing), holding squealing swine as throats were sliced, hauling away the offal from the slaughters, chasing the ever-present vermin from dragging morsels off into weedy place... She had been past ready for this new position of lower house maid.

From near her fourteenth birthday, her duties had included laundry, scrubbing floors, window cleaning, hauling ashes, and taking whatever orders were cast her way by those above her station—which appeared to be most everyone. The uniforms and bonnets she'd so lovingly envied were as-yet non-existent to her status. Would she ever glean such a seemingly unattainable situation? Presently, having not long ago passed her sixteenth full year on this earth, she rested from the labor of scullery. Her friend, Biata, who was much older than she, had nearly been let go because of circumstances beyond her control. Biata had lost her husband. Then her grown son and his wife took over her little house in the village and had informed her that she could sleep in the street for all they cared. Biata had begged the housekeeper Constance to keep her on in any capacity whereby she could have a cell in which to sleep each night.

Constance put her own head on the block to keep Biata but had to lower her from upper house maid to scullery to keep Lady Alice from finding out. It was evident that the sister and brother-in-law of Master Harry were consistently removing servants that Lady Alice considered excess. Teresa, having overheard conversations, believed that those two were systematically undermining the structure of the house, as well as planning for the vacancy available as soon as Master Harry died.

But having been raised from birth to the hardships of the world by her lone mother, Teresa had been rather prepared for her strenuous life. Teresa's family home was but a largish formation of stones which, from eons past, had been cast up to rest against each other in a large cone shape. A natural fissure provided a hidden entrance into a sheltered space which had provided them with protection and some no-little comfort from the natural elements of the seasons.

Out of the necessity of living by their wits, the child, from her birth, had been given an education few others could have received. She was introduced to the imperative uses of everything God had supplied for their livelihood. Seldom did her mother warn her away from something as having no use to her survival. Consequently, Teresa had developed her keen mind to absorb each vestige of information she was privy to observe or hear or feel. Seldom did she speak, but instead held information cataloged in the files of her mind where it was easily accessible.

By her unobtrusive life, she had become almost invisible when others were in conversation. Thus, she learned that the lord of this house was in dire straits. From gleaned listening, it seemed to her that he was just on the upper side of being dead, and so Teresa had begun to consider that possibly her mother, Gretchen might know what it would take to heal him.

She, herself would, if given the opportunity, ply him with a tea of black walnut shells. But wait, perhaps that might be too strong and carry him over the edge. She determined that she best see her mother this night.

Teresa slid off the buttress and left the warmth of the kitchen but glanced back to bid the pale specters farewell for now and stepped into the deserted back passageway; she involuntarily shivered from the onslaught of the frigid air. *Too cold and dark for the ghosts to roam out here,* she thought. Taking her heavy cape from the peg, she flung it about her shoulders and pulled up the hood. Nestling her form into the scratchy folds of the worn garment, she smiled at the remembrances elicited just by the heft of the fabric and its attendant odors. She recalled Gretchen had come in that night long ago with her arms full of "gleaned" property from some nearby manse. How proud she had been as she joyfully wrapped Teresa in this wonderful gift. The night she received it had been well over ten years ago. In fact, her mother had stitched a deep fold into the bottom to preclude it from becoming too soiled. This cape had been hers from the year she was six.

If she cared to look now, she might well see where Gretchen had removed those loving stitches. Smiling inwardly, she absentmindedly stroked the hood and felt the soft rabbit fur through her mind's eye. The fur had long since been removed, and the nearly bare hide had then been used to line leather boots.

Tying the worn cord snugly beneath her chin, she pulled open the right half of the heavy door leading to the kitchen gardens. Glancing about for any sign of another soul and seeing none, she quickly made her way toward the back gate which opened to the sloping meadow with stables beyond. Never heeding the slight discomfort of the icy dew against her bare feet, she headed away from the open field and kept to the high rock wall that ambled to the east side of the mansion. Drawing her small form deep into the folds of the cloak, she blew her breath out into the frigid air to watch as ghosts of a different hue were freed from the bondage of her body.

Knowing at this point in her service that she may be missed, still she was bound to heed her inner instincts that bade this foray back to the rock house this night. She had completed all her daily assigned chores. Biata, her roommate, was probably abed, and so she felt her chances of being sought out for anything extra, would be nil. Consequently, this little escape was worth the risk.

Once she found herself closest to the edge of the dense forest, she ran directly toward the majestic fir which was her guide to an unseen path. Upon reaching the cover of the shadowing woods, she stopped to catch her breath and peered ahead to allow her eyes to adjust to the darkness. Soon the hidden path became evident to her eyes and she stepped quickly toward her destination. Receiving comfort from the exquisite night sounds she had grown accustomed to as a child she instinctively knew there was nothing to harm her—which was quite the opposite of everything she had been warned of by those who feared the dark forest.

The air was easy to inhale but definitely colder and caused her breath flow out in smoky streams. She smiled to herself as she anticipated the coming exchange with Gretchen. Breathing an unspoken prayer for the answers to the blaring problem facing her, she began to run.

The darkness deepened, but within a few more minutes she perceived a pinpoint of light flickering in the distance. She increased her speed, then skidded to a stop a few feet shy of the low door set into the side of the large rock formation. A thin stream of gray smoke rose from somewhere above and ascended straight up through the black trees.

Teresa knocked firmly one rap upon the door, and immediately the palm-sized grille was slid open and Gretchen said, "Come in, child."

The door opened on silent leather hinges as Teresa slipped into the warm room. Enfolded gently by Gretchen's arms, Teresa kissed her mother's cheek as she wiped the silent tears of joy that came at the sight of her. Drawing her child in closer to the fire, Gretchen removed the cape and laid it across the back of a vine-woven chair.

"Here, child. Sit and warm yourself. Our Heavenly Father has decided to provide a nice chill for us tonight in anticipation and preparation for the coming winter." Taking a seat in the other well-padded chair, Gretchen continued, "... and the fuzzy caterpillars wear dense fur coats as well as all the forest creatures. We can expect to have fewer insects next spring to raid our gardens."

As Teresa sat back into the cushions of the chair, her mother said, "You cannot know what a joy it is to see you again. It has been much too long, child. But I know they keep you busy... which is a good thing. No one ever needs to have unproductive hours in which to hatch mischief."

Before Teresa had her thoughts together to expose her reason for this visit, again Gretchen spoke: "Are you keeping up with your lessons? Do you need a new tome or two? Tell your mother what you have need of my darling."

"Truly, mother, I do read every night. In fact, I have had to glean candles from other places because I use my allotment too quickly, and I care not for anyone knowing of my studying every night. And besides, Biata sleeps so soundly she's never aware I read well on into the night." Glancing around the snug room, she stood. "Mother, you know I have not come here this night to discuss my studies."

Smiling, Gretchen nodded. "I know, Sweeting. You came because your lord is very ill, and indeed, lies presently outside death's own door."

"Yes. Now the question is... do you know some formula whereby he has the best chance at living and recuperation?"

Lord Harry Martingale had been lying abed for nigh onto a fortnight with some malady for which he had been bled, fed, starved, cosseted, and posseted by his two physicians with not the least bit of improvement.

Teresa explained what she knew of his troubles, even going so far as to quote the words heard discussed by the staff. Her mother listened quietly, asking nothing, but nodding periodically.

Finally, Teresa sat back, folded her hands together, and watched her mother.

Gretchen got up from her chair, stoked the fire, added another log, and sat back down. She gazed off, nodded a couple of times, and spoke as though reading from a book:

"Once you see the blood-red stalks of the poke berry bush, on the next full moon gather fifty-one stems of the white-flowered nettle." She paused and turned to gaze lovingly toward her child. She then continued, "Pull each stem straight out of the soil, being careful not to bend or break any. Lay them on a sheet and bring it here. We will boil the nettle for one full day and one night. Then we'll strain it up from the cauldron."

Glancing toward a high shelf arrayed with an assortment of bottles and boxes, Gretchen mused, "I may use some of the powdered black walnut shells for good measure."

Teresa smiled at her own earlier thoughts.

Then looking back at her daughter, she continued, "From what you have told me, I believe your master is infected with a possible putrid bowel. Or it could be some sort of infestation of parasites. In any event, I do believe our brew will do the trick without snuffing out his life.

"But you must be careful. You will need to count the number of times his countenance draws in pain within a quarter-hour. If the pain comes three or less times, then he is strong enough for the purge. If the pain comes on him more than three times during that time, then I fear he may be too far gone to recover. Your master may well be on his death bed. But we'll commence with the remedy in the anticipation of him being strong enough."

Teresa stood and began gathering her cloak. "Mother, I'll get the nettles tomorrow as the moon is now in its full stage; I'll bring them tomorrow evening."

"Yes, Darling. You will need to take the brew into the manse two nights hence. We'll use that lidded bucket." She pointed to a large keg with a heavy metal lid strapped across its top. "You must keep it safe where only you will know of its whereabouts. He must ingest one teacup full every two hours. It is imperative to make sure no one feeds him anything, or that he gets anything by his own request, for three days. After the initial loose defecations, his body will only need to void as often as necessary. The liquor will pull all the poisons out through his bladder and must be expelled quickly. By then, the troubling bowels ought to be rid of their poison."

"I'll do my best to try to save his life," Teresa said. "After all, there are so many people dependent upon the master for their livelihoods, not to mention us!" She leaned to kiss her mother and quietly slipped out the narrow door into the black night.

All the way back to the manor house, Teresa worked over in her mind all the possible ways open to her to take charge of her master's care. An impossible task! Nothing came to her for the accomplishment of such an implausible situation. Him, the Lord—her, newly promoted to lower house duties and the least recognized of his lower servants. She must come up with some way to cure him, else she would lose her position by his untimely death, and then what would become of everyone dependent upon his benevolence? As it was, she was convinced that Lord Harry's sister and her husband were primed to take over this massive establishment. Suddenly she wondered if possibly they could be poisoning him! She prayed not!

The path was literally disappearing beneath her bare feet as the heavy darkness descended upon the land. Inside the thick growth of trees, from which she would soon emerge, the light was not. Steadily walking onward, she noted the trees thinning and could ascertain the open field ahead.

Suddenly, the upper lights of the manor house came into view, and from her position, she presumed it must be Lord Harry's room ablaze with candles as shadows moved through the space of his chambers. The Doctor's Bristleman and DuBuque, were surely in attendance tonight, along with Lord Truluck and Lady Alice.

Teresa could envision the staff being sent on first one errand and then another as all avenues of medical attempts were made to cure him.

She knew they had run out of options and were even now chasing after any idea short of giving up.

Hanging her cape on the peg, she slipped into the darkened kitchen with candle stubs on her mind; however, there were two large pots still half-filled—one with broth, and the other with a savory beef stew. On a spit were hung well-cooked meats. From what she could surmise, everyone had been fed and the large cauldrons would be kept at a simmer all night. Tomorrow's meal would be heartily enjoyed by the servants since the gentry would be fed freshly assembled foods. They had no idea how delicious was the goulash that was kept simmering for days until every morsel was ingested. Just the odours permeating the air set her mouth to watering.

The tables held the crockery that had been cleaned by Biata and herself from the meal eaten by the kitchen staff, but she found a small amount of mead left in an earthen jug, from which she poured the last drop into a small pewter chalice and drank. Reaching over she stripped several juicy chunks of beef shoulder from the hanging carcass over the fire. With a drizzle of grease slipping down her chin, she turned as Elizabeth swept into the room. "Well miss!" she cried. "Where've you been? Calvin's been lookin' for someone to see to the changin' of the Masters' linens! 'pears everyone has disappeared for the night, so I guess it'll be you this time. My advice is for you to get a stack and head up there now!"

"Yes, mum, I'm going, but you must direct me to his chambers as I've never been," said Teresa. She grabbed a small lantern, lit it with a straw from the hot ashes beneath the dripping beef, and ran out into the cold hall and headed to the laundry area. She found a stack of folded bed linens as well as swaddling clothes. She picked up a chunk of soap, toweling, and a bathing cloth, as well as a bundle of dried lavender, and hurried back up the stone stairs to the kitchen.

She quickly spied Elizabeth busy slicing and dropping chunks of beef into the huge pot. "Tell me the fastest way to the master's chambers."

"Come here... out into the back hall." She pointed to a short stair and said, "Behind the door at the top there you will find a long hall. Stay on course until you come to the last door at the very end. Through that door is a stair which will wind past three landings. Take the fourth landing and you will enter the hall just outside his bedchamber. The door will be directly there on your left. Knock on it and then enter as Mister Calvin shall be waiting for you." She stepped back. "Now girl, do you think you have it?"

"Oh, yes ma'am. I will have no trouble. And I assume to return the same way."

"Wait! Take this kettle too. Can you carry it all?"

"Yes, Ma'am. I have got it. Just open the first door for me, please."

Teresa trembled with the seriousness of the task at hand as well as the blast of cold drafts pummeling her scantily clad body. So! Here she was heading to the bedchamber of the Master of Martingale. She had only seen the tall, dark-haired gentleman a handful of times from afar off and really had no idea of what sort of man she had been tasked with trying to help. But if her mother's purge could only be applied, there was an excellent chance he would make it.

She had only needed to set the kettle down twice to open doors on her way. Finally arriving, she knocked gently on the door to his chamber and without waiting for an answer, opened it. The stench struck her nostrils, and she knew as sure as tomorrow would come that he was dying in his present state.

"Bring the linens this way, girl," demanded Calvin. "Lay them there!" He pointed to a low stool standing by the bed.

"Yes, sir." She did a slight curtsey. "My name is Teresa Lyons." She directed her eyes at the Valet. "You might know of my mother. People speak of her as Gretchen-the-

Witch, sir. She is also known as The Healer." With that, she stepped toward the bed.

Scrutinized by the Doctors as well as Lord and Lady Truluck, Teresa moved to her master's bedside. Noting his pallor and the strong odor of death, she whispered a wordless prayer for help in the successful planning of her intervention with his diet.

Stealthily looking at the mantel clock, she noted the time and began watching her master's countenance as she placed the bed linens first,

then laid the swaddling clothes on top and placed the lavender sprigs in a deep fold of the tapestry curtain. Calvin had taken the hot kettle from her hand and set it on the hearth.

Asking Calvin for his help, she threw aside all the covers while Calvin placed the folded blanket over Lord Harry's upper torso. Teresa, working quickly, poured hot water into the bowl, and laid the lye soap into the water. She wrung out the washcloth and washed his thin, shivering body. Calvin turned Lord Harry, first one way, and then the other as the cleaning and removal of the soiled linens was accomplished.

Working quickly, she wrapped fresh linen around Lord Harry's lower torso and secured it with gauze ties. Noting how emaciated was his body brought to her attention the dire present circumstances of her lord. Constantly praying for him, she worked diligently so he would not become chilled.

Calvin pulled the warm blanket down the length of his Lord's body, and with a slight grunt, gently lifted the man from the bed. Teresa swiftly tore the bed apart and sprinkled some of the lavender blossoms over the mattress.

During the process, Teresa felt confident that she had caught each time Lord Harry had drawn into himself with a pitiful groan. Within the allotted time she counted his pains as having come upon his body just four times. That was one more than Gretchen had told her was safe, but to Teresa's thinking, noting the way he was able to move within Calvin's arms, he seemed strong enough to take the cure that had been planned. Her efforts may not save him, but to do nothing would surely see him in his coffin.

Within a very few moments, Calvin laid Lord Harry back into the freshly made bed and Teresa placed the small bundle of dried lavender at the top of his pillow, and Lord Harry watched her every move, as did the other five.

Once Teresa had left the chamber, Harry motioned for Calvin to send everyone out of the room except himself.

With much complaining and foot-dragging from Lady Alice and Lord Benjamin, finally, Calvin was able to close the door behind the quartet. Hurrying back to the high bed, Calvin leaned over to attend to his ill lord. Noting that he was struggling to speak, he moved closer to ask, "Tell me what you need sir."

Turning with some little difficulty toward his man, Harry asked, "Where did our little maid escape from?" Sighing, he went on. "She surely was raked from the bottom of the barrel. Why on earth is it that it was she who was sent on her mission tonight? Could not someone a tad more presentable have come?" Closing his eyes, he sank back into the pillows.

Smiling, Calvin nodded in agreement, as the wiry and wild-haired young maid was definitely not of the upper house staff. "I suppose she might have been at hand at the time, sir." As he pulled up another comforter to snug around the ailing man, he spoke on. "And, she is the daughter of the healer, Gretchen Lyons, Sir."

With eyes flying wide open, Harry moved toward the sound of the voice. "Is that child in service here?" His query bordered on the incredulous.

"Evidently, sir. I am convinced that she is utilized below stairs and possibly was found to be available to come when I rang." Calvin was busying himself with straightening the bed covers, to stay close to his Lord. He did not want to miss hearing what might be needed of him. With the weakness, his Lord's voice was barely audible.

"Did you say her mother has some healing powers?" whispered Lord Harry.

"Indeed, sir."

Becoming more animated, he moved upward upon the heavily embroidered pillow casing, opening his eyes a bit more, he asked, "Well, do my Doctors lay any credence to the woman's powers?"

"I truly do not know, sir. Should I ask them what they think of Gretchen's powers? She is truly well known hereabouts for accomplishing the impossible, sometimes... And then, m'lord, there are occasions when nothing done seems to help in the least."

Mind made up, Harry slipped downward until the comforter covered his chin. "Send ... what did you say her name is?" asked Harry.

"Her name I believe is Teresa Lyons, Sir. You want me to send for her?"

"Yes, now." He reached up to pull a few sprigs of the lavender toward his face and closed his eyes. He pulled into himself as another wave of pain dragged itself through his torso and shuddered as a tear slipped from his tightly closed eyes. *I fear it may be too late for a recovery from this deadly plague. Pray not.*

Calvin strode to the front wall and pulled the long tapestry belt.

Having just returned to the kitchen and intent on locating a piece of candle to take to her room, Teresa was intercepted by the cook. "Git on back up there. Now, girl. You have left something undone. See to it!"

Calvin opened the door as she approached from the cold hallway. "You sent for me?" asked Teresa softly.

Harry heard the soft, feminine voice in his head, but for the life of him could not recall why she should be there. "Who are you, girl?" He spoke from behind the bed curtains.

Stepping toward his bed, Calvin pulled back one of the tapestried panels and held it, she said, "Your servant, Sir. My name is Teresa Lyons, and I've been in your employ for some six years and a few days more, sir," she answered.

He opened his eyes and stared at the dirty, unkempt urchin trembling before him. Harry took in her wild hair—very blond, nearly white by the light of the many candles ablaze within the room. He was not able to catch the color of her eyes but was impressed by the sweep of her lashes when they caressed her cheek as she lowered them in deference to her master. He thought she needed to be cleaned up a bit. Young ones ought to be taught early on to take better care of themselves. Moving somewhat beneath the heavy bed linens he spoke. "My man tells me your mother is a healer, is this true?"

"Yes indeed, sir, that is true," replied Teresa with another mild curtsy.

"I command you bring her here so she can work her magic on my malady. Go now and bring the woman here."

"Oh sir, she cannot come." Teresa bowed low and shook her head sadly.

"And why, pray God, not?" demanded Harry with as much power as his pitiful body could elicit.

"Please forgive her, Lord Harry, sir. She cannot leave her hovel in the forest. She has been a recluse for almost twenty years now and no force in heaven or hell could bring her out. She was once very beautiful and attracted the advances of some devil who was incensed with her refusal to his unholy desires. He destroyed her beauty with a hunter's knife, and while she was unconscious, he raped her." Drawing in a quavering breath, she continued, "I am the result."

"Who is that man? If he is still alive, he shall be made to pay!" blurted Harry as forcefully as he was able.

"No, my lord. Mother has never revealed his name, and consequently I don't know if he's alive or not. And what good could come of it now... after all these years. She has learned to be content where she is and does much good for anyone who needs her help. She has passed on much of her knowledge to me and in fact..." She hesitated but only a moment before she gathered the determination to reveal her mission. "...has given me the recipe to heal your body. Would you feel content for me to apply my mother's healing for your benefit?"

Lord Harry almost sat up, instead he waved his arms in agitation, "Why are you standing there, girl? Get to it. I fear I have not long to live if something isn't done to turn this around. I am so weak and empty. I have very little will available within me. Do what you can, girl." Harry looked past her and spoke to Calvin. "See that the girl has everything she needs and send for the slop they've been plying me with. I can hardly bear it, but I am starving and feel it's the only thing keeping me alive."

Teresa reached out to touch Calvin's arm. "Wait, sir. If I tend to the Lord, then he's to have nothing to eat for two full days before I begin my regimen of healing."

"Don't you think I'll be dead from starvation by then?" asked Lord Harry.

"No sir, you're stronger than you believe yourself to be and plenty able to have food withheld for two days. In that time, you are to visit the water closet as often as needed. You can lift yourself from your bed with your valet's help. Keep him by your side." Turning to Calvin, she said, "Move a pallet or cot into this room and let no one else enter. When the kitchen sends up food for him," nodding toward Lord Harry, "discard it into the slop jar, and you eat yours out of his sight. Go into the clothes-press room if need be. Do not be tempted to give him anything solid. Ply him with lightly salted, boiled water drawn three times a day from the kitchen well. Nothing else to drink... especially not wine."

Teresa paused long enough to send a silent prayer heavenward for the ease with which God had come through for her to be able to help Master Harry. Heading for the door, she turned to Calvin with one last order. "Keep the door locked. Let no one in... particularly not his doctors. I shall let Missus Constance know what is going on. She is well acquainted with my mother, and she can break the news to the good doctors and other family members. I'll return in two days' time." Moving back to the bedside of her lord, she said, "Meanwhile, concentrate on what you'll be wanting to do first once you've beaten this poisonous disease."

As ill as Harry was, he took her suggestion seriously. He smiled, and Calvin wondered what Lord Harry was thinking.

Calvin himself considered Lord Harry to be on the verge of madness simply by his unhealthy state and the look on his face as Teresa left them.

She headed to the lower regions of the manor in search of a piece of boiled linen in which to place the nettles that her mother required. The candle stubs could wait.

"I just received word that we are not to be granted access to my brother! What do you make of that, Benjamin?" asked Alice, emphasizing the "we."

"'pears to me there just may be some mischief afoot." He turned and lifted his snuff-box, shook it, and clicked open the tiny lid. Sniffing loudly, he sneezed with force into the dusty air of their bedchamber. "Mayhap someone of import has become privy to our plans, wife. Do you know of other kin who might have heard of Harry's possible demise and are ardently seeking to take over?"

"Upon my word, I know of no other. I alone am his only blood kin." She strolled over to swing open the west-facing window to allow some of the dust to dissipate. "Are you sure you've left no stone unturned in your takeover of his holdings?"

"As assured as can be ascertained at this juncture. My solicitors have set in place everything possible at this time, in anticipation."

"Good! That is the main reason I want to be at his bedside. I want this inheritance secured for our family. Darling Matthew is counting on this—but I wonder if it was such a good idea of you apprising our son of his ascension to this level?"

Smiling, Benjamin answered as he strode about, waving the ornate little snuff box to watch the light play upon the gold. "A young man of Matthew's character needs to live with the pride of hope. I believe he'll become equipped to the high standard I shall set before him."

"Well, just be careful and don't set his hopes on something that could fail."

"No fear. They have not been successful thus far with his healing, and I do not expect any miracle to be forthcoming. Harry may well be passed as we speak."

Shaking her head sadly, Alice said, "Not like when Father died. His passing was such a shock... Harry away at school, and you—relegated to an occasional foray bade by Father for business." She turned and slipped her arms around the waist of her husband. "I'm so looking forward to this manse being fully ours in every way, and besides, Harry was too young and inexperienced as it was. Circumstances were propitious for him to appoint you to hold the reigns until he'd finished his schooling... and now nothing can be done except the obvious."

The pair smiled and kissed. "Yes, dear Alice, we shall finally be at the top of our social ladder with purses to match."

CHAPTER 2

# GATHERING HOPE

WEARING A LONG-SLEEVED tunic with the hood snugged over her hair, Teresa was unobserved in the moonlight gathering the tall nettles. Her hands were becoming raw and had begun to swell from the onslaught of the prickling hairs attendant upon every part of the weed she was gathering. Knowing this unlikely plant held the properties to save Master Harry made the burning-itching bearable. She pressed on until she had gleaned every one of the number of stems needed; then, pulling up the corners of the white linen, she deftly tied two knots to secure her prize for conveying to her mother.

Reaching the abode upon silent feet, Teresa was not surprised to see her beloved mother swing open the door at the instant of her arrival. "Come, darling. Let us get this labor of love begun."

They opened the linen and inspected each stalk of "hope" before dropping it into the simmering water. Once that was done, Gretchen spoke, "Now come, child, let us tend to your healing." Gently taking both hands of her beautiful daughter into her own, she turned them this way and that. "Oh," she declared, "this won't be difficult at all."

Teresa was made to lie upon the cot on her left side with hands extended over the side where her mother could ply her healing powers.

As the girl slept, Gretchen stroked the affected skin with soft sand, pulling much of the hair-like prickles loose. Then, over an empty receptacle, Gretchen slathered warmed beeswax, fanning it until it became as hardened as possible. Using a dull blade, she gently scraped off the wax, letting it drop into the pan below. As dear as beeswax was, she would never waste one gram. It would be melted and used again and again; even though it now contained all the residue from the nettles, the wax was completely benign, allowing for any use Gretchen desired.

Dipping a strip of hemp fabric into heated rose water, she cleaned away all evidence of her ministrations. Immediately upon patting her daughter's hands dry, she rose and began measuring out a few dips of powdered black walnut shells to stir into the simmering cauldron containing the now-limp nettles. Glancing back over at the girl that she was privileged to love as her own, Gretchen began to cast back into the past to recall exactly how this child became her responsibility.

# CHAPTER 3
# SECTIONS 1 - 7

### -1 THE PAST

THE LYONS FAMILY gypsy band had again made their yearly visit to Gravelstone when Gretchen had just turned seven. She recalled standing next to her mother, Stella, and being so impressed by the sheer size of the Constantine dwelling. From her vantage point just inside the kitchen gate, she gazed up toward the sky to observe birds nesting in the crenelated windows. Above that even higher, she could hear the snap and pop of several large banners as they whipped in the winds.

As her older brother Doyle was busy sharpening the blades of assorted knives, Auntie Marjorie was instructing someone how to braid narrow ribbons into the tresses of a little blond girl. Before Gretchen knew it, her mother had her hand upon her elbow and was leading her away from her musings toward the pretty little girl. "Gretchen, this is young Mistress Melanie. She would very much enjoy your living here with her and being a sister-companion."

"For how long, mama?"

"Forever, my Sweeting."

"But why would I want to do that? I think you might miss me too much."

Kneeling before her youngest child, she took her into her arms, and with welling tears floating on the edge of her lids, she spoke very seriously. "Gretchen, any girl as beautiful as you are needs to have every advantage in life. Here, with young Melanie, you will be given exactly what she is given. You shall be taught everything she is taught. You will have the same clothes she wears." Standing up, she continued, "And, I believe you will never suffer again from being hungry, or from being chased out of some village, or of being misunderstood."

"Mama, do you believe life for me will be better with the little girl than it will with you and our family?"

Nodding as the tears dripped down her sun-browned cheeks, she said, "Yes. I believe this is something I will be proud for you to do. And if it is possible, we shall see you next year when we return."

Holding Gretchen's hand, Stella walked toward the child's governess. "I believe Gretchen will prove to be an excellent companion to your charge." Looking directly into the eyes of the governess, Stella asked, "Can you promise me that she shall be given the same care and concerns as young Melanie?"

"You have my assurance of such. Her mother, Lady Sarah has been very concerned for her daughter needing someone she feels will not run away... as has been the case in the past. She has suffered the loss of two girls previously who were simply too old and became enamored of being away from the constraints of Gravelstone."

Nodding gravely, Stella turned to gaze at her beautiful child. "Very well. Our camp is set up in the black forest about thirty minutes away by foot. Might I have this night with my daughter? I shall return with her tomorrow. She will be prepared by then to take on her new life as the companion to your Melanie Jane Constantine. Too, I shall prepare a written contract for the signature of her parents' agreement to this arrangement. Will you abide by this?"

Bowing slightly, the governess smiled. "Yes. Tomorrow, bring yourselves through the front gate by the carriage lane. You will be brought in to meet Lord and Lady Constantine. I shall apprise them of your stipulations."

By the campfire that night Stella spent the bulk of the time in constant instruction, advice, spiritual guidance, and deep prayer. Even as Gretchen slept in her mother's arms, Stella spoke words of wisdom and the passing of deep truths and age-old knowledge into the hearing and mind and heart of her beloved child.

## -2 DANIEL STEADMAN BORDEAUX

Beatrix Steadman Bordeaux birthed six children, only one of which lived. Her husband, Peter, blamed his wife for having animosity against him, thereby losing all his would-be heirs. Peter had at the beginning taken it upon himself to gleefully name each of his children—three sons and two daughters—who disappointingly perished before they were walking. When Beatrix gave birth to her sixth child, the midwife announced the child's arrival to his father and asked for his chosen name for the boy. Peter stalked out of the room, declaring, "Let his mother provide the name that'll be carved upon his tombstone! I don't care!"

His mother christened him Daniel Steadman, named for her father. But the child's own father, Peter, would have nothing whatsoever to do with the boy. After all, he would soon join his siblings in the cemetery behind the chapel on the steep rise above the village.

Much to Peter's chagrin, the boy grew. He was terribly spoiled, filled with self-love, and became more incorrigible as his teen years came upon him. Being sent away to school was very much to the liking of both son and father. There, the boy learned many useful ploys with which to throw suspicion toward his classmates whilst he himself appeared the forgiving and benevolent victim.

Upon graduation and returning to Covington Court, he began to rule his domain with the full appreciation of his mother, Beatrix. She relied totally upon her son now because Peter was bedridden from injuries that would not heal. His body had been too broken and sustained internal injuries from having been thrown from a newly purchased steed. After months of suffering, Daniel's father finally passed. His death was spoken of as a "sad release." The day his father was interred, Daniel Steadman Bordeaux celebrated by deciding to find the most beautiful girl in the territory and pay her court.

He faced no problem in the attempt. Steadman was now-not only handsome, but the very wealthy Lord of Covington Court. Knowing any father would be thrilled to have himself show definite interest in his daughter, he was anxious to be about this satisfying business of choosing a damsel worthy.

Sixteen-year-old, blond, and beautiful, Melanie Jane Constantine of Gravelstone Abbey, the only child of Sarah Hashbrooke and Leopold Flanders Constantine, happened to be the ill-fated object of Steadman's affections. And surely her dowry would be nothing to sneeze at—a rich prize, indeed.

Through several visits with her parents, he was able to talk them into forgoing her debut and promising her to him the day of her seventeenth birthday.

*Good god! A whole year! I shall have her before then, or my name is not Daniel Steadman Bordeaux! Just you wait and see!*

Every time the sun shone it seemed that Steadman was arriving with gifts of one ilk or another for the pretty girl.

Young Melanie was completely smitten by the superfluous attention from the tall, handsome stranger, and was overly anxious to be away from the confines of her "prison."

"But mother! Why do you insist on waiting for my Birthday? What difference will a few months make anyway? And think of the money that will be saved by foregoing my debut." Melanie stomped her dainty foot upon the turkey carpet and continued, "Besides, Gretchen will be with me and you know how diligent she is! Why she will watch Lord Daniel like a hawk! Please, mother."

Finally, Sarah was overcome by the pleadings of her only child and gave permission for Melanie to be away with Steadman if Gretchen was with them.

Lady Sarah spent several determined moments of instructions to both young ladies. "Never be out of sight from each other! Comport yourselves properly as is due your station." Turning to Gretchen, "You are completely in charge of this jaunt and will be held responsible. Do you understand me?"

With a quick curtsey, "Yes, Ma'am. You need not worry about Mistress Melanie. I shall lay my life for her in a heartbeat.'

"This is against my better judgement however I do realize Melanie feels a prisoner here does need a tad of entertainment. With your promise, I shall expect the best."

Before the two girls were allowed to depart Sarah took her child off to the side and reminded her to dress comfortably and to "be sure to wear the medallion beneath your undergarments."

"I shall, Mother. And please do not worry. Gretchen will be right with me all the while."

As the two girls descended the stairs, Sarah had a chill of foreboding, but brushed it off and said, "Now you be careful, Lord Daniel, and take your outing with my daughter seriously."

"Of course, Lady Sarah. I agree to nothing less! We shall take a small jaunt down to the river where we three shall enjoy the small repast that I have brought. Please, have no fear. I am forever in your debt. Melanie shall have a wonderful time. And we'll be returning before the sun is halfway to setting."

"Thank you for your assurances, Lord Daniel." She turned toward her daughter and her companion and said, "Now, you young ones have a sweet outing, and do be careful. The sky looks a bit threatening. If the weather turns, you must hurry back. You understand?"

Steadman spoke up. "Don't worry, madam. The young ladies are in my care, and I'll have them home before you know it."

### -3 THE ACCOSTING

With clarity, Gretchen recalled the horror of that afternoon.

No sooner had she laid out the linen and placed all the delectable foods upon it than she heard muffled screams. Rising up from the blanket she ran toward the sounds. Coming through the tangled underbrush, Gretchen came upon Lord Daniel tearing at the clothes of Mistress Melanie. As she approached to try to shove him off her mistress, he stood, his trousers agape, exposing his bloodied phallus. He took three steps toward her and slashed her face with the knife he had held to the throat of young Melanie.

By the time he stepped away to try to get back to his victim, Gretchen threw herself upon his back, dragging him down the incline toward the water. Both tumbled into the current, and as Gretchen was being swept downstream, she saw Melanie on the bank stumbling and running toward her. As if happening in slow motion, she watched as her mistress too slipped, fell, and sank into the turbulent stream.

Not really knowing where her mistress was, Gretchen grabbed a low limb and pulled herself up, half out of the water. She then saw Melanie hanging onto a sharp rock just a few yards beyond. Back into the water she dropped and tried to maneuver herself to reach her mistress. Struggling mightily against her binding clothes, she forced, by sheer will, to head in her direction. Soon she bobbed up right next to the bedraggled maiden. With very few words, they helped each other swing back out and on toward a small embankment holding a pristine white sand bar at its base.

Pulling themselves onto the warm sand, Gretchen began to assess their situation. Looking skyward, she surmised that with the assuredly approaching storm, she would need to find shelter somehow. "You stay right here. I'll have a look-around to see what I can come up with for us to shelter in and be a little more comfortable until we can make it back to Gravelstone."

"Oh, Gretchen," Melanie sobbed, "you're so terribly hurt. He cut your sweet face because of me. I am so sorry. Can you ever forgive me for causing this terrible thing?"

"Now Miss! Do not concern yourself. You rest and I'll be back before you know it. And keep an eye out for your attacker. If you see him, scream as loud and hard as you can." Gretchen reached and swept up a handful of wet sand. "Here, throw this in his face if he comes near. I will be right back."

Leaving the sandbar and climbing upward to the crest of the embankment, Gretchen came upon an unusual and very large rock formation. Going around and round the structure, she saw where one might just squeeze through and be completely out of sight. *Maybe we could stay here until we know that Lord Daniel is gone or something, so we can be safe and get dry.*

Returning to help the shivering girl mount the bank, they soon arrived at the rock formation. Gretchen pushed Melanie through the narrow opening between two of the larger stones.

They found themselves housed, as it were, in a roomy area, protected and completely dry. At least for the time being. They sat and held each other for a few minutes until Melanie finally spoke up. "What shall we do now, Gretchen? Mother and Father will be so concerned if Lord Daniel goes back home without us."

As the two girls commiserated, they divested themselves of their outer clothing and laid it about to dry.

"As soon as I can, I'll make a fire to help us get more comfortable. We cannot leave here for quite a while. You see, we have no idea if Lord Daniel is alive or dead or what. And you have been ruined by that devil! You will never be able to marry now as no self-respecting gentleman will have you. We must stay here. I'll take care of you until we can find out about him and what has become of him." With bravado far outreaching her inward assurances, Gretchen felt her mettle rise and with it came a will of iron. She could—would do this thing!

"Oh, Gretchen, I hate to mistrust you, but exactly how are we going to take care of ourselves? We have no clothes, nor food, nor any help at all. We must return home if we are to survive."

"Mistress Melanie, you'll need to trust that I can take care of us. I know a great deal about gathering foods and about getting clothing made. You'll soon learn that I'm very capable." Not allowing even a niggling thought of failure, she pressed onward. "We shall survive, and we shall thrive!"

Sitting back against a large stone, Melanie shrugged her small shoulders and nodded. "I guess I'll have to, Gretchen. I certainly cannot help us, now, can I?"

The girls sat dejectedly in thought for a while, then Gretchen spoke up. "Can I trust you to stay here while I go gather some needed supplies? And I'll find us a necessary place while I'm at it."

"Yes! I need to go even now. Might I come outside with you?"

"Come on." Gretchen held out her hand to young Mistress Melanie to help her to her feet.

They stealthily left the sheltering rocks and crept through the brush until they came upon a small hidden glen where they relieved themselves. Standing and adjusting their still-damp underclothes, Gretchen reached to stroke the arm of her charge. "Young miss I'm so very sorry for what damage has been done to you. But I give you my solemn oath: I shall do everything in my power to care for you until you can safely return home. Now, go on back into the shelter. I'll be in soon enough."

Melanie was fast asleep upon the dry earth when Gretchen made her way back into the stone enclosure. With a dearth of movement, she soon had a fire blazing in the center and was roasting a spitted rabbit. For dessert, she found half a dozen locust pods from last fall. There was water brought from the river in a sling of bark lined with leaves to slake their thirst.

While her friend slept on, Gretchen was busy. Laying all the pine rosin she had gathered onto a small, thin slab of shale, she placed it atop a rock in the center of the fire, where it warmed and became spreadable. Attempting to hold her severed cheek together, she swabbed the sap across and down the wound as much as possible, in the hopes it would aid in the healing and not allow the scar to form so badly. *At least this will preclude infection*, she thought.

Bringing half of the roasted rabbit over to wave beneath the nose of her mistress, Gretchen said, "Wake up, sleeping beauty. Your dinner is served."

"What? Where am I? Why am I here? Gretchen, what has happened to me?"

"It's all right, miss. Sit a minute and you'll remember."

"Oh, no!" cried Melanie. "Did he truly destroy me, Gretchen?"

"I'm afraid so. I just hope he is drowned dead by now. Last time I saw him, he was going under downstream from where we were."

The girls ate, relieved themselves once more, and settled in for the night. As Melanie began to breathe in soft, even breaths, Gretchen knew she was fast asleep, so she arose and went back out into the night to search for whatever was available for their upkeep for the near future.

## -4 ADAPTING TO CONDITIONS

Having been born into a Gypsy family of healers, seers, and prophets, Gretchen had the ability to charm, thereby obtaining game rather easily if it happened to find itself in her vicinity. Through the quickly passing weeks, she labored diligently to accomplish and put to use all that she knew—as well as learning and inventing as she went.

Remembering how Doyle taught her to see with discerning eyes, she could spy exactly the form of limbs to ultimately become useful for crude furniture. Interlocking the branches, she soon formed a sturdy table upon which they took their meals, using stones to sit upon. Leaves were piled high over near the wall for their bed. Sleeping nestled within each other's arms provided warmth after the fire dwindled. Gretchen kept every bit of hide from the game she took and soon had enough for a somewhat ragged cape for Melanie. Through the next few weeks, Gretchen became more adept at using nearly every part of the animals for different projects. The sinews were dried and stretched and used to attach one section of hide to another by means of holes punched by the large thorns from the locust tree. Sharpened stones from the river's edge became knives. Hollowed rocks were used as bowls. With an abundance of fish available, they had enough to dry for future use. Wild roots and berries also were plentiful this time of year. Gretchen and Melanie stayed busy gathering everything available.

The rock room soon took on the look of a snug home. They had lined the walls with branches they wove to make the area nearly windproof. There was a natural outlet overhead where the rocks were separated which allowed the smoke to ascend and escape. When the rain did come, it trickled harmlessly down the crevice near the entrance, and soon Gretchen had fashioned a leather bucket to catch every drop for future use. Everything was going along smoothly until Melanie suddenly became sick. She was in the middle of a meal when she stopped eating, looked at Gretchen, and quickly ran out to vomit into the grass. Wiping her mouth, she entered the room and began to cry. "Gretchen, what have you fed me? I feel so sick! I think I need to go back outside." She did.

"Miss Melanie, we'll need to wait and see if you get better. We've both had the same foods, so if you are the only one to get sick, then it must be something other than the food."

"What could it possibly be other than the food?" She began to weep.

"It's been nearly three months since that devil hurt you. I fear you may be increasing." Pulling no gentleness, she spoke assuredly.

"Increasing? Increasing? You mean like with a baby? Surely you are mistaken. I pray you are mistaken, but if what you say is true, then we must find a way to get back home and get Father to make him marry me. Nothing could be worse than having a baby without a husband." She was crying in earnest. Large tears formed and streaked down her flushed cheeks.

"Surely you don't mean that you'd actually expect that dog to marry you! Hopefully, he is dead and if not, then I'm sure he's found his way out of the country, thinking he's caused your death."

"Then what am I to do, Gretchen?" Melanie wailed loudly.

Gretchen took her arm and shook it. "Hush! Hush! Let me think. Let me think."

## -5 STEALTHY REQUISITIONING

With little effort, Gretchen was able to find her way through the deep woods late that evening, trekking across meadows and even finding a place with enough rocks that she could ford the river without being swept away. At last, she spied Gravelstone Abbey in the gloaming. Holding back, unseen, she stood until all activity from the servant's hall had ceased. The only light now seen was that bathing the kitchen from the immense fireplace.

Entering the house from the rear kitchen door, Gretchen found Milford asleep on a bench, basking in the comfort of the dying fire. Shaking him awake, he jumped up and asked, "Who you be, woman?"

"Don't you recognize me? Gretchen. I'm Gretchen."

"No! Ye ain't lookin' like no Gretchen I ever knew. You look like some haint or other. Somebody done gone and cut you fierce-like, and yer hair is all matted and yer clothes is all ragged and filthy. Ye cain't be Gretchen, no more'n I am."

"Sorry, Milford. But it is me. I've been through a terrible ordeal, me and the young Mistress Melanie."

"What? Miss Melanie? Why she be dead! That Lord Daniel come home 'bout three months back with a tale what'd lift the hair offn' yer neck! Said her and you—Gretchen—done drowned in river Woffard. Said he searched and searched for ye, but said he finally decided y'all be gone. The family be still in mournin' for their loss. They is had folks after folks searching everywhere. Everday. For weeks. They finally gave up a month or so back and it's done been spread around that you two is departed this earth for a better place."

"Do you know where Lord Daniel is now?"

"Not rightly, but I did hear talk of him writing to some of his folks from some foreign place they spoke of as Indie. Whatever or wherever that is. But I cain't believe he is gone nowhere, bein' as how I think it was him that I seen t'other day comin' outa a tavern down by the channel docks. He 'peared plenty rough too, and nobuddy wuz messin' around him."

"Thank you, Milford. That bit of news helps me a great deal. Now, I want you to forget that I was ever here. I want you to go back to sleep and when you wake, this encounter will simply have been a dream." She gently shoved Milford back down onto the bench, stroked his bald head, brushing her hand ever-so-slightly over his forehead and eyes, while murmuring low in her throat. Within a few seconds, she was overjoyed to hear his deep, snuffling breaths.

Not one to waste time, she found the way clear to streak through the halls and passageways gathering necessary items to hold herself and her charge in relative comfort through the fast-approaching winter. Exiting the wide kitchen door with a huge bundle slung across her shoulders, she lifted a large wooden keg from the sideyard.

*This will surely come in handy. The gardener will blame his carelessness for its loss. One day, I shall make it up to him, and to the house as well. Everyone will look at everyone else supposing they are the guilty party for the missing items. Cannot be helped. One must do whatever one must to hold body and soul together. And I have the young lady to think about. She must be protected. I will see to it that she suffers for nothing. God, help me.*

As the months passed, the two girls made quite a comfortable life for themselves. Gretchen had been able to keep them fed and warm. The only drawback was Melanie complained constantly as she became heavier with the child. "Can't you do something to keep me from getting any larger, Gretchen? I feel I'm going to split wide open way before this baby is ready to be born."

The rape had taken place mid-August. The month—if Gretchen had calculated correctly—would now be about April. She counted the crocus for February and March, and now the daffodils for March and April. She expected Melanie to have the baby within a few more weeks. She began pulling in the necessary items to have everything handy for the time she began labor. *God help us* became her mantra.

With the onset of the more temperate weather, they noticed more game worthy to be trapped for food. Gretchen knew they had need of more meat to maintain better strength for increased foraging and for the lactation of Melanie for her babe. Gretchen could easily see Melanie's breasts were large and heavy. She would be able to keep her baby satisfied and growing.

The girls had long since discovered their little rock abode was near to another large house. Neither knew its title nor anything of the folks there, but its proximity made it handy for the needed supplies beneath the cover of darkness. Gretchen had been there so often that the mastiffs had begun to greet her in silence, wagging their entire bodies with joy at her approach, knowing they would be given special treats upon her departure.

## -6 HAIL AND FAREWELL

Coming back into the stone room with her arms filled with clothes, Gretchen was stunned to find Melanie hunched over by the cot with legs spread, a puddle of water soaking into the sod floor.

Running to throw the clothes over on a chair in the corner, she bade Melanie come to the bed and lie down for a rest.

"Oh, Gretchen! I cannot rest. My back and belly are hurting something awful and I feel as though my innards are wanting to force themselves out." She paused and raised tear-filled eyes toward her companion. "What am I to do? I do not want to do this! Can we stop it now? Please..."

Grabbing one of the two chairs to drag over to the girl, Gretchen bade her sit. "No! I cannot!" Melanie screamed. "Help me, Gretch! Help!" And with that, she sank to her knees.

Throwing a quilt onto the sod between Melanie's knees, Gretchen drew up Melanie's muslin skirts and tied them across her lower back, and watched in awe as a little, red, squirming baby dropped gently onto the quilt.

*My God! The babe! Help me, Father, to know what to do now.*

Seeing the squirming infant was still attached to Melanie by a bloody rope, Gretchen reached and tugged firmly upon it, and a slithering mass of matter fell upon the child. Gretchen assumed it must be separated from the baby, so she pulled the child from beneath the mass, and in so doing the baby began to cry.

"Is that my baby?" Through racking sobs, Melanie began to recover and asked to know if it was a boy or a girl.

"A girl! Melanie! You have a baby girl! And now you lie down while I get her cut away from this thing and get her cleaned up. You be ready to nurse her in a few minutes."

"Here, Gretchen, get my skirts loose. I feel ready to fall. I need to pee. Help me to the bucket."

Leaving the crying infant still attached, Gretchen helped a staggering Melanie to void into the commode-of-sorts and wiping her bloodied privates with one from a stack of boiled linen cloths, she helped her over to their bed, tucked a wad of linen between her legs, and bade her rest.

Wiping her bloodied arms and hands, she reached to lay the blue cord upon a flat rock, tied it with a fine white cord a few centimeters from the belly of the baby, and then severed it neatly with her sharpest knife. "Have you decided upon a name for your baby?" asked Gretchen. Hearing no answer, she glanced up at Melanie and noted how silently she lay. *Must be worn out. I have heard that childbirth is almost like death.*

Continuing her ministrations with the baby, she had her presentable in no time. But Gretchen was literally covered in blood. Paying no attention to herself, she brought the silent infant over to the bed, Gretchen realized that Melanie was deeply asleep. As Gretchen touched her shoulder, Melanie roused and whispered, "Teresa Jane. Keep this for my Teresa Jane, as proof of her birthright." And she drew from inside her blouse a long narrow ribbon, upon which there flashed a large, flat, gold seal.

Gretchen took the medallion in her hand and in so doing lay a bright smear of blood against the gold. She saw that it was imbedded with rubies upon a raised crown in the center, atop a heart pierced through with three arrows. On either side were dragons in relief. Three feathers were molded as though emerging from the center of the crown. The letters etched across the top edge spelled out "Constantine," then at the bottom was a quote: *"Deus, Honor et Gloria."*

Hefting the heavy talisman in her palm, Gretchen asked, "Melanie! Why have I never seen this before? Have you had it all along?"

"Dear friend. My dearest friend. I now believe my blessed mother had some premonition before we left home because she made sure I carried this identification in case of an emergency. I've not wanted anyone to know of it until there came an absolutely necessity." Pausing momentarily, she continued, "Until now. The time is here. I know in my heart of hearts that I've only a few more moments until I meet my ancestors, and I want to assure my little baby inherits her lawful due."

Staring in disbelief, Gretchen glanced back at the child, "Teresa Jane. We've got an awful road ahead, but God will see to us, I know."

Turning back to comfort her friend, Gretchen said, "Sweeting, you cannot die! Who will care for your Teresa Jane?"

Pointing a wavering finger toward Gretchen, she breathed, "You." Melanie closed her eyes as death bade her soul away.

### -7 NOTHING IS IMPOSSIBLE

Gretchen collapsed upon the dirt, raised her eyes to heaven, and cried, "Oh, my God! How am I to care for this babe? Help me!" Inexplicably, a dampness began seeping into the fabric of her blouse. She looked down as two wet rings enlarged, and she felt warm liquid begin to run down her chest. *Is this possible?*

Sitting upon the warm sod at the feet of her deceased mistress, holding the motherless infant in her unbelieving arms, covered with the blood of her mistress, Gretchen wept as she opened her blouse. She was overjoyed as she lifted the silent baby to her left breast, and within a few seconds the rosebud lips opened and took in the proffered nipple. With the baby's eyes open and fixed upon her new mother, Gretchen and baby Teresa forged a bond that could only be broken by death—if even then.

Once, fully sated, the newborn was nestled within the quilts at the bottom of the bed below her birth mother's feet. Soon Gretchen exited the home to bathe in the stream and then to search for the perfect spot in which to lay the beautiful young mother.

After digging for several hours, she was summoned back to the room to provide another feeding for little Teresa.

So, it went for well into the next day: feeding the baby, consuming a mouthful or two when time permitted, and digging the grave deep enough. Once it was ready, Gretchen bathed the body of her young mistress as she sobbed deeply. *Lord, no wonder she died. With this much blood loss, no one could have survived. I need to remember this. If I had not spent all my youth with my head in books, I might just have learned what was expected in birthing. God help me, though. I shall do my best.*

Wrapped in white linen, seventeen-year-old Melanie Jane Constantine was laid to rest. Gretchen doused the entire length of the body with scoop after scoop of the white lime that was used daily over a section of their "necessary" in the hidden bower.

Gretchen had brought lime with each return from the big house. Such a needful item for the control of vermin that always wanted to congregate wherever human waste or rotting of any sort might be found. She desired to protect the body as much as was humanly possible.

Within another month, she had carved out a cross to place on the site. The grave area could not be easily found by anyone except Gretchen.

## CHAPTER 4
# THE STRENGTH OF A MOTHER'S LOVE

EVEN NOW SHE could see it in her mind's eye as she sat and rocked to and fro, gently weeping for the loss of such a wonderful girl—Teresa's birth mother, Melanie Jane Constantine, her companion and best friend.

Of course, the woods had grown tremendously, and several trees had incorporated their roots deep into the grave. She often would talk to the great trees as though Melanie could hear her voice. There were times when Gretchen "felt" the words of Melanie entering her heart. *"Remember, Gretchen, just who Teresa is. Keep the golden medallion safe until it's time."*

*One day I will be forced to expose exactly who this precious child truly is, and I will need to show her where her true mother lies beneath the sod. Pray God to alert me when exactly that must be.*

The sun was rising when Teresa began to stir. "Mother, what is that I smell? It's delightful, and I'm hungry."

"There you are, my lovely. Arise and prepare for your breakfast. I will have it on the table by the time you return. Now, go quickly."

Teresa exited the rock room and headed off to the "necessary." Upon exiting the leaf-strewn bower, she washed her hands and face and patted down her disheveled hair. Then noticing her hands were not swollen, nor were they stinging, she thought with a smile, *I've the most wonderful mother in all the world.*

Finding her seat at the table, she waited with bated breath for her mother to present the wonderful foods. Fruits, hot bread, goat cheese, and dandelion root tea. Nothing tasted as good as Gretchen's food. All the things provided from the country estate of Martingale Manor could never come close to the flavors of the earth available here.

"How is the nettle brew coming along, Mother?" asked Teresa.

"Exactly as it's supposed to. Give it just another few hours and we can let it cool to dip it up ready to be taken to your patient." Gretchen stopped momentarily and glanced over at assorted herbs drying from the poles wedged across from one rock crevice to another. "Think I'll also send along a poultice of eucalyptus you can tie around his chest, front and back. I will grind the leaves and mix in a little lard for you to heat before the fire until it's warm. If my guess is correct, he may have too much fluid in his lungs from inactivity. The concoction ought to cause him to cough. Make sure he does not take it off. He must cough a lot to clear his lungs to provide the fresh air to help heal his body. Everything works together for good health. If it cannot, then sickness is the result."

After their breakfast, they exited the room and began foraging for berries and roots, as well as checking on the land and river traps. Living as they did, this gathering was a constant effort to ensure survival. Teresa found nothing at all unusual about her life with Gretchen. Indeed, she found manor living to be something difficult to adjust to. The stringent demands. The cross words. The thankless commands. However, she was grateful for the opportunity to begin a civilized life, simply because Gretchen told her it was an absolute necessity in her upbringing, and that one day she would need to know everything about this "civilized" living.

Teresa's education had begun immediately after birth. Gretchen taught all she knew the same way her own mother had imbued knowledge to her. Without awareness of any formal process, the child developed abilities far beyond a classroom setting.

Gretchen deemed Teresa was prime to enter service when she reached her tenth year and knew far more than most adults by that time. Gretchen had brought the child to the rear gate of Martingale Manor directly to the groom, John Hatfield. She was well acquainted with John and his family as they regularly came to her for cures and advice. She felt he would be amenable to taking her under his tutelage or else hand her over where he felt she might be best utilized. Thus, she entered service through the lowest position—that of killing fowl and preparing them for the kitchen, of gathering eggs, of cleaning offal from where the slaughters took place.

Personal cleanliness was practically non-existent. Working the slaughters as she did, she became so filthy that her initial foray back to Gretchen's caused her mother to shriek in horror. Even though the water was freezing, Gretchen had dunked her daughter into the drink—clothes and all. She quickly stripped away the rags to let them swirl downstream. She pulled Teresa out onto the bank and threw a quilt around her small, shivering form, and led her back to the house where she scrubbed her with soap and warm water until her young form was pink and shining.

"Don't you have anywhere to wash up?" Without waiting for an answer, she continued, "You'll need to do better than this. At this rate, you'll come down with some malady for which I may not have a cure!"

"But Mother, no one will allow us to get near to anything to get cleaned up. Boyd and I are the two that work the slaughters and he's as dirty as me... maybe more so."

"Alright then. You must make a way to find a source of water, be it warm or cold. Train your mind to locate the most convenient source and hold that ready until you are free to take advantage of it."

"I'll do my best, Mother. And mayhap I need to enlist Boyd to help us both to do this. What do you think?"

"Yes! Two heads are infinitely better than one... that is, if there are a modicum of brains in at least one of those heads!" And she smiled broadly. Teresa laughed.

Every task given to the child was performed with diligence and with a happy countenance. Little did anyone know that she was brought up in such an environment by Gretchen, that she and her mother had literally "lived off the land." Teresa Lyons had spent two years in the initial back-breaking labor she was allotted as a ten-year-old child. What she gained was strength and an innate ability to know when to keep silent.

From the heavy, filthy outside labors she was taken into lower house service to fill in for a poor soul who had died as she attempted to take the ashes from the kitchen hearth to the soap-making area. As she fell, some of the still-active coals had caught her skirt on fire, and before anyone could rescue the old woman she was engulfed and burned. Men were called from outdoors to remove her body to be taken to the village and the hovel of her daughter (who herself was paralyzed from an accident years ago—which was the reason her elderly mother had gone back into the only service for which she was capable). So... Teresa became adept at such tasks and thereby increased her knowledge of the myriad jobs attendant to the 'running' of such a manse. She held the remembrances of each of her birthdays attached to whatever she happened to be doing on that date. The date the elderly woman fainted and burned to death was May 10... Teresa's twelfth birthday. That had been four years past.

## CHAPTER 5
# ACQUISITION

WHAT WITH LORD Josiah dead and buried it seemed to Teresa that the estate was becoming somewhat derelict. Young Teresa knew Lord Truluck and Lady Alice wanted to assume ownership of this grand estate, but with Lord Harry still alive, their plans could not proceed.

Covington Court had been taken over by Lord Josiah when he married the widow of Lord Peter Freedmon Bordeaux. Josiah renamed the estate Martingale Manor at Hampshire. This was to distinguish it from Martingale Manor in London, where the family had previously lived.

Josiah Martingale's first wife and mother of their two children, Bessie Mae LeMons, died in '55, and Beatrix Steadman Bordeaux lost her husband, Peter, that same year. Knowing of his passing, Josiah immediately sought out the widow, and with profuse condolences he commiserated with her as to his own loss. They found much in common sorrow, and even before the period of mourning was past, they formed a bond. Sworn to marry as soon as it could be considered no longer vulgar, the two were wed and leaving the London house behind, Josiah moved his daughter, Alice, with husband Lord Benjamin Truluck and their four children, along with his youngest child, Lord Harry, into their new home in Hampshire. The magnificent edifice was near enough to the Channel that it could easily be seen from any of the forward towers.

Josiah assumed that Lady Beatrix had no living children, for she never spoke of any. However, he did seem to recall there may have been a young boy, it was said, who lived after the couple had lost so many in early childhood deaths. Now, with no mention or knowledge of such a son, Josiah was thrilled to realize that Harry would automatically inherit this grand mansion one day, with all its attendant revenues. Until that time, he was the consummate and attentive husband to Beatrix. Their union was happily appreciated by both Josiah and Beatrix. They spent much of their time together travelling to London, Bath, and Stratford-upon-Avon. Beatrix did enjoy Shakespeare's theatre.

However, their joy was short-lived. After only three years of wedded bliss, tragedy struck. Returning home late one evening along the coast track, one of the horses stumbled, and the careening coach was unable to right itself, tumbling over a cliff.

They were found two days later. Every life was lost except one horse, which had to consequently be put down. It took nearly a day and a half to get the bodies brought up. The laborers simply shoved the equines into the roiling surf, after the removal of their gear. The trunks had been destroyed and clothing was scattered everywhere. The driver was nowhere to be found, and it was assumed he had been flung into the sea and drowned.

The news was brought to Covington Court, the country estate of Martingale Manor, late in the evening two days after they had been expected to arrive home. The manse was in deep mourning for well over a year. Lord Benjamin stepped up to take the reins and saw to the running of the estate until young Harry completed his studies at Cambridge.

## CHAPTER 6
## PRECARIOUS HOMECOMING

THE SPRING OF young Harry's arrival home was bittersweet. The absence of his father's overbearing personality crashed upon his heart so much that he became somewhat vacillating when expected to make decisions. He was truly unsure if he would be capable of overseeing such a magnificent estate, and so begged his brother-in-law, Benjamin, to continue as before until he could fathom his way through the myriad intricacies of such an endeavor.

Dogging Benjamin's every step and action, Harry was beginning to understand most of the burdens of the estate. He soon found out that much of the estate was in the hands of solicitors. There were three men whom Benjamin called upon frequently, or who contacted him with advice as well as with problems to be settled.

The eldest of the three was Sir Edward Phillips, with his uncle, Sir Doyle Preston, and Preston's eldest son, Skylar Preston. This trio comprised the company of Solicitors for Martingale Manor at Hampshire as well as London. As far as Harry was concerned, he felt Skylar to be the most proficient at understanding the extensive workings of both.

No sooner had Harry begun to assume the full role as Lord of the Manor than he began to experience weird inner-body problems.

Initially, he thought it must have been something ingested that did not agree. Mistress Collier had been known for some unusual meals, particularly when trying to stretch the food to feed more than it ought. At first, he had lauded her frugality, but if this malady was the result, then he must see that she had better and more quality foods for the upstairs meals. He determined then that she must be sent for before the next market day outing.

By the following Saturday, Harry was in the throes of a full-blown bowel crisis. Doctor Bogart Bristleman, as well as Doctor Clifford DuBuque, had seen to his health, with no improvement whatsoever. They had tried bloodletting, even though both felt sure this was not the best procedure. Both men bade the cook to prepare poultry broths, beef bone soups, calf's foot jelly, and teas of all sorts of well-known plants. Nothing alleviated the deepening problem. It so happened it was at this time that Teresa was sent for to bring the fresh bed linens and boiled rags to be used to diaper the young Master of Martingale.

And now, upon being ordered to bring the healing potion from her mother, Teresa had spoken to Mistress Constance Williston and related the errand she had to accomplish for Lord Harry. Constance understood perfectly, realizing that Gretchen was probably the only person on earth capable of any hope whatsoever for the recovery of the Master of Martingale. She simply said, "Take whatever time you and your mother need. I'll see that the staff fills in for you and that Lady Alice understands the seriousness of her brother's condition."

Constance considered that Gretchen was the final bastion available to Lord Harry. Lady Truluck could deal with the Doctors. They would surely back off since they had tried everything in their bags, and nothing had worked. Why he had not rallied even one time since he had become ill. "Now you hurry along, and don't worry a bit."

"Oh, thank you, Missus Constance. Just please see to it that he gets plenty of freshly drawn water several times a day and be sure to boil it and add just a touch of salt. Tell the kitchen to not send up trays for him until I can get back. I will let you know when and what he can eat. Later, that is." She headed toward the back stairs, stopped, turned, and came back to embrace Constance in an unexpected burst of appreciation. "You're an answer to prayer!"

# CHAPTER 7
# HELP ARRIVES

COMING INTO THE back hall with her arms full, Teresa saw Patricia scurrying toward the laundry landing. "Here, Patricia! Please, take a moment to help me," cried Teresa.

"I'm in a bit of a hurry. What's you need?"

"Hold this bag until I can find a place to lay these other items where they won't get lost or damaged. I must see Missus Williston immediately. Do you know if she's around?"

"Give it here. You put those things over on the bench and see if she is in the lower dining room. I think I heard her there a few minutes ago."

"Thank you. I'll be right back."

Patricia let curiosity get the best of her, and she began opening the bundles and bags and was about to open the lidded bucket when Teresa returned. "Don't open that! Do not mess with these things, Patricia. They must not be contaminated. Please. Did you touch anything inside the bag?"

"No ma'am! I never. Why are you acting so high and mighty? I wouldn't touch your pitiful packages if my life depended on it!"

Putting her hand out to touch Patricia, Teresa said, "I'm so sorry. I did not mean to sound so bossy. I never want you to think I ever feel superior or anything. It's just that these things are assembled for the curing of Master Harry, and they must be as strong and pure as we can keep them to do the work of making him well again."

"Well, if I'd known that, it would'a made a difference. I just thought it might be something special to eat or something."

Teresa reached to hug the girl and said, "I do thank you for guarding the things for me. I have found Constance—Missus Williston, and now I am going up to see Master Harry. Pray that the things I have brought will cure him and make him right as rain, all right?"

"Sure. I do hope he gets better soon. That sister of his sure does get her nose into everything. She keeps the house in an uproar, what with the Lor' bein' so sick and all." Patricia smiled.

Gathering everything she could hold, Teresa started toward the stairs leading up to the kitchen level.

"There you are, girl! I've just heard you were back and thought I'd come to see if I could be helping in any way."

"Hello, Mister Calvin. What a sight you are! It's so good to be back." She stopped and handed him the heaviest of her burdens: the bucket holding the dear nettle brew. "Take this and try to spill as little as possible. Gretchen tried to buckle the lid on as tight as she could, but some still manages to slosh over the top. We mustn't waste any, as the Master will have need of every bit, I'm sure." Not slowing, they exited the stairs and made their way on toward the center of the wing heading to the Masters' apartments. "What's the latest on his condition, Mister Calvin?"

"I must say, Miss, he seems a tad stronger despite no sustenance whatsoever. Maybe the fresh water has done it." Smiling just a little, he continued. "That is, made him meaner than a wet hornet! He is getting a bit overbearing which isn't his true nature, from all I've known of him these past few years. Maybe your presence will temper him a bit." Looking up as they ascended the stairs on the last leg of their journey, he continued, "Pray your ministrations will do the trick. I certainly don't want to face trying to live in this place without him at the helm."

"We shall see shortly, then, won't we?"

Calvin unlocked the door, and they entered the silent room. Teresa noted that the odor was not nearly so overwhelming as the first time she'd entered his quarters. Stopping Calvin by her eyes, she asked, "Has anyone been in here at all?"

"No indeed. You can rest assured your orders have been completely adhered to."

From the shadows surrounding the bedstead, Harry cried, "Who's that whispering over there? Come here into the light. Let me see your faces!"

Teresa, setting her bundles down on a table nearby, turned into the light and smiled. "It is I, m'Lord. Teresa Lyons. I am here with the promised cures this night, sir. And if you think you are up to it, we'll begin shortly."

Noting the cleanliness of the girl, he wondered if this might not be the initial girl he had seen before. But how could anyone else have the white-blond hair of this maid? "Well, girl. I was beginning to think you were some sort of apparition since Calvin here never seemed to know anything about the hour of your return. I'd begun to think him trying to starve me to death, so I've fought like the devil to keep body and soul together in the hopes I really did remember what you promised." Straightening himself somewhat upon the soft mattresses, he patted his belly and said, "Give me the healing food straight away! I'm literally starving to death."

Laughing lightly, Teresa began dispensing a cupful of the nettle tea.

Calvin laid a napkin beneath Lord Harry's chin.

Teresa handed the cup to Calvin. He lifted it toward the lips of his master.

Sitting back, he looked at them, from one to the other, and asked, "What in God's name is that?"

"Why, this is the brew to begin the healing process, sir."

"Oh no! You go and bring real food here." He flung off the bed linens and drove his body out of the confines of the high bed, where he promptly fell into a misshapen heap of arms, legs, torso, and wild-eyed, wild-haired, pale-faced panic.

"Quick, Teresa. Get hold of his arm... Help me get him back onto the bed."

Just as she sought to take hold of one of his arms, he reached out and grabbed her wrist and bit deeply into her hand.

Teresa never made one sound, but she drew back her free hand and slapped her master's pale face with all the strength she could muster.

Both men were stunned! Staring bug-eyed at this pariah, they withered.

"Now." Looking directly into the not-so-wild-eyes of the ailing man, she continued, "You get yourself back into that bed and prepare to take the cures that I've brought, or, so help me God, I'll leave this room, this house, this land, and you'll never have another opportunity to take advantage of my sweet nature again!"

Totally chastised, Lord Harry, rump shining, climbed back onto the bed, turned around, and sat with hands folded in his lap, watching as both Calvin and Teresa once again commenced with his treatment.

With barely a tremble to his hands, Calvin held the cup up to Lord Harry's lips. Harry had his eyes clapped upon the countenance of the defiant girl as he drank. *See. I can drink it all,* he thought.

Within just a few minutes, he had drunk every drop of the tea. She then bade him remain still as she drew up his bed gown and began to place the warmed poultices on his back and chest to begin to elicit coughing. She explained exactly what the poultice contained since he was curious to know. "Ground up eucalyptus leaves with a bit of lard. It is to be worn beneath your gown, and you must lie still to keep warm."

"And if I must void?" he asked.

"You tell Calvin. Your commode is empty and right handy. Void as often as you can. But I must warn you, sir. You will more than likely need to defecate soon." Seeking out Calvin's face, she continued, "As soon as you hear his first groan, be prepared to help him to the chamber pot." And then, "Don't take him off too soon. I expect his body to evacuate two or three times between doses of the nettle tea. Even though his stool will be mostly water, it is imperative that you examine the pot each time, and if you see anything unusual, remove it for his doctors to see. There'll be no harm in whatever you might find, as it shall be dead." She turned to head to the door.

Aghast at the words just spoken by the girl, Harry nervously asked, "Aren't you staying here with us?"

"Yes! I need you to be here to help me," cried Calvin.

"I shall be back soon. I must get down to the laundry and bring back a load of fresh sheets and bedding as well as night clothes for the Lord." She did not look back as she headed toward the door.

"Do hurry, Teresa," they chimed together.

## CHAPTER 8
## AMAZING DISCOVERY/RECOVERY

THE FOLLOWING WEEK found the only activity in the vicinity of the main door to Lord Harry's apartments was just outside in the wide corridor. Piles of filthy linens and night clothes were picked up several times a day. However, by the end of the third evening, Matilda Goodale found only two sheets and no gown. The sheets had no appreciable staining. *Must either be a bit better or else there ain't nothing left o' poor Lord Harry,* she thought.

Every morning found Doctor Bristleman and Doctor DuBuque with heads together commiserating about their patient—without effect, however. It seemed that Lord Harry had fallen under the spell of that witch and had succinctly forbade anyone to enter his chambers except for Calvin and Teresa Lyons. However, as soon as Calvin sent word for the two doctors to present themselves, they ran as though in competition with each other to be first to arrive. Met at the door, they were handed a container without one word, and the door slammed shut in their faces.

Taking the porcelain pot to the end of the corridor to where a beam of sun shone through the stained glass, they took their first glimpse of a pile of what at first appeared to be small entrails. "Here, Bristleman, let's get this outside into the light and examine it better."

"My thoughts exactly."

Finally, word was sent to the kitchen. "Bring a tureen of chicken broth." Elizabeth Collier was ecstatic. "Lord Harry's recovering!" she shouted to those within earshot. "Quick, get those hens what was brought in this morning. We are going to fix chicken every way we can. I just knew Teresa and Gretchen would bring him through." She grinned, happily. "Now, hurry, everyone."

Seven days after the treatments were begun, Teresa sent to the kitchen for a fresh loaf of bread, warm out of the ovens. As soon as it was delivered, she took it over to the table in front of the open window, where Lord Harry sat, wrapped to his chin in robes with a woolen hat upon his head. He was pale and thin, but his eyes sparkled with good humor. He kept his mind upon his pretty savior wherever she moved within the large bedchamber. Seeing her in this element gave Harry the opportunity to latch onto every innuendo of her actions. She was sparing of excess movements, accomplishing the necessary chores quickly and precisely. Hourly his admiration of Teresa grew, and a bond formed without awareness from either Lord or servant. Harry did not fail to take note of her attire. The only change from what she wore the first night she had entered his chamber was the fact that the rough, gray, ragged skirt was now clean. Her brown tunic was now cinched with a broad piece of white fabric. Harry was sure it had been torn from a castoff bed sheet. Her white gold hair was combed and held by a like band of white linen. He considered that if he were an artist, she would certainly make an interesting study.

Sitting in the warm sunshine streaming through the window, Calvin was amazed to see how quickly Lord Harry had improved once the offending malady had been overcome. He saw his young Lord in a light never before viewed as his usually withdrawn character was suddenly cast away and an appreciative and self-assured man surfaced. If there were a metaphor for this event, it might be spoken of as clouds parting and sun breaking through. Calvin smiled.

As Teresa spoon-fed him the clear broth, she dipped a small chunk of the warm bread into the soup and watched as he took his first solid food. As soon as he swallowed, he primed himself for the next bite, but she shook her head.

"What do you mean? I don't get any more than one bite?"

"Lord Harry, we must not be too hasty. We need to wait to see if your stomach rejects it. If you do not retch it back, then we may proceed with another small bite. Just give it a few more moments." She observed him swallowing several times as if trying to keep the food from regurgitating. He was successful. "Here, another small mouthful."

Watching her every move with hawk-like fierceness, he spoke his thoughts, "Tell me about yourself, Teresa."

"Whyever would you want to know anything about me?" She peered at him quizzically.

"It appears you possess more intelligence than any young person I've ever met. I'd like to know how you became so knowledgeable and wear your bearing as if raised in the highest society."

She tittered gently. "You are gravely mistaken, Sir. I am an earth child. Born in the forest, raised by a lady known generally as 'the witch'. My mother was of a Gypsy tribe but separated herself from them, for what reason I never could know. She never divulged exactly why she parted from her heritage." Pausing a moment to gather her thoughts, she said, "But, I believe that after the rape she sequestered herself to await my birth in the attempt that the man would never find her and his offspring."

*I will attach myself to this girl come what may. She is my life's blood. And beautiful to boot! I cannot seem to recall when this child went from an ash-coated urchin to this exceptionally beautiful girl.* He counted her every move and felt himself becoming stronger by the hour. His heart yearned toward her as though toward a life raft in wild seas. *I must do something special for young Teresa once I am back in command of my house.* Smiling, he entertained himself between delicious bites with fantasies outlandish.

So went the next number of minutes. Both patient and caretakers were extremely satisfied with the progress being made. "Tomorrow do you suppose you might enjoy a bit of beef broth?" asked Teresa.

"Am I ready? I wouldn't want to do anything to upset the advancements we've made." He grinned like an idiot, hoping for a like response from the girl. He was disappointed.

"I'm sure, Lord Harry, that the cause of your illness is long gone, and it'll only be a matter of a few more days and you'll be strong enough to try a more extensive selection of foods. Why you might even feel up to taking a meal downstairs with the family. Calvin could see you down and then back up here to your quarters to rest. What do you think? Would you enjoy that?"

"Only if you will join me, Mistress Lyons. Only if you will join me."

"I thank you for your magnanimous outreach, sir, but I fear that would cause a great stir amongst your family as well as your staff. I simply cannot feel that would be a good step to attempt. No, sir, I cannot."

"I am the master of this establishment, Mistress Lyons, and it is your duty to obey my orders, is it not?"

"It is sir, *if* the orders won't cause disorder. What you suggest is asking for trouble for both of us. From what I understand," she glanced over at Calvin, "there are factions within your circle that would wrest the ownership of this house from your hands. And your illness gave them more power to entice weaker personalities to their cause. You surely do not want to do anything to give them more ammunition to use against you. Be reasonable, sir."

Turning to look at Calvin, Harry asked, "Is this so, Calvin?"

"I'm not at liberty to say, sir. It simply isn't my place to 'stir the pot,' if you please, Lord Harry."

"Oh, come now, Calvin. Surely you, as well as most of the household staff, hold a plethora of information about this manor. In fact, I would wager you hold more understanding of the innuendoes of living here than anyone else, me in particular. So, until I am able to coerce you into divulging your knowledge of this household and its personnel, I shall bide my time and keep my eyes at half-mast, and my ears wide open."

Both Calvin and Teresa smiled.

"I must be about the business for which I was hired, sirs. It is back to the lower parts for me—not the least of which is to pass information as to your diet, sir, to Missus Collier. She'll see to it that whatever is placed before you for consumption is safe and healthy." As she reached for the large doorknob it turned and opened, nearly knocking her in the face!

Pushing through the door was Lady Alice with eyes flashing with distrust and sweeping around the room to catch mischief at play.

"Why did I not hear a summons before you so rudely flung open my door, sister?"

Drawing a deep breath to provide enough time to conjure a believable excuse, she said, "I'm truly in error, brother, but in my defense, both Benjamin and I have been at sixes and sevens with concern for you. I felt we were being singled out to be ignored by you and your 'inner circle'!" She deliberately raked her eyes over the girl. "Even your doctors are off conferring and allowing no one to come near to their investigations." Alice ceased her prattle and posed with a shy and pitiful air. Whining, she continued, "Dear brother, you have kept us, most particularly me, your own flesh and blood, in the nether regions as pertaining to your malady, and now I see, as to your recovery."

Harry, heart suddenly touched, reached out and bade his sister to come sit by him. "Dear Alice, I have no defense except that had it not been for these two here..." Looking about, he saw only Calvin industriously folding linens and wiping up specks of the remains of the bread from his past meal. "I see Teresa has left us."

"For the time being m'Lord," whispered Calvin.

"As I was saying, if not for Calvin and Teresa I would assuredly be lying beneath the sod. You must show your indebtedness for my health to them."

"Of course, Harry. Of course." She quickly went on, "Seeing you are recovering, when can Benjamin and I expect you back at the reins of Martingale? I'm not pushing you, understand, but Benjamin has several projects in their initial stages and wants desperately to see them through."

"Fine! I am grateful for his availability. And yours, too, my dear."

"Since my presence is evidently superfluous here, I shall see to other more pressing matters. Good day, brother."

"Good day to you, Alice."

Turning toward Calvin, Harry said, "I believe you must port me to my dining room this eve. I want to take my place at the head of my table!"

"Yes! Sir! We can do that! I, as well as the entire staff, will be overjoyed to see you once more where you belong." Calvin wore his biggest smile.

"Contact Teresa and have her make the arrangements with the kitchen. I know Alice and Benjamin will be happy to see me back at the helm—if only partially—until my full strength returns." His smile was verging on the diabolical. Then Harry motioned for Calvin to come near. "Sit here!"

"Sir!"

"I said, *sit*!"

As soon as Calvin was situated in the same chair vacated by Alice, Harry leaned forward and asked, "Benjamin and Alice are my enemies, are they not, Calvin?"

Balking and coughing and turning red, Calvin spoke haltingly, "Truly, sir, I ought not be the bearer of such tidings. It is not for me to say. What if I am mistaken? Then look at the damage that could come from such a revelation. If untrue, it could tear at the fabric of this great and auspicious family."

"But I know there are undercurrents of unrest in this house. I cannot glean that it comes from any of my staff. Even though I have been very out of the stream of the daily living of this mass of people, I am still able to 'read' emotions extremely proficiently. I know you, for instance, are an open book, as is young Teresa. Another equally understood individual is Constance Williston. She runs a tight ship, as it were, and, I believe, probably knows more than all of us together."

Suddenly, slapping his hand upon the arm of his chair, he said, "That's it! Send for her to come at her earliest convenience, will you, Calvin?"

"Will you be enjoying your repast downstairs in the formal dining room this evening, Sir?"

"Dare we attempt it, Calvin? Teresa said another few days did she not?"

"She did; however, I do believe the kitchen will now have the foods that are best for your plate, and I can see to it that you're taken there and back. What is the difference—eating your food in this room, or in your own dining room, sir?"

"I say, let's get on with it!" Then thinking, he continued, "But I will definitely want Missus Williston summoned to this chamber early tomorrow. Privately. I must attempt to syphon out knowledge and information that even she may not be aware of, as it were."

The contentment of both men rose to heights not felt in much too long! A plan was being formed for the security of Martingale and the recipients of its vast benevolence.

"We shall leave no stone unturned, indeed, sir." Bending over to help his master, Calvin aided his rise from the chair and said, "Time to get bathed and prepared for your outing to the dining room."

Below stairs, Elizabeth glanced up at the row of bells as one rang that had been silent for quite a while. Startled at first, she then quickly decided to send Teresa up. "Look here, girl, get yourself up to the Masters' room now. Haste!"

"Yes, mum. On my way." She flew up the stairs, taking two at a time. Calvin had hardly returned to his master's side before he heard the soft tap upon the door.

"Come. We are here in the salle-de-bain. Who's here?" asked Calvin.

"Me, sir. Teresa. A summons brought me here, sir."

"Come, girl. The lord's in his bath. He'll speak for himself."

Teresa walked to the open chamber and stood just out of sight beyond the door. "Yes, Lord Harry?"

"Yes, my dear. I have decided that this night will be my entrance back into the leadership of this family. I do not want anyone but you and a few of the staff to realize that Calvin is bringing me down to the dining room." He drew in a quavering breath. "Now listen carefully. I want you to alert the kitchen to prepare and hold my food, and you are to let the diners understand that I am simply not well enough to come down this evening. Make sure they are comfortably aware of my absence."

Back in the kitchen, Teresa conveyed the directions to Constance and Elizabeth, then left.

Later, the dinner gong was sounded, and the family gathered quickly into the large dining room. The males stood silently as the seating commenced—first Lady Alice and the children's tutor, Mistress Meredith Lindenberg. Then Benjamin motioned for young Matthew, his eldest son (eight years old past January), to take his seat, as usual, at his father's right. The three younger children were aloft in their beds. Alice kept the far end of the massive table, directly within sight of Benjamin, who claimed the head seat. His was the highest-backed chair. This auspicious chair was carved and inlaid with fine stylized chips of brass and ivory. Many considered it to be fine enough for a king. And, indeed, Benjamin assumed the airs of royalty every evening as he presided over those within his realm.

As soon as he lifted the pristine napkin from the table and laid it on his lap, the rest of those present did likewise. He then smiled benevolently and spoke, "Enjoy the bountiful fruits that Martingale Manor has provided for nearly four hundred years. Enjoy!"

Benjamin neglected to mention that this edifice had only been spoken of as Martingale Manor for just over fifteen years. Indeed, for well over four hundred years this manse saw to the security of the surrounding area but was (and by many still) known as Covington Court on Wofford of Hampshire. The previous and auspicious family in residence had been the Bordeaux clan. Lord Peter had married Lady Beatrix Steadman, whose ancestors could be traced back to the era of Henry VII.

Most of the staff of Martingale Manor were keenly aware of the arrogance of Lord Benjamin and his self-centeredness, both being openly encouraged by Lady Alice. And their children were being brought up to embrace this dangerous fallacy. Such activity was rife with the certainty of failure before too much longer, they were certain. Or hopefully so.

When Calvin heard the distinctive clink and clatter as the diners dove into the meal, he gently tapped upon the door. At this sign, Constance opened the food service door, and Calvin helped the Master of Martingale into the room. Silence! Every fork was stilled. Every wine glass caught mid-air. Every chew was arrested, and Benjamin quickly—maybe too quickly—leapt to his feet.

He stammered, "Welcome, brother. We were not apprised of your imminent arrival." Then coming out from his place, he went to the far end of the table to pull out a chair. "Here, Calvin. Let him sit here, near his sister."

"No, Ben. I shall take my rightful place at the head of my table." Turning, he commanded the plate of Benjamin be removed to the place beside Alice, and his own food placed where it belonged.

As soon as Calvin stepped back from seeing his lord at his rightful place, applause was heard from those serving within the room as well as from without.

In stone silence, the meal began once again. The only sounds were those of silver against china and the ring of crystal.

"Where is all the conversation I was privy to before Calvin brought me in? Does no one want to talk?" After a few moments, he tried again. "Since no one seems to want to share thoughts, then it seems I must open the dialogue." Glancing at Benjamin—ever vigilant, seated near the side of Alice—he said, "First thing in the morning I'll see the books. All of them. And..." still with eyes full upon his brother-in-law, "I'll be in my office before nine. If there are any problems or questions to be seen to, I shall address each one in turn." Sitting back to ease the ache inside his torso, he continued, "Do not expect me to hide away any longer. With Teresa as my personal assistant, and Calvin as my bodyguard—and the faithful staff of this magnificent home—I shall once again be Lord Harry Martingale, Master of Martingale Manor, Hampshire and London!"

"Father, you said that I'd be the Master of Martingale!" spouted young Matthew.

"Shut up, Matthew!" yelled Benjamin and Alice together.

The staff present that evening were all smiling, and if one listened deeply enough, they would be able to hear the backslapping and toasting coming from the nether regions of the house as the news filtered below stairs.

Nodding and smiling, Calvin needed no further assurances.

At this juncture, there was no one below-stairs that did not know of the miraculous recovery of Lord Harry through the efforts of young Teresa. Thus Constance had been apprised by Calvin that Lord Harry wished Teresa to be groomed for service upstairs. Catching Elizabeth, Constance confided, "I've decided to see that young Teresa is brought into upper house service. I know I can count on your help to see that she is educated in every possible way from kitchen to salons. Place her education wherever you deem will produce the best results."

Nodding seriously, Elizabeth agreed, "Yes ma'am. I will be more than proud to see the young lady promoted. I shan't fail you." Not but a few hours later, Elizabeth caught Judith coming down the steps with a heavy silver tray from upstairs. "Child, I need your attention as soon as you dispose of your burden in the kitchen. See me in our dining hall."

Curtsying slightly, Judith said, "Yes, mum. Right away."

Seating herself across from the Head Cook, Judith asked, "What do you need, ma'am?"

"I'll not waste our time. How are you at grooming someone who desperately needs it into suitable service for upstairs?"

"Well, I don't rightly know, Missus Collier. I never been tasked with an assignment such as that before. But since you thought enough to approach me about it, you must think I could do it. Is that right?"

"Right you are, Judith. Your upbringing was rather stringent, being as how your father is Squire Venderly. You are imbued with talents and deportment of which I am sure not even you are aware. However, that is beside the point. Would you be willing to take a young girl beneath your wing and provide her with everything you've been blessed with by your upbringing by your gentle mother and father?"

"Yes, mum. I am willing, but I don't rightly know exactly how to go about it. Would I need to have her next to me all the time, or would I need to just tell her what will be expected, or what?"

"I'll let you determine the strategy. You'll need to be introduced to her and you can figure how to approach your instruction then." Standing she said, "I'll see to it you meet your charge as soon as possible. For now, though, continue your duties as usual."

Working scullery duty had been one of the dirtiest jobs inside the kitchen. By right of her labors, Teresa was ever beset by blackened grease and powdered by the ashes she dragged outside to the soap-making areas. But, not to be deterred, by the time Judith had the seamstresses measure Teresa for her two uniforms and produced the initial one, Judith had introduced her charge to the tubs and soaps available after hours for those with the foresight to utilize them for their benefit. Once Teresa was comfortable with how it all worked, she might be found at her ablutions at least weekly. She had never experienced such luxury—always before her bodily cleansing had taken place in the frigid waters flowing near her mother's rock home. And during the winter months, she simply swiped the few areas that desperately needed attention as often as possible.

Too, she was now assigned a private cell which held a narrow cot, a small chair, a smaller table for a candle, and a dry sink that sported a large porcelain bowl and pitcher. A small trunk held two linen bed gowns, two underdresses, and personal items. She proudly hung her new uniforms on pegs. There was no window, and she found that keeping the door closed, a modicum of heat could be built up with the addition of a ceramic flue placed around a lighted candle. Teresa began to feel she had "arrived" and vowed to accomplish every chore so well that Judith, nor indeed anyone else, could have any complaint of her work. Thus, she was seen pressed and dressed in the dark dress of the upper house maids and sporting the pristine white apron and simple mop cap. Gretchen had supplied tatted lace which she stitched around the separate white collar that Teresa wore on occasions she deemed special—which was often.

Judith proved to be an excellent teacher and advisor as to the innuendos of upper house duties. Teresa needed only one time to be told or shown and the job was satisfactorily performed. Too, she counted her promotion as a well-earned gift, never negating the fact that she had paid dearly for it through the long years of strenuous labor and extreme circumstances. She knew she had triumphed, and Gretchen would be proud. Her mother had ever strengthened Teresa's backbone with encouragements of "you will do this," or "never say never," or "there's nothing you cannot do if you make up your mind." Consequently, her character formed, blossomed, and grew, producing a female of unquestioned abilities and intelligence, forbearance, and commitment.

# CHAPTER 9
# EXPOSING DECEPTION

STANDING BEFORE LORD Harry, Bristelman said, "I hate to bring it up, Lord Harry, but mine and DuBuques' creditors no longer want to see us. Our apothecary runs to hide when we attempt to enter his establishment. Our wives cannot pay our cooks, nor anyone else. I shall be forced to lay off several of our best people."

"Why have I not been apprised of this situation before now?"

Doctor Bristleman simply looked his patient in the eye.

Nodding silently and lowering his eyes to attempt to cloak his mounting ire, he opened the stationary drawer. He became more incensed upon learning that neither of the good Doctors had received compensation for their attendance upon this manor and its residents in far too long a time. The house ledgers had been sloppily kept, with days or weeks between entries. Harry spent several hours unraveling the fraying threads of income and creditors, of payments promised, payments deferred. *My God, how much damage can be accomplished in such a short time. I must get to my solicitors.*

"Of course." Grabbing a sheaf of vellum from the drawer and dipping the quill into the black ink, Lord Harry nodded to Bogart, "This will be taken care of immediately." Looking behind the good doctor to catch Calvin's eye, he said, "Bring the chest!"

Calvin was gone but a few moments before coming back into the office with a very non-descript, small wooden chest. He placed it on the desk in front of Lord Harry.

Opening the lid, he grabbed a stack of money, made a mental note of the amount contained in the bundle which he handed over to Bogart, saying, "Share what you can with DuBuque. If either of you have need of more, come back. Until then, speak of this encounter to no one. You and DuBuque may inform your wives that you have just received your back pay. I pray this will again give you both access to your apothecaries and get your servants happy again."

Bowing greatly, Bogart said, "I thank you, m'lord. Cliff will be ecstatic over this turn of events. We were becoming fearful of your demise and the shoddy conditions now prevailing at Martingale. And I humbly ask you to convey our sincerest appreciation to young Mistress Teresa and her mother. We now know exactly from what stemmed your problems and will be better armed if we ever run into it again." Backing out of the door that was being held open by Calvin, the doctor again said, "Thank you."

Scratching off a letter to his solicitors, Lord Harry had young Rodney Milburn cycle it to the post only seven miles away.

In the attempt to close all gaping holes whereby Benjamin and Alice might be usurping his authority, Lord Harry left instructions that all mail received would forthwith be brought straightway to him alone. It mattered not to whom it was addressed. Harry would see to it first. He began to suspect that more interference in his life was in place than he could have imagined. He must get to the bottom of this attempt to unseat his rightful place. With his official standing and education, he knew too that he should take his place in the no-nonsense running of this establishment. No more playing the idiot expecting someone else to step into his shoes. That had been a huge mistake. In fact, he really was the one to blame for Benjamin and Alice thinking they could take over. He was sorry about that, but now was the time for him to become a man—a responsible man—a "take-charge" man—fearless and fearsome at the same time. Pray God, he had the gonads to hold fast and learn the lessons that were surely in the offing.

Since the public promotion of Teresa, her below-stairs duties were relegated to others, and she soon became aware of much-needed upstairs work left undone for the lack of someone to have the time to do it. Taking the chore upon herself, she spoke to Constance about what she perceived to be a dire need. "Would it be possible to hire on more hands?"

"Lady Alice would not allow it, even though this dearth of help makes all of us less efficient," she said.

"Do you think Master Harry might allow it?"

Mistress Williston was quite aware that Teresa was summoned almost daily into the Master's presence on some excuse or another. The upper help gossiped that Lord Harry had been put under "a spell" by the pretty young witch. Thinking to herself, *if anyone can get through it is you,* but said, "Feel free to ask him. All he can say is yea or nay."

"I'll find out. Pray that he shall."

Every day that the mail was delivered, the young postman had received instructions that the mail was to be laid directly into the hand of either Calvin or Master Harry himself. There had been only a couple of instances where someone else had tried to coerce him into giving them the letters. And then there was one time when Lord Benjamin had tried to run young Gordy Hammet into the ditch. Gordy had been sure the deed was on purpose, but with his determination and agility, was able to protect himself—and then was delighted look back to see the trap swerve and nearly overturn.

As soon as he arrived at the manor house, he informed Calvin of the encounter.

"Thank you for the information." Reaching into his vest, he brought forth a coin and placed it into the hand of young Gordy. "Keep up the good work, son."

Taking the mail into Master Harry's office, Calvin said, "Young Gordy was near to being run over this morning by Lord Benjamin. I fear you may be getting close to exposing the extent of this mutiny, sir."

"Yes. Makes me more determined than ever. And is young Gordy alright?"

"Indeed, sir. He is fine but will certainly be on the offensive for his safety."

Reaching for the stack of mail, Lord Harry began shuffling through, then stopped. "This is what I've been waiting for. Maybe I'll soon have some answers." Looking up at Calvin, he said, "Thank you. You may relax for a while. Take some time with your wife. Come, though, if I ring."

"Thank you, sir." Smiling, Calvin thought, *Now, won't Libby enjoy me interrupting her schedule! I'll just inform her that it's orders from on high.* And he stepped lightly toward the lower reaches to attempt to locate his wife and share of cup of tea, perhaps.

No sooner had Calvin sat down with Elizabeth in the lower dining hall than Constance called out to Elizabeth. "Better send your Calvin back to the Masters' office. His bell is ringing."

Smiling and tweaking his wife under her chin, Calvin said, "Duty calls. Enjoy both cups of tea, dear, and think of me."

Arriving quickly, Calvin tapped and opened the door. "Yes, Lord Harry, I'm here."

"Come in and close that door," he commanded. "Send for Teresa. And you, see to getting the coach ready. We are headed to London. Get Rodney right away. I have important errands ready for him. He will be needing to prepare to get to London right away... leaving now. There is not a minute to waste. See that no ear can be privy to this plan. They are free to figure it out after it's begun, but without help from anyone else." Rising from behind the desk, he said, "Now help me to my room before you set out."

"Yes, sir." And he quietly closed the door behind him as he aided his master's ever-strengthening legs up the stairs to his room. He busily catalogued all the chores set before him in the order that they must be done. First, up to the chamber with Lord Harry.

Tapping lightly, Teresa opened the door, stuck her head in, and asked, "Sent for me, sir?"

"Yes, my girl. Come in." Standing in his night shirt by the fire, he began. "You, Calvin, and I are headed to London at daybreak. Tonight, you will pack what you need for a little while—possibly as much as a fortnight there. You are to have Missus Collier pack the proper foods to hold us until we arrive. It will probably take us three days if the track is not too rough. I'd like to get there as quickly as possible if you can stand the inconvenience."

"I'm sorry, Lord Harry, but exactly why am I going to London?"

"Why, my dear girl, you've come to mean more to me than anyone else—other than Calvin. You and your dedication returned my life back to me and I intend to see you fully compensated."

"What makes you believe I might expect any compensation? Lord Harry, the only requirement I might be willing to accept is for me to maintain my position as servant to this house."

"Very laudable, child, but I have a much greater vision for your life. I intend to adopt you as my official ward. You shall take your rightful place as though a daughter born to this inheritance."

Teresa backed up and as she turned, she shook her head. "No, sir. I cannot accept such. I would be ostracized by every individual below stairs as well as above stairs. Your idea would jeopardize my comfort and freedom. I simply cannot agree to this."

"Never mind, then. I shall proceed with the adoption without your signature. It matters not what you will or will not do. I shall not be deterred in this endeavor."

Teresa lowered her head and tears flowed down her cheeks. "Might I speak to my mother about this proposal, sir?"

Without hesitation, he said, "Only if you get it done before we hope to leave ere dawn. I want you with us, child." Reaching to aid Calvin in slipping him into a heavy robe, he looked up at her and said, "You deserve more than even I can give you. Now, get moving, and hurry back. We'll meet at the kitchen door as dawn breaks."

It took Gretchen a few seconds before she opened the door to her daughter. "What brings you here at this time of night, child?"

"Oh Mother, I need your advice. Please tell me what to do."

Sitting in the semi-darkness of the snug home, Gretchen had her eyes on the dwindling fireplace in the center of the room. She kept her gaze there, but her mind opened and accepted every word spoken by her daughter.

Teresa proceeded to explain exactly what Lord Harry had in mind. After a few indrawn breaths, Gretchen spoke. "You must go with your master this night. Your future is unfolding even more rapidly than I imagined. But unfolding it is. This gift of your wardship is something that I saw in your future. You must embrace this fully. Accept everything offered, as this is your destiny. I did not expect it as soon as this, but I cannot discount the time. You must go and receive this inheritance."

"Mother, you're not thinking clearly. He desires me to attend him in London for several days."

"Yes? And what is the problem with that?"

"I have no clothes that will be acceptable in such surroundings."

"Oh! Is that all?" Gretchen smiled. "You are aware that through the years I've confiscated items from this manse, and they are stashed in trunks beneath my cot. Come, help me locate a few pieces that might make you a little more comfortable during your jaunt to the big town." Gretchen handed a pair of leather shoes to Teresa with, "These might fit pretty well." And after finding two linen skirts and two tunics, a pair of underdresses, and gray cotton stockings, she folded and tied everything with a slip of white linen that could be used as a sash.

Gretchen reached for her child and enfolded her in strong arms, kissing her cheeks. Stepping back, she gently pushed Teresa toward the door. "Go with God, Darling. Go with God."

Coming through the woods with the items of clothing carried close to her chest, Teresa was mincing along in shoes that pinched. How she hated the confinement of these items of torture. She determined immediately to wear only her shoes that had been provided as an upper maid. At least they were comfortable if not stylish.

# CHAPTER 10
## TERESA'S INHERITANCE

THE MANOR WAS still asleep, except for the groomsmen and the kitchen crew when the low-slung coach pulled out of the back drive that morning.

Sitting in relative comfort and snuggled deeply in the fur quilts which deterred the cold morning air from penetrating, the trio tried to sleep. None of them had gotten one minute of slumber during the night hours.

Their attempts proved too difficult and they each in turn began to glance around at the others. Seeing eyes open, they all sat up straight and laughed. "Guess we'll sleep tonight, then."

Harry, with his elevating consideration of the pretty young lady, began to picture her attired as would befit her in her new element as "Ward of Martingale-Covington Court." His imagination drew forth elaborate fashions draped upon her frame—and her hair! That gorgeous hair! It was a fact he had never seen a more beautiful shade of blond before, and he mentally smiled as he pictured his hands removing the pins and loosening the tresses to watch them tumble free upon some dark pillow in candlelight.

As he scrutinized the girl, he suddenly saw her seated in his box at the Theatre Royale. "Have you ever been to the theatre, Mistress Teresa?" asked Lord Harry.

"Now, really, sir. When would I ever have had the opportunity for such an adventure?"

"Forgive me, child... not thinking, am I? But since we will be in London several days, it is reasonable that we ought to take advantage and attend whatever is currently playing."

Laughing, she said, "No, sir... you definitely aren't thinking. I am too simple a country girl to even consider myself worthy of such an endeavor. Besides, my clothes are inadequate. Why they'd send me to the back to sweep the street outside the doors." She smiled at the silliness of his suggestion.

"Harrumph! Let me assure you, young lady, you are more than worthy! Why I've watched you since that first night you came into my chamber, your carriage and demeanor are more ladylike than many high-bred women of my acquaintance." Looking at Calvin, he said, "Isn't that correct?"

She smiled, inwardly remembering the incident of her slapping his pale cheek, wondering if he had forgotten. Certainly, a most unladylike happenstance.

"Yes m'lord, I do believe you are correct about the girl. She has breeding somewhere in her background, I'm sure of it."

"See? Calvin agrees. How many young ladies of your status have your ability to read and write? Tell me. You are far above even my own sister. You had to have received instruction from someone with great intelligence and forbearance. Why, in my mind's eye, I can see you dressed in the fashions of today and could put you in any setting. There'd be no one to think you weren't brought up on the highest rung of society."

Not to be outdone, Calvin then suggested, "And she can sing, M'lord. Like a nightingale. Prettiest voice I've ever been pleased to hear."

"Truly? Why then you must sing for us now."

"Heavens, no. I cannot assail your ears with my squawking. And besides, I don't believe Mister Calvin has ever heard me sing anyway." Looking directly at him, she asked, "Have you?"

Knowing full well Teresa would be able to tell if he lied, he cleared his throat and said, "Well, I must confess I have not, but Elizabeth wouldn't waste her time telling me about your beautiful voice if it were not so!"

"Now, see? I insist! Please sing something for us. It will make the time pass more pleasantly. Please."

"Well, for the sake of Mother Mary! All right. Is there anything special you might want to hear? Now do not come up with anything too new. I only know the old songs."

"What about 'Brown Robin'? My mother sang that to me when I was but a toddler. She came to the nursery at bedtime and sang to me. Do you know that one?"

"Yes. I hope I recall the words." And she opened her mouth and began. The coach filled with the most beautiful and melodious soprano the men had ever had the privilege to hear. They were mesmerized. No sooner had the last words left her lips than they began naming other songs.

She sang until her voice began to fade. "Gentlemen, I fear I must stop ere my voice leaves me completely." Laughing, she said, "But maybe that's your ploy. Getting me to where I will be forced into silence!"

They laughed and swore it was not so.

They made London early the morning of the third day. Arriving at Martingale Manor in the Saint George district, they were pleased to find the place already astir. Molly and the others were busy with preparations for the day. She was expecting to leave shortly to glean the markets for the special foods from a list she had been supplied by young Rodney.

The upstairs and all the lord's rooms had been aired, cleaned, dusted, and polished, bedding sunned and beds remade.

"Oh, it's so good seein' ye again, Lord Harry. 'Tis been far too long, but yer home's awaitin' and ready fer yer welcome. If ye finds anything out'a place, or if ye needs is not met to yer satisfaction, all's ye needs do is mention, and it'll be put to rights."

To young Molly, her master was the most wonderful of men. Tall, and so very handsome, even if a bit thin. If truth be told, she would kiss his feet. Blushing at her thoughts she continued to wonder what it might be like to be held in his arms or gazing into his deeply set brown eyes. Just seeing him again was like a burst of sunshine on a cloudy afternoon. *Blessed will be the lady this 'ansom Lord picks 'n' thet's fer sure!* she thought.

Harry chuckled at the adoring "spaniel eyes" of Molly as she gazed up at him. "Thank you, Molly. Apprise every one of our arrival, please, and send someone to see to our baggage." Reaching for Teresa, he led her forward and said, "And Molly, this is my ward, Mistress Teresa Lyons. I'll be needing her taken as soon as possible 'round to Madame Alexandra's establishment. I'll send a message as soon as you find yourself able to accommodate this request."

Bobbing a quick curtsey, Molly nodded, "Yes m'lord. Very soon I'll see it done. Now let me go and see to getting everything of yours settled and in place. Yer rooms is all ready."

Nodding, then turning to reach for his "ever-present" help, Harry said, "I'm afraid I shall still require your help, Calvin, in mounting these steep stairs. I never did appreciate this house for that very reason." Looking upward, he said, "One of these days I believe I'll call in a good architect and do something about them. Now come."

At the top of the stairs, Harry pointed, "Teresa, your rooms are here on the second floor across from mine. See here, I shall show you." He opened the door to sweep her into the beautifully appointed chamber. "Come rest and recuperate until Molly sees our breakfast brought up. We'll wash off some of the road grime before noon repast... as soon as sufficient water can be heated."

Mid-afternoon Molly had sent Daniella to show Mistress Teresa to the shops of Madame Alexandra. The two girls arrived home just as the evening meal was about to be brought into the dining room. When the young ladies entered the foyer, both Lord Harry and Calvin were stunned to see Teresa in a sky-blue wool overcoat and matching bonnet.

"How beautiful you look, Teresa. Your coat is stunning, and it's warm?" *Heavens! This girl is more beautiful every time I see her. She takes away my very breath.* Both men were taken aback at the utter transformation of this young house maid. Harry found himself being drawn into a web of need he had no desire to fight. *When did this transformation occur? I know this is the trembling urchin that first entered my space when I was lying on my death bed. But, my God, look at her now.* Shaking his head to clear his thoughts, he became aware of her speaking.

"Oh, yes! It is wonderful. I've never had such a gift as this. I thank you with all my heart, sir. I'll be indebted to you all my life for these fine outfits." Turning around, she swung the bonnet away from her blond tresses and opened the several buttons running down the front of the coat. She slipped it off and revealed a lovely dress beneath. "Madame Alexandra had this dress and coat already on display. I was deeply grateful they fit so well. Why the dress only needed the hem let out to make it right." And she continued, "But, Lord Harry, I beg this to cease. I cannot feel right about being gifted this way when it feels like I am being bought and paid for, for reasons I've yet to ken. This largesse makes me feel under great obligation, and I do not want this. Please."

"Nonsense, girl! Madame Alexandra takes her orders from me, and you shall be gowned as befitting my ward. As to your obligation, why there is not enough available in the whole of London to begin to pay the debt I owe for the giving back of my life. Not only my very life but the life of Martingale Manor. Without the intervention of you and your mother, I certainly am not stupid enough to believe I'd not be dead by now, and my brother-in-law at the helm.

"I am the one to be ever in your debt, my girl. You are the only reason I'm alive." Reaching to take her hand, he brought it to his lips, then pulled it into the crook of his elbow and led her into the dining room. Standing behind a chair, he seated her. He then called for warm damp toweling brought so Teresa could cleanse her hands before the foods would be served.

As soon as Calvin seated his Lord, the doors opened, and foods were brought in and served. Harry noticed an entirely different flavor in the beef stew. Looking to Teresa seated to his right where he had insisted she be—he asked, "Do you perceive a different flavor than usual?"

"It is a surprise, sir. I had your cook incorporate a little burgundy into the stew to give a boost to your blood. Is it agreeable?" she asked.

"Indeed! Why it's the best I've ever tasted, and you say it's burgundy? I must always remember that. We must alter our recipe at Hampshire as well!" Thinking for a moment or two, he asked, "Does this mean I may now imbibe in an after-dinner drink, my dear?"

"Only one small glass of dry red wine, perhaps. And not ever on an empty stomach. If you imbibe, do it immediately after dinner, or, if you prefer, you may have that one glass now, with this meal."

"I believe I shall anticipate that glass more after this meal, and in the comfort of the salon. Before a raging fire, possibly." Turning slightly to glance back, he asked, "What do you think, Calvin?"

"My sentiments exactly, sir."

After a few minutes in total enjoyment of the foods Harry asked, "Did Madame Alexandra take your measurements, and did you select fabrics for several gowns?"

"Indeed. She told me to come 'round tomorrow afternoon for a try-on. She also informed me that she would have the cobbler bring several pairs of slippers for my investigation. And too, there are plenty of underthings and night dresses available that she believes will fit well, and so won't require having to be made up for me." Continuing, she again iterated her uncomfortableness with being forced into this situation of feeling like a "bought woman."

Her concerns never registered with Harry as he asked, "Did you remind her that I require evening attire for you as soon as possible?"

"No, sir. There was no 'reminding' the lady of anything! She produced a veritable list of items per your specific request. So, yes. She helped me choose the fabrics for that. She told me that the dress must be very simple with little fuss about it, as I am still too young for dazzling my many admirers." She laughed at what she perceived to be utter ridiculousness.

The men did not. "I can understand her insight." They glanced at each other seriously.

The next morning the trio crammed themselves into the hansom. Calvin was not going to be the cause of his lord's tardiness at his meeting this morning. When he had sent Billy for a cab, he'd failed to stipulate the occupancy of it, and so he felt it his fault when the two-passenger, smart black hansom was pulled to the door.

As the company of three seated themselves, with Teresa in the middle, Harry was very aware of the sensation of Teresa's thigh pressed against his own. A shiver of delight ran through his chest. He smiled and enlarged his thoughts.

"Good day! Lord Harry. What a most pleasant meeting! Especially since we thought you dead and buried! We were most surprised to greet your young man when he brought news from you. And even happier to hear you were arriving today."

"We've much to discuss, but I want to introduce you to my companions." Harry indicated his valet. "This is Mister Calvin Collier, my right hand. And this," bringing forth the other, "is Mistress Teresa Lyons, my ward, or soon shall be, with your officiating."

Skylar was immediately affected by the beauty of the young woman—and not only by her looks. She was a rare girl, particularly in that she was so open and not the least bit coy or shy or coquettish in any fashion, like so many young ladies her age. He believed he was smitten and wondered if she had made her debut. He determined to make it his business to find out.

Stepping forward, Skylar took Teresa's arm and led the way down a short hall to open a door. There he indicated, "Here, let us take a seat in the conference room." Five found places around a shining mahogany table while Calvin stood off to his master's right. Sir Edward spoke first. "Needless to remind you all that this firm was defrauded by your brother-in-law and sister. Our firm was contacted by their man, Sir Zachary Franklin, several weeks back. He informed us that you were dying, and they wanted to make the transition as smooth as possible to promote goodwill in their assumption of power.

"We agreed to send your files over as soon as we might get confirmation of your demise. We sent letter after letter but never received anything that might give us the hope that you were alive. Consequently, we gathered all our files on both your properties and handed them over to Franklin. The only files we kept were your personal files and we stored them in the attic; however, since hearing from your man, we retrieved them and have them all here in front of you. What is your pleasure now?"

*My God! How close they came to ousting me. Thank You, Father God, for Teresa and her mother.* "As quickly as possible, get all my property returned to my control. You know what procedures must be adhered to. Which Barrister to approach... what is needful to solve this quandary. I shall not press charges for the sake of my sister, but she and her family will no longer have access to either of the properties.

"Then again, neither do I desire to cast my family into penury. So, you must come up with some sort of monetary favor to be paid out yearly for a comfortable upkeep. Nothing extravagant. Just their basic needs to be met. Maybe Lord Benjamin will find employment of some sort. He'll no longer be able to live off the Martingale wealth."

Pushing back from the table, Edward stood. "Tomorrow afternoon we'll have the legal binders in place for your signatures. We can get to work and solve this dilemma with little effort. I will talk with Barrister Sedgewicke as soon as possible. Maybe even this afternoon. I'll send round and see if he's available."

Reaching for the crystal decanter settled upon the buffet between the windows, he offered, "Now, gentlemen, and lady, shall we have a toast to our success?"

Shaking his head, Harry said, "I'd love to do so, but in my precarious condition, I'm afraid the only refreshment my glass could hold would be water, at that must first be boiled." He smiled.

Going to the door, Sir Doyle called, "Mary, bring fresh glasses of water, please."

"Now," said Skylar, "I'll get the forms and we'll get the adoption of Mistress Teresa Lyons as your official ward completed."

"By all means yes!"

## CHAPTER 11
## NIGHT OF DRAMA

THE WEATHER WAS crisp and dry. No fog tonight. The smoke from a thousand chimneys rose up and away, into the atmosphere. One could see the stars brightly shining, as well as observe breath expelled in thin streams of condensation, as the trio talked on their way to the Theatre Royale.

The New Ward of Martingale Manor delighted in the foreign sounds emanating from the hard heels of her beautiful new brocaded slippers. As the small company kept together along the walkway, Teresa stopped momentarily and performed a quick jig for her own entertainment. All three laughed gaily as surrounding strangers also heartened by the ebullience of the young girl, smiled in appreciation.

Entering with crowds of like-minded, they soon found their way upstairs to the Martingale box. Calvin had seen to it that it had been dusted and prepared for their arrival this evening.

Once they were in place, Calvin drew open the heavy velvet curtain, exposing the interior of the palace to the wondering eyes of Teresa. She was dizzy from trying to see everything at once.

Listening as the orchestra was tuning with discordant noises, she could see young dark-clad boys scurrying off stage carrying unidentifiable objects. Directly down below there were no-few people busy at finding their assigned places. Teresa watched it all in a fit of awe.

Letting her gaze wander undirected, she stopped as her eyes came to rest on a man standing in the box directly across from where she sat, his mouth agape, staring at her. She turned to see if Lord Harry or Calvin saw the person, wondering exactly in whom he was so interested. Neither of her companions were interested in looking toward the cavernous room, let alone eyeing anyone across the way. She turned back, and the man was now seated but had opera glasses up to his eyes. She could feel her skin crawl. Something was dangerously wrong.

"Lord Harry. Please, sir, do you know the man across from us in that box?" She indicated the place where she had seen him, but it was now vacant. The man was gone. A chill came over her.

"I see you are disturbed about some man you perceived to have been looking directly at you, is that correct?" he asked.

"Yes. At first, he was staring, and then he held his glasses up to see better. And now he's gone."

"His actions are well understandable, my dear. You are not aware of it, but your beauty is overwhelming. Especially when seen at first glance. He probably is out now trying to find out who is the lady seated with Lord Martingale. Don't let it disturb your enjoyment of the play."

"I'll try, but I only have these feelings when there's danger. I have lived with this type of premonition for far too long to not pay attention when it occurs. But I'll see if I can overcome it this time."

Harry leaned over to whisper into the ear of Calvin. Teresa did not notice as Calvin left the confines of the dark box. The curtain was opening—opening a new world for Teresa Jane Lyons.

She prattled all the way back to the manor house, keeping the two men accompanying her filled with laughter and joy at her excitement.

"My dear, we must get you to every new play that the troupe presents. I find that I am enjoying it more than I considered I might. What say, Calvin?"

"Indeed, m'lord. It is a rare pleasure to witness such delight."

Once the group entered the house, the men sought the comfort of the library, as Teresa bade them good night and mounted the stairs to her rooms.

As the men entered the library, Harry bade Calvin sit. "Now, tell me what, if anything, you gleaned tonight of the stranger."

Nodding, Calvin spoke. "He seems to be newly returned from a foreign field. India, I believe. He appears to be simply lurking about for some reason. I found that his father died a while back and his mother remarried not long after. I hear that even she has since deceased. Her new husband took over his family's estate, so I suppose he is determined to wait it out. His driver informed me that he does not expect to visit his home while he is on leave at the present time. He will be leaving at the end of the month to head back for his duty post."

"Did you get his name, perchance?"

"I believe it might be a Major Steadman, sir."

"Give his name to our solicitors and have them look into it. They may desire to use a private investigator. See what they can come up with." He sat silently for a minute, then spoke again. "You see, Calvin, I completely trust young Teresa's intuition. The fact that you found him trying to determine exactly who she is gives credence to her trepidations. We don't want to treat this lightly, but neither do I want her overly anxious, so we shan't broach the subject again in her hearing."

"Understood, m'lord."

"Let's finish our drinks... wine, and you, your brandy. I shall be more content later when I am able to close out my evenings with a good brandy and a fine cigar. Remind me to query Teresa in the morning as to when something a tad stronger than red wine might be incorporated into my evening regimen. I seem to be gaining strength every day, and she has enlarged my list of agreeable foods." Standing, he bade Calvin see him up the stairs. "I think I can make it on my own this time but stay with me. Let us see, shall we?"

Ascending the narrow stairs, he continued, "On the morrow, you will hire a couple of detectives for me. Obtain the best you can locate. They will surreptitiously guard my ward. Understand, they must be ready to travel wherever she happens to be. Until this situation is proved to be of no consequence, I shall expect them to remain in my employ."

"Understood, sir."

## CHAPTER 12
## CHANGES MADE

RODNEY ARRIVED BACK at the Hampshire Mansion in the early afternoon two weeks after Lord Martingale, Mister Collier, and Mistress Lyons had left there. He left his horse at the stable in the good hands of his elder brother, Jimmy. "Give 'er a good rubdown, Jim. She's been through lots these past days and needs a rest."

"Yer headed to see Da?"

"I'll see Da after I've taken care of a little business for th' Lord, n'all."

He strode to enter at the ground level hall at the gardens. He glanced around to see if his father was anywhere near, but not seeing him, he entered the house. Walking through, searching for the first friendly face, he came upon Gladys with her arms full of turnips. "Ere. Let me help ye."

"Thank you, Rod. Yer a good boy."

"Could ye get me through to Missus Williston? I must git a message to her from Lord Harry."

"Come on. I'll see what I can do fer ye."

As soon as they entered the exterior well-room of the kitchen where all the vegetables were washed and prepared for cooking, out walked Edith Bloomsbury. Gladys spoke. "Edith, child, will ye help me a tad. I need to get word to Missus Williston that young Rodney here needs a word with her as soon as possible. It's from Lord Harry, so you know it's important."

The girl turned and headed up a short flight of stairs toward the servant's dining hall.

"Golly, Gladys, I sure wish ye hadn't told her that. No telling what she is apt to do. I ever see her in the company of Lady Truluck. And I sure ain't thinkin' she's supposed to know what Lord Harry is a-doin'. Ye may have just flung dung into his plans."

"Well! Ye never let on a'tall that ye never wanted me to open me mouth! If anything is amiss, it'll sure lay itself at yer own doorstep, Rodney! Why didn't ye warn me afore hand? Huh?"

"Too late now. I'll just need to lay that bit of snag into me news for her."

"Rodney! Come up to our dining hall," called Edith. He ascended the few stairs and found the head housekeeper waiting for him. He leaned forward and whispered, "Can I speak to ye in private, ma'am?" All the while, Edith was loitering nearby pretending to sort through some silverware.

"Of course. Isn't where we are alright?"

Shaking his head and leaning in to whisper, he confided, "No ma'am. Edith has ears bigger'n a' elephant. I need for no one but you to hear this. Please, ma'am."

"Oh, all right. Come into the pantry and we can close the door."

The two entered the sunless room and shut the door. Rodney could see sunlight filtering in below the bottom of the door and pointed to the shadow of two feet that had taken the space in an attempt to hear what was about to be relayed.

Quickly, he jerked open the door, and Edith nearly fell into the room. He slapped her before he even considered he may lose his trusted position for it.

However, Mistress Williston spoke up and said, "Edith, if there's one thing I despise, it's a spy. You go pack your things and clear out of this house before you take another step! And feel free to let your papa know exactly why you've been let go."

The squalling girl ran out and down toward the servant's quarters.

"Mary! Come here, now!" called Constance.

The girl came running, breathlessly. "Yes, ma'am?"

"Get yourself down to Edith's room and see that she packs everything that belongs to her, and not one jot or tittle that does not! No go and let me know when she's cleared out."

"Yes, ma'am."

Then taking Rodney by the shirt sleeve, she led him over to a chair and sat beside him. "Now, talk."

Drawing a lungful of air and expelling it, he began, "Lord Harry is on his way back from London. In fact, his carriage may get in as soon as tomorrow, or the next day for sure. Anyway, he wants you to have all his rooms ready. And most especially, an apartment for Mistress Lyons. You c'n believe it or not, but she has become his ward. He's seeing to her coming out an' everything. He's kinda adopted her, but for what it's worth, I think he's in love with her. Now, that's jes me a talkin'. So, don't spread that around none."

"Gracious, Rodney, you certainly can come up with a lot in just a few seconds, now, can't you?" She smiled.

Taking another gulp of air, he continued. "But I ain't finished! The worst part—maybe the best part—is that you must pass this letter on to Lord and Lady Truluck." He withdrew it from inside his jacket. "I don't rightly know, but I believe he wants them gone a'fore he gets back here. That's jes me a' talkin' again. Comin' from overhearin' stuff and all. Anyway, they'll read what's in it."

He paused to gather his thoughts afresh, then proceeded. "And then, on top of all that, yer to begin to prepare for a celebration of sorts, a kinda debut for the new ward. He's gonna introduce her into society as soon as her next birthday. First here in Hampshire, then they wuz speakin' to return to London and do it again there. At least, that's whut they wuz all talkin' about."

Putting her hands on either side of her gray head and rocking her ample body back and forth as though attempting to comfort herself she said, "Rodney, me boy, my head's a-swimmin'! But! Let me get up from here and get started." She left the room and began calling names right and left to attend her immediately, as she waved the sealed letter in her left hand.

## CHAPTER 13

# DANGER NEARS

GRETCHEN DRESSED AS carefully as she could, but still felt like a fish out of water. She forced herself to slowly walk the distance through the deep woods, taking the unseen path up toward the back of the mansion. The dew had wetted the lower half of her linen skirt, but she held the shawl close around her shoulders and over her head to protect herself from the shadows invading her heart. She prayed.

She had received word that now was the time for "the revelation." She had been praying since word came to her last night concerning this mission. She placed her hand in the pocket of her apron, around the gold medallion protected within the folds of a finely woven handkerchief. The ribbon had long since rotted, but she maintained the vestiges of it still. The pale green shreds embraced the metal as old friends, each as dear as the other.

She had no fear for herself, but great trepidation for her darling daughter. No! Her beloved was no blood of hers. Now, having seen that evil devil walking through Lord Martingale's woods yesterday, it made her blood boil to realize he was the father of her beautiful, vulnerable Teresa. But thank God, he never saw her nor her hovel in the rocks.

He was whistling along as if he owned the place, swinging his cane. She watched and followed him to see him circle the manor all the way around. He spent quite a while kneeling in the graveyard beside the chapel on the small rise above the house. And she observed him talking to the stable hands and the gardener as though they were old friends. After about an hour of snooping, he finally left for the cliff road, where she saw him mount his horse and ride away.

That was when the voice came and bade her do it. Now was the time.

## CHAPTER 14
## THE REVELATION

THE LETTER GIVEN to Missus Williston contained not only instructions to the Truluck family, but also a gift of enough money to get them settled somewhere out of Lord Harry's territory. It took three carriages to get everything Alice declared belonged to them. Not willing to argue, the servants helped load it all and were collectively relieved to see the family go. Grateful, the staff was happy this inconvenient family was out of sight long before Lord Harry's entourage came into view.

The servants, from youngest to eldest, were waiting with gleeful anticipation for the arrival of the Lord of Martingale Manor. The only worry niggling in the brain of Constance was that Gretchen was waiting in the library to speak to Lord Harry as soon as possible. She just could not understand how Gretchen surmised that the coach would soon be rolling in from London today. They say that for every ray of sunshine, there will be raindrops! Well, today she prayed it would not be a deluge.

The afternoon was wearing thin by the time the trio arrived. As the family stepped from the carriage, the staff applauded and welcomed all three of them home. Elizabeth was so happy to see Calvin! Three weeks was far too long apart.

From inside, Gretchen watched the activity out front and was rewarded with the sight of her beautiful girl. *Oh, pray God I handle this well so as not to hurt this child.*

"Get me up to my room, Calvin, please, I feel truly exhausted. I must lie down for an hour or so. Leave the sorting out until later. Just let me rest quietly for a little while."

"Of course, M'lord. Come... I shall help you. I do fear you may have overdone your activity while we were away. Trying to see to every detail has been too tiring. I'll see that you aren't disturbed until you are ready to ring the bell."

"Thank you, Calvin. Please bid Teresa make herself at home and see that Missus Williston has appointed a lady's maid for her."

"Yes, sir."

By the time all the hullabaloo was done, and everyone was trekking off to their own business, it suddenly came to Constance that Gretchen was still in the library. Moving quickly in that direction, she spied her standing in the open doorway. "Have you forgotten me, Constance?"

"I do fear you are correct. I was so wound up in trying to settle everyone and everything until I have just this moment considered your presence." Stopping to face the scarred visage of this healer, Constance asked, "Can you return tomorrow? Lord Harry is abed and cannot be disturbed. He may not arise for possibly an extended time, due to his weakened condition."

"A condition with which I am well acquainted, Constance."

"Yes, I forgot momentarily."

"Your memory seems to be off more than on right now. But be that as it may, I shall remain here until I am permitted to see him privately. It is of urgent importance and cannot be postponed."

"In that case, would you care to convey your message to Calvin, or perhaps Teresa? They both are in his confidence completely. Those three seem to read each other's minds. What one knows, they all know."

"I'm sorry, but no. I must see the Lord initially. If he cares to bring in the others, that is his business, but I am determined that he hear this information first. Privately."

"In that case, make yourself comfortable. I shall bring refreshment forthwith and show you to the privy if you need it. Meantime, sit. I'll close the door on my way out, to deter prying eyes."

Gretchen nodded and walked back to sit in a chair near the stone-cold fireplace.

Turning at the door, Constance said, "I'll send 'round the man to start the fire right away."

"No. No need. I'm not the least bit cold or uncomfortable." She suddenly lifted her hand toward Constance. "Wait. On second thought, maybe it would be better for it to be warm in here for when Lord Harry does come in."

"Yes, I agree. Now, do you need the privy?"

"That won't be necessary. I am fine. Thank you."

Constance closed the door quietly and left for the rear of the silent house.

Gretchen then roused herself from the chair and began scanning the shelves of books until she found what she was looking for: **A Compilation of Great Britain's Family Coats of Arms, With Attendant Histories.**

*I would love to find the one that belongs to Teresa.* Carrying the large tome, she placed it in the center of the desk, lit the lamp, and opened it to the index. *Constantine.*

The fire was burning brightly. Some man had been in twice to stoke it down and lay on fresh logs. The heat was beginning to be appreciated as the day wore on and darkness was drawing close. Constance had

# THE MEDALLION

come to pull the heavy drapes and to offer food, but Gretchen had denied it. As soon as she had left, Gretchen realized she was hungry, but would not ring for her return. Time had flown and Gretchen gleaned much information on the targeted family crest.

The history of Gravelstone Abbey was rich indeed. Teresa would inherit the largest estate on the Channel coast. The castle was located at the lower west edge of West Sussex. Construction had begun over four hundred years ago. It had been altered as well as added to through the ensuing centuries.

A sect of Carthusian Monks had quartered there until Henry VIII had them murdered and their buildings confiscated. Since that time, it had been given variously to first one favored individual or another until it came into the hands of the Constantines.

The quarters that Teresa's mother—along with Gretchen, Teresa's grandmother, and grandfather had utilized was on the third floor of the wing and tower facing inland, as they did not care for the view of the cliffs and channel, preferring instead the placid landscape of low rock enclosures and grazing sheep and cattle.

The medallion, presently held in the pocket of Gretchen's linen skirt, was featured, time and again, in the pages of the disclosure of Gravelstone Abbey. *I wonder if there might be a place for me where Teresa will ultimately call home, or will she be incensed over the fact that I've lied to her all these years, and kept from her the knowledge of her rightful inheritance?*

The door to the library silently opened, and Harry saw the woman who provided the miracle to save his life. He spoke. "Don't let me frighten you. I was just now told of your presence here. Please forgive my tardiness." He stepped quickly toward the little woman and reached for her hand. Noting the long black plaits woven with small ribbons, and the sparkling black eyes so diametrically opposite to those of her daughter, he wondered at the vagaries of nature that such a dark and swarthy individual could birth such a pale, blond child with brilliant blue eyes.

She curtseyed and said, "Perfectly all right, Lord Harry. Might I introduce myself, since we have never met? My name is Gretchen

Benchley Lyons, formerly companion and maid to Mistress Melanie Jane Constantine of Gravelstone Abbey." Gently withdrawing her hand from his, she asked, "Do you feel well enough to take some rather extended information?"

"I do believe so, Mistress Lyons. I understand you are the gracious mother of our beloved Teresa. That is correct, is it not?"

Smiling, Gretchen said, "Might we sit here by the fire and allow me to begin at the beginning, sir?'

"By all means. Have a seat."

Gretchen took her seat near to her host and held the large book opened, upon her lap. She was silent long enough to gather her thoughts. *Where ought I begin?*

Lord Harry had left word that he was not to be disturbed, because not even the man entered to stoke the fire. Gretchen kept up with it. No one came and knocked on the door. He listened without any comment, or even a sigh or sound, as Gretchen unfolded the dramatic life and beginnings of the lovely Teresa.

She began her exposé from the earliest times she had memory of: Her being given over as a child of seven into the house of Constantine to be raised along with the daughter, Melanie, an only child of three years of age, at the time.

Using facts so recently gleaned from the book in her lap, she desired to impress upon Lord Harry the ancestry and importance of the dynasty surrounding Teresa.

Finally, she brought out the folded handkerchief and placed it on his palm. "Here is proof of exactly who our girl really is. Also, I can take you to the grave of her mother, as well as her past ancestors who lie in the enclosure at the Abbey Chapel." Reaching over to touch the back of his hand, she forced his eyes to intercept her own. She needed him to understand the gravity of the situation.

Harry uncovered the heavy gold talisman and wondered at the deep rusty smear that was swiped across the surface. "This looks like blood." He gazed into the face of this little gypsy.

"You are correct. It is the birth blood of our Teresa. I did not desire to remove it. But you are free to follow your desires concerning the stain." Gretchen drew herself up somewhat and continued, "Teresa's life is in grave danger and has been since her untimely birth. Hence, the imperative deception of her identity. But, you see, she has grown into the image of her true mother. She is her exact copy... That alone poses great threat from the one who now knows of her existence. Every facet of her face is as if Melanie has returned to life. They are nearly identical in every way. In stature, bearing, voice, and especially in tenderness." Gretchen paused just long enough to assure herself that Lord Harry was indeed absorbing the seriousness of the situation that prompted this exposé.

"I have brought Teresa up to become very self-sufficient. I taught her everything I know." Sitting up, Gretchen gazed into the crackling fire. "Everything I've divulged is nothing but pure fact. Truth. My ultimate fear is that her father may want to claim her to get his claws into her inheritance. I saw him yesterday. Here. He was here and sweeping around like he owned Martingale itself. I think he must suspect that the girl is living here."

"What did you say his name is?"

"Daniel Bordeaux, but I believe he is known by his middle name of Steadman, which was his mother's maiden name."

Lord Harry was silent, struck through with the news. "My God! If this is true, my own father married his mother. We never knew that there was a child from her marriage to Lord Peter Bordeaux. Father was under the impression that she had lost all of her children at young ages.

"So now, wherever he has been keeping himself, he's back and looking for trouble. I believe we had an encounter with him in London. And I do believe he tried to reach Teresa. Especially since you say she looks so much like the young girl he raped."

Rising from his chair, he went to the desk and brought out a sheet of vellum, opened the inkwell, and prepared the nib. He began to write. He scratched away at the paper for some minutes before he finally stopped. He handed the paper to Gretchen.

She read it. Twice. Then looking up into his countenance she said, "Well, let us hope and pray this will do it. I would hate to see him benefit, in any fashion from all the dastardly deeds he's done. He needs to pay! His rape of Teresa's mother caused her death as surely as if he murdered her that afternoon."

"It's the least I can do. I must do all in my power to protect Teresa, her property, and her good name. And too, I certainly would not want to lose this..." he waved his hands around in the air, "to some evil clown who might decide that Covington Court is his birthright." Bringing himself back to sit next to his guest he said, "And, I am expecting a pair of detectives I've hired to arrive very soon with the specific duties to guard our Teresa 'round the clock."

He reached out and placed his hand over that of his healer and stood. As she rose from her chair, he spoke. "It's so late and dark and cold—would you consider staying over the night here where you'll be more comfortable? There are plenty of rooms available. In fact, you could sleep in with your daughter."

Bowing somewhat and shaking her head, she said, "Thank you, Lord Harry, but I shall head back to my little rock-hovel. You must come visit sometime. Teresa can show you the way. It is not easily found for which I am grateful. I love my solitude, especially since my face is so disfigured and few enjoy my company. I do rather well with the little wild animals who visit regularly. We have formed a bond few creatures enjoy as I do."

Reaching to hug the lady, he kissed her cheek. "You, Mistress Gretchen, are the most beautiful creature in this world. God has gifted you with more innate sense than any fifty others. I owe you my very life."

Heading toward the door, he paused, held her gently again, and said, "We shall see to the safety and protection of Teresa. Never fear. All possible shall be done to obtain justice for injustice. Come, I shall see you out. Are you sure you can find your way in the dark?"

"My eyes will adjust quickly, and my feet will find the path with no trouble. I shall pray for you as you break the news to our girl. Somehow, I believe she shall seek me out as soon as you convince her of her ancestry. She will need me to seal the information to her satisfaction. Please, take care of her. Protect her." Moving lightly down the wide steps, she turned and said, "Thank you."

Harry stood watching the little woman until she disappeared from his sight. *I knew Teresa had to be someone very special raised by someone very special.* He stood silent, gazing upward toward the upper reaches of the great house, and considered all that his ward must face. Wondering at the tremendous changes in the offing that would vie for her attention. *Will I even have a place in her heart? This child has suddenly risen beyond my own status, by God. Dare I consider my earlier thoughts now that she has surpassed me?*

## CHAPTER 15
## RIGHTING A WRONG

LORD MARTINGALE GAVE Rodney the task of taking this important letter all the way to London. Rodney knew exactly where the offices of Phillips, Preston, and Preston were, as he had been there before.

As soon as he was shown into the office room, he was invited to seat himself as the three lawyers went over the information. Finally, they conferred privately over in a far corner out of earshot.

Skylar soon came to tell Rodney to go get a bite to eat, and that they would have something for him to take back to Martingale as soon as he returned.

When Rodney entered the office an hour later, they handed him a large, sealed envelope and asked him not to tarry.

The round trip to London and back to Martingale was record-setting. Rodney was back before anyone expected to see him. Striding into the hall behind Calvin, he met Lord Harry and the trio entered the library.

Harry accepted the package, reached into his vest, and retrieved a coin. Laying it into the palm of the youngster, he said, "Rest a while, son. You've earned it but be ready if I need you again."

Grinning and nodding deeply, Rodney backed out of the door, where he turned, clicked his heels, and whistled as he departed the house.

Seating himself behind the desk, Harry unsealed the large envelope and a number of pages fell out across the gleaming mahogany. Harry restacked them and began with the uppermost one.

For nigh on to half an hour he was in deep study of all that he had before him.

At last, he sat back and said, "We've a massive undertaking before us. But with these suggestions and the legal guidance held herein," he held the papers up, "we shall correct a wrong that has affected both this house and those who previously held her, as well as the estate of Gravelstone Abbey." Glancing over at the unopened book that Gretchen had left in the chair she had vacated several nights ago, he said, "May God help us to be successful in this dire attempt."

## CHAPTER 16
## UNSTABLE HEART

WHILE A PRIVATE investigator was on the trail of a so-called Major Steadman, the law offices of Phillips, Preston, and Preston were in the throes of installing a Mistress Teresa Jane Lyons-Constantine into the legal ownership of Gravelstone Abbey. Teresa insisted her new title-cum-name contain the name she truly identified with- Lyons. That name was the essence of who Teresa felt herself to be. Her new ownership of the property would henceforth be identified as Lyons Gate at Gravelstone Abbey on Wofford-West Sussex.

As for Lord Harry, his home of Martingale Manor was now a title of the past. Everything was reverting to the original, historical legally-binding identification of this ancient area. Covington Court became the home of the Martingales. Its identifying title was now Martingale Manor at Covington Court-Hampshire.

Teresa would remain as the ward of Lord Harry until her marriage. Upon that contract, she would take residence at Lyons Gate.

Teresa herself was continuing to be a child lost in her new world, lost to a status not altogether to her liking and comfort. This life brought with it heavy burdens she was not willing to face without her mother by her side.

Daily? No! Hourly! No! Moment by moment, she could imagine the "iron stays" of her status, ever-tightening, drawing into her flesh, constricting the flow of blood within her life-sustaining veins. Crying as silently as possible while she was alone in the cooling waters of her bath, she felt the overwhelming need for Gretchen to come and make everything right again.

"...But Mother! I need you now more than ever! You must come. I cannot make it! I cannot face all ahead without your presence, your visible-viable presence. Can you not understand? I shall never claim another mother, no matter how many times I am asked to sign away my heritage with you." She was crying with body-wracking sobs, kneeling before Gretchen upon the sod floor of the room.

Gretchen's heart began to crack. Initially, a lid slivered open to allow one tear to fall. It found its way to land upon the face of this daughter of her soul. She bent over to lift her child into her arms. "I'll come. I promise."

Laying within the strong, comforting arms of her mother, Teresa's sobs soon turned to soft snubbing. "Mother, I'll send help to get you moved straight away."

Gretchen pushed her back and stood, "No, darling. Please allow me to move in my own way, at my own pace. I want to keep much of what I have right here for future needs. But I will promise to live most of my days in your presence." Hesitating but a moment, she continued, "Now you must get back before they all come looking for you."

"Oh, they're right outside now. I couldn't get away without someone coming with me."

"What? You mean you brought someone with you?" cried Gretchen.

"Yes, Mother. Lord Harry and Calvin are outside waiting."

"Good heavens, child. You left the Lord outside?"

"Well, yes, Mother. I felt you might not accept my pleadings with them in attendance. And besides, they offered to remain outside as lookouts."

Opening the door of her home, Gretchen bowed low and asked, "Will you forgive my rudeness for not inviting you gentlemen into my humble home? However, I beg benevolence. You see," she said, smiling, "our daughter became somewhat thoughtless in her haste to present her case to me. Are we forgiven?"

Both men laughed heartily and nodded. "Without doubt!" spoke Lord Harry. "But was she successful?"

Grinning, Gretchen answered, "Without doubt!"

## CHAPTER 17
## UNWANTED CHANGE

IT DID NOT take long before the entire household was aware of the proximity of Gretchen the Healer. It seemed she was ever sought out for advice of one sort or another. And, with this evident acceptance, she began a routine of sorts: daily seeing to the pressing needs of the sick and ailing, to the selection of herbs for drying suspended from the kitchen beams, to sorting through her supply from the rock house to the planting of certain herbs, thereby becoming acquainted with Sydney Milburn-estate gardener as well as father to young Rodney, and his older brother, Jimmy. Gretchen was rapidly becoming a viable entity in the fabric of Covington Court and found herself not only content but downright happy. The most wonderful aspect of her new life was seeing and being near the daughter of her heart, if not her body.

Growing more beautiful and vibrant and knowledgeable each day, Teresa was becoming proficient in etiquette, conversations, deportment, fashion, two foreign languages, history, and ear-splitting practices upon the pianoforte.

*She will make an indelible mark in her world before too much longer,* smiled Gretchen.

Constance was in her element with the planning and execution of the upcoming debut ball for "the soon-to-be" Mistress of Gravelstone

Abbey, as well as being the ward of Lord Harry, here at Covington Court. She convinced Lord Harry to go the extra mile and send for London's best seamstress and designer.

Madame Alexandra had been persuaded to pack up and come all the way out to *"God knows where that place is!"* to perform her best talents on a gown extraordinaire. Beneath her demeanor of inconvenience lay a heart ultimately thrilled with the prospect of the endeavors before her.

With her entire entourage housed close at hand and at her command, she became increasingly productive in her ideas for designs. She came up with not only the ball gown for Teresa's debut but also designed a veritable wardrobe fit for a queen. Now all she had to do was convince Mistress Teresa that every stitch was necessary to her status in the realm. Oh! Joy!

Being fairly easy to sway by reason of necessity, Teresa acquiesced to every suggestion by Madam Alexandra. "However, you must also prepare a fine gown for my mother. I shall not wear a stitch before I see my mother in a new gown. And not only one new gown—she is to have a complete wardrobe. Do you understand?"

Gleefully, Madame Alexandra agreed. However, this news assured her that a shipment from London was imperative and must be done as quickly as possible. She must make a list! No time to waste.

The kitchens were busy, as usual, but more so with the addition of the new hires. Constance was ever trying to get her subordinates to train them. They were being sent here and there, losing their way, getting in the way, doing unnecessary tasks.

Finally, she called Calvin. "Don't you have a sister in the house of Sir Ansel?"

"By last word, yes. She has been there quite a while. Probably near to retiring."

"Exactly what is needed here! Do you think Sir Ansel—or better yet, Lady Barbara—would be willing to lend her to us for a few weeks? "

"I shall go at earliest convenience to inquire. We ought to have their answer before tomorrow noon."

"Thank you, Calvin. I'm in your debt."

Wednesday afternoon Constance welcomed a Missus Helen Collier-Smyth. She was short, rotund, red-cheeked, and jolly, which belied her strength. She was soon found to be a hard-driving taskmaster. Within four days she had all the new help assigned to the jobs to which they were most proficient and performing tasks with ease. Now she had to educate Constance and Elizabeth exactly how to relegate those tasks for the highest efficiency. Within a two-week period, the entire house was running along like a well-oiled machine.

Later, Constance approached Helen, assuming she would soon be returning to the Ansel establishment.

"But I was under the assumption that I was to remain here. I brought most everything I own with me. Now you want me to leave? I'm sure I don't know where I'll go, Missus Constance." Her face began to crumble in the process of weeping.

"Oh! No! Helen. Then you are to stay here, I am sure. It is I who am mistaken. Never let it be said that I messed with the plans to have you here for good. No! This house is too large as it is, and there is always a need for good people to tend to her. You are more welcome than you can ever ken. Please, allow me to dry your tears and assuage your fears. Consider yourself a viable and most necessary member of Covington Court, my dear." With that, Constance gave the little lady a snug embrace. "Now, it's back to work with us."

Two new forever-friends entered the kitchen together, one to head out to the well-room to oversee the cleaning of the vegetables and the other toward the upper levels to see to the proper setting of the tables and preparations taking place in the ballroom.

Gretchen and Sydney were industriously tending to the outside gardens and lawns. They had also visited the stables about the need for clearing the nearby grounds to hold the expected carriages, coaches, and conveyances while the horses were tended to during the hours of the upcoming ball.

Gretchen was slowly coming to trust the gardener's attention. He seemed to never notice her scars. Particularly, he did not fear her eyes. He always met her glance with tenderness and understanding.

Gretchen was not cognizant of the fact that Sydney also had scars. His, however, ran deep beneath the surface of his skin. He had lived a life of abuse by parents that had been addicted to drink, which left him to his own devices to raise himself. Instead of becoming mean and vindictive, Sydney found early on that kindness brought him more than obstinacy. He had come to Covington Court as a boy, and finding himself a niche in this grand house, he did all in his power to stay true to it.

And now, here he was thanking God for bringing such a wonderful woman into his life at this lowest ebb, while he was facing the loneliness of a barren future. Before Gretchen came, he had begun wondering what would become of himself once he was too old to be of use to this house. Knowing the probability of solitude, coupled with an aged body and nothing left but memories and thoughts of his early childhood, he considered that he would be truly better off dead.

And then into his life walks this woman. A woman who knew his heart. A woman he could discern was a kindred spirit. A woman who finished his sentences as he searched for the words he needed to complete them. Life for Sydney was glowing with promise. Happier than he had ever been in his life, he silently prayed that God would protect Gretchen, himself, Covington Court, Lord Harry, and all its attendant souls. Looking up, he and his companion were surprised by a sudden shaft of sunlight breaking through the deeply clouded sky. Looking over to the uplifted face of Gretchen, Sydney leaned over and placed a soft kiss upon her lips—her first kiss from a man.

Coming down the steps, Teresa and her maid, Virginia Haviland, toured the ballroom and then opened the vast doors to an outside cobblestoned area overlooking the grounds. There in the near distance was her beloved mother hard at work with the gardener. Suddenly, Teresa was shocked to witness her mother being kissed by Sydney Milburn! Retreating sharply, she ran back into the ballroom, past the crew that was cleaning the huge chandeliers, through the long reception hall, into the vast rotunda, up the west steps to the landing, on up to the hall, and beyond the turn into another hall where her rooms were.

Entering her room, she slammed the door in the face of the breathless Virginia.

The child stood silently until she could decide whether to open the door or not. With breath-holding trepidation, Virginia turned the handle and shoved the heavy door ajar just enough for her to peer around inside the vast room.

She spotted Mistress Teresa standing at the grilled and leaded window, gazing outside to the scene below. Knowing her mistress was in some tremendous mental disarray, she kept quiet and entered the chamber on silent feet, hanging back at the door until she might be summoned.

After some moments of inactivity, Virginia saw her mistress turn. With tears glistening upon her cheeks and in her eyes, Teresa spoke. "How could she! How could he! Unseemly! A travesty! Not possible! It simply cannot be! I shall see to this fiasco! I'll put a stop to this!"

And she stomped toward Virginia, who side-stepped quickly to allow Teresa free passage. Racing behind her mistress, Virginia fought a battle to maintain pace. When Teresa finally slowed to a steaming saunter, Virginia found her tongue and asked, "What happened, miss? Where're we bound?"

"Don't you worry about it! I am off to find my mother. And I shall as soon as she can find her way inside. I suppose she will enter at the kitchen garden door. We're heading in that direction."

Finding themselves in the servant's quarters and the business section of the old mansion, Teresa suddenly realized she had them both lost. Standing still to listen for sounds, she kenned them to be where she had grown up. She was near the laundry where she spent many hours in labor, and she suddenly smelled the scents of her childhood. With it came the memories flooding her soul. She thought. *Who do I think I am? Why should I want to deny my own mother the joy every woman seeks? What if her contentment is found in the arms of a gardener? Isn't a man of the earth the perfect match for such a soul as Gretchen? And I-I myself hope to one day hold my love close to my heart. Does he ever think of me other than as his ward? Would that I could be strong enough to advance myself. But! No! Society dictates we females* must remain aloof and chaste! Well, never let it be said that a woman cannot pray! And pray I shall. I shall one day see him returning my ardor, or my name isn't Teresa Jane Lyons Constantine!*

Coming to herself, she said, "Here, Virginia, let us return to our places beyond this section of our source of supply. We find ourselves in the nether parts of a world far away from the life that has been set before me. I thank God He allowed me to return, if only for a moment in time, to the place of my origins. I must never forget these hard-earned lessons from my past. I know they will stand me in good stead for all the future God has planned out for me."

"What do you have need of Mistress Teresa?" asked Elizabeth as the pair exited the well-room.

"Nothing really, Elizabeth." She was cognizant of her lie when she said, "We were just drawn here by the delectable odors wafting through the place. I became nostalgic with the remembrances of our time together when I first became caregiver to Lord Harry. Does my presence here upset you?"

"Never, Mistress Teresa. You are welcome to wherever you decide to put your foot!"

Teresa reached to hug the chef, who smelled wonderfully of bacon drippings.

Stopping short of the stairs leading to the servants' dining hall, Teresa turned to Virginia, "Please go on up and prepare a bath for me. I shall be there in a few minutes. I want to take a moment of solitude in the herb garden, and then I need a bouquet of dried lavender from the drying room downstairs. I won't be more than ten minutes."

The girl curtseyed smartly and turned to the stairs, "Yes Mistress."

Teresa entered the drying room first and sought out a nice-sized bunch of lavender. Holding it gently to protect the bundle from losing any of the tiny, crisp flowerets, she left the kitchen and walked slowly in the warm sunshine toward a vine-covered trellis on the west wall, where she seated herself there to drowse momentarily. Inhaling the pungent odors of the herb garden, she smiled and closed her eyes. She needed this respite from the hubbub of the last few weeks, and to contemplate the direction in which she must abide for her future. A vibrant vision of Lord Harry emerged behind her eyes, and she smiled.

## CHAPTER 18

# GONE

VIRGINIA ENTERED THE kitchen to interrupt the beehive of activity as myriad platters were being assembled for upstairs. "Has anyone seen Mistress Teresa?"

Seven pairs of eyes turned upon the girl. Elizabeth Collier spoke first, "When? You mean recently? How recently, girl? I saw her out with you in the gardens early on this afternoon."

Virginia began to wring her hands. "No ma'am. I mean in this past half hour! I left her getting a bundle of lavender, and she was coming right on up for her bath that she sent me ahead to prepare! She never came!"

Silence! Then a cacophony broke out with everyone talking at once. The voice carrying the most weight happened to be Gladys. She took a spoon and racked it against a copper pot. "Listen to me! First things first! I shall go tell Gretchen now. She will know what to do. The rest get back to the chores at hand. This house cannot come to a standstill. Get back to work. I'll be right back."

And with that, she swept quickly out the door and headed toward the gardens. She was striding with long rapid steps, just shy of running. Her eyes were searching the landscape for the couple that had done so very much to make the grounds and gardens come alive. Rounding the east wing, she spied the pair. Raising her apron high, she waved it and called to get their attention. "Here! Gretchen! We have an emergency. Come quick."

Both Sydney and Gretchen dropped the gardening tools and ran across the turf as quickly as possible. The first words spoken were by Gretchen. She said, "She's gone, isn't she?"

Gladys nodded. "We don't know, but she didn't come in about half an hour ago when Virginia was expecting her."

"Come, let me talk to Virginia."

Standing at the back gate, Virginia was bawling loudly. Gretchen took her arm, jerked it, and said, "Stop the blubbering now! Look at me. Tell me exactly where she was and what she said the moment you two separated."

Snubbing and attempting to calm herself, Virginia relayed word for word the exchange between herself and her mistress. "She just wanted a minute to relax and be alone. That's all."

"Thank you, Virginia. You may go inside. Find something constructive to keep busy with and do not blame yourself. This was bound to happen. I knew it in my heart." She turned to Sydney, "I'm going to my home in the woods. Do not come."

He silently nodded.

She touched his face and said, "Be sure to stash the gardening equipment for tomorrow."

Harry was beside himself with recriminations. "I ought never have taken her to London! She should never have been put on display! What have I done? She never deserved this sort of danger." He slammed his body into the leather desk chair and threw his head into his hands.

Calvin poured a brandy and placed it before him. "Drink this, sir. It'll help you to think more clearly and to approach her rescue in the best way possible."

"Yes! Calvin, contact Paul and Earl. Have them come! Now!"

## CHAPTER 19
# THE VISION

IN THE GLOAMING, Gretchen entered the rock home. Her heart kept reaching back into her childhood for whatever reason God willed. She built a small fire and placed the kettle upon it. She then stripped off all her clothes and prepared her bath. Still, the small voice continued. Snatches of words floated before her eyes. Standing, naked and vulnerable before His Spirit, she deliberately washed every portion of her body, including her long black hair. Finally glistening, and clean, she lifted her face and arms toward her Heavenly Father and recited the words her earthly mother had spoken so often until Gretchen was able to repeat them fully without prompting.

"*O Lord, Thou hast searched me, and known me. Thou knowest my downsitting and mine uprising, Thou understandest my thought afar off. Thou compassest my path and my lying down, and art acquainted with all my ways. For there is not a word in my tongue, but lo, O Lord, Thou knowest it altogether. Thou hast beset me behind and before and laid Thine hand upon me. Such knowledge is too wonderful for me; it is high, I cannot attain unto it. Whither shall I go from Thy Spirit? Or whither shall I flee from Thy presence? If I ascend up into heaven, Thou art there; If I make my bed in hell, behold, Thou art there. If I take the wings of the morning, and dwell in the uttermost parts of the* sea; Even there shall Thy hand lead me, and Thy right hand shall hold me. If I say, surely the darkness shall cover me; even the night shall be light about me. Yea, the darkness hideth not from Thee; but the night shineth as the day; the darkness and the light are both alike to Thee. For Thou hast possessed my reins; Thou hast covered me in my mother's womb. I will praise Thee; for I am fearfully and wonderfully made; marvelous are Thy works; and that my soul knoweth right well. My substance was not hid from Thee, when I was made in secret, and curiously wrought in the lowest parts of the earth. Thine eyes did see my substance, yet being unperfect; and in Thy book all my members were written which in continuance were fashioned, when as yet there was none of them. How precious are Thy thoughts unto me, O God. How great is the sum of them. If I should count them, they are more in number than the sand; when I awake, I am still with Thee. Surely Thou will slay the wicked, O God; depart from me therefore, ye bloody men. For they speak against Thee wickedly, and Thine enemies take Thy name in vain. Do not I hate them, O Lord, that hate Thee? And am not I grieved with those that rise up against Thee? I hate then with perfect hatred; I count them mine enemies. Search me, O God, and know my heart; try me, and know my thoughts; And see if there be any wicked way in me, and lead me in the way everlasting. Amen."

She dressed in clean clothes, doused the fire, and stepped outside into the dark. Walking with sure steps she strove toward the resting place of Melanie. Once there, she lay near to where she could feel closest to Teresa. "Father. Take my Spirit upon Your Spirit wings to our daughter. We beg Your protection and comfort as You lead us to her rescue."

There came a light as Gretchen was taken from her prone form and ported to a dark and stinking room. Standing next to a narrow cot, Gretchen realized the room was near to a brackish pool, or stagnant water, maybe a pigsty. "Father, help my soul to understand where I find myself."

A door opened and a woman entered bearing a candlestick, which she placed on a shelf above a narrow bed. There upon the bed lay Teresa. She appeared to be asleep. "Wake up, mistress! Wake up.

Ye've slept long enough now. Time to rise and shine fer yer father. He's done paid fer yer victuals. So, wake up now." She stepped to the bed and slapped both cheeks of Teresa, rousing her somewhat.

"Where am I? Who are you?"

"Ye'll see soon enough. Now, come on, get up and use the pot if need be before I take ye down fer yer breakfast."

Ever one to do the bidding of whomever was in charge, Teresa sat up, albeit a tad unsteadily, and finally slipped off the cot and onto the cold ridge of the porcelain chamber pot. Soon, as she was adjusting her clothes and shaking out her skirts a bit, she said, "I fear someone struck my skull rather badly as I've an awful pain here." She gently stroked the temple of her head; bringing her hand forward, she saw that it was covered with dried clots of blood.

"Here. Let me clean that a bit." Taking a rag from beneath the washstand, the woman wet it and wiped several times to remove as much as possible without causing the wound to begin bleeding again. "There, that's better. It ain't too bad, and'll heal soon enough. Th' young always heals quick."

"Very well and thank you. I'm ready to see whomever it is you speak of as 'my father.'"

Descending the narrow stairs, Teresa felt as though there was someone holding her elbow and gliding along beside her. Thinking maybe this phenomenon might have been brought about by the deep sleep of head trauma and laudanum, she did not attempt to rid herself of the feeling. Stepping from the lowest stair, she was met by a tall man, dressed in fine clothing. She realized he was the same man she had seen at the Opera House in London. He took her hand and kissed it. "My child! At last! I lived many years without even knowing you are here. But this wrong shall be righted!"

Teresa felt a firey burn emanate and travel up from where his lips had touched her hand toward where the "apparition" held her elbow. As soon the collision occurred, the man dropped her hand with force and glared at her! "Are you ill? Your hand is burning up!" Turning, he said, "Here, Lisle. Feel her. I think she's sick."

The red-headed, buxom woman came around from behind Teresa and laid her hand upon her brow. "She's fine. Ain't nothing wrong as I can tell. You're just imaginin' things... Take her on in to eat. She's probably past hungry by now."

Somewhat maddened by fear she was ill, he reached and jerked Teresa by a limp arm. Muttering, he mouthed into the air, "Damned girl. You best not get sick. Not now!" Nodding, he led the way into a noisy room where a table was laid for them in the furthest corner. He slammed the injured child into the nearest chair while spitting out, "Your spoiled days are past! Once we have settled, you'll be taught what obedience really means."

Teresa remained still and quiet to gather as much information of her whereabouts as possible. She deemed they were inland somewhat as there were no seafarers; most of the diners were villagers and farmers. She listened as keenly as she could, trying to catch a word hither and yon that might give a clue as to the whereabouts of this place.

"Eat, child. You'll need the strength for the journey," prompted Lisle.

"Where are you going?" she asked, looking at the woman.

"No! You mean where are *we* going?" he smiled. "We've passage from London next week. I shall be taking you to live with me until such time as I am able to prove your mother loved me and since her parents had given their permission for us to marry, she heartily agreed to our coitus that resulted in your birth. I soon shall take into my personal possession my own inherited property as well as Gravelstone Abbey." He bent low over his platter shoveling in the victuals. Then he glanced at the disheveled girl and continued, "And you'll bring a pretty penny from the man I'll have the privilege to pass you over to."

Teresa felt her body vibrate with fear and tension. "I'm not going anywhere with you. You raped my mother and caused her death."

He threw his head back and laughed raucously. "Who on earth told you that?" He shoveled in a mouthful of food and waved the spoon around. Laughing, now gently, he said, "Dear daughter. Your mother was in love with me and me alone. She defied her parents to be with me. And you are my flesh and blood." He sat back a tad and took another bite. "It is very unfortunate that she died, and not knowing you existed, I was so broken-hearted when I heard of her death that I left for India. I was able to purchase a nice commission and have spent the bulk of these ensuing years there... only coming back to England a few times.

"But when I spied you in the box at the Opera, I knew immediately who you were. You are my Melanie made over."

"Well, sir, I simply refuse to add to your fantasies about me. I shall see to it that you hang for the rape of Melanie and her ultimate death."

Laughing loudly, he asked, "And exactly how do you think you can prove such an absurd conjecture?"

"The truth never dies. Even though my mother has been gone from this earth, her blood cries out for truth to surface and debts to be paid." She stood and looked fearlessly into the eyes of her father. He blanched at her piercing blue stare. A veritable chill forced its way down his spine. "Truth cannot be destroyed. Remember that."

He watched as she strode toward the stairway and ascended them smartly. "Follow her and lock her in... and keep her dosed with the laudanum. I don't need trouble from her." He nodded to Lisle.

Once the two women were upstairs in the room, Lisle locked the door and began dispensing the dose of laudanum. Teresa spoke up, "Wouldn't you like to know the truth about the man you've attached yourself to? He's a master of deception and you probably think he intends to take you under his wing to care for you... am I correct?"

"Oh, ye're a little spoiled girl and know nuthin' of life. If'n ye were in my shoes, ye'd be a'tryin' to catch up wif summ'on to git yer hooks into deep enou' fer it to catch. I perceive th' Major has yer bes interes' in his heart. Ye need to be a'countin' yer blessin's, child."

"Would you be averse to hearing what I have to say? That is, before the laudanum? I would hate for you to end up as my mother did, and too there is nothing on earth that will force me to think my rescue isn't well on the way as I speak. You would do well to aid my escape. It's inevitable, you know."

Lisle shook her head. "Ain't no power on this sod can swap my mind from th' Major. He's my ticket to a better life." She opened the bag and nodded her head. "But you go right ahead, Miss. I'll listen whilst I pack th' case but, first, here take this spoonful of dreams."

"No. Please. Let me speak first. Please." Noticing the hesitancy, immediately Teresa gave as much of the complete story to the wondering ears of the red-haired Lisle, who nodded all the while, and periodically could be seen stopping her labor to gaze into the eyes of the young blond girl. Once Teresa reached the place in her unbelievable life where she had been abducted, she stopped her story.

"I'm ever so sorry luv. Ye'v 'ad an extra difficult life, But what kin I do? I swore to th' Major I'd stay and be yer mum 'til India. And I wuz 'opin to stay on there with him."

"Will you agree to omit the dose of laudanum this time? I promise to pretend to be sleepy, and I swear to not give you any trouble. But just maybe I might see a way where I can escape and get help to get back to my home." She paused, "Please, say you'll help me."

"Alright, I'll leave it off this time, but mind, now, no trouble out of ye." As Lisle left, she said, "But, I'll just lock th' door fer yer protection."

Gretchen awoke and spoke to Her Father. "Thank You. Now, guide my steps to aid in the rescue of our daughter." She quickly made her way in the dark back to Martingale Manor where she found the kitchen staff running this way and that in an attempt to aid in any possible way to placate Lord Harry. He was seen stalking the halls and ranting at anyone venturing near about how he needed to be throttled for his thoughtlessness in porting the girl to London, too entangled in his own self-indulgence about the girl: How he, the great Lord Harry, was going to be lauded for discovering this pearl of his universe and set about getting her the recognition he now knew was her due.

Elizabeth trotted over to Gretchen and opened her plump arms to enfold her, in the hopes of conveying her sorrow and sympathy at the kidnapping of darling Teresa.

Gretchen suffered the embrace, and as she removed herself from the arms of the cook, she said, "Elizabeth, please do not be so upset, dear. You might ruin the stew, and this group looks to you alone for guidance for the preparation of nourishing meals—particularly at this inopportune hour. Now, possibly more than ever before you will need to maintain a level head and get on about your daily chores. Leave off the desire to drop everything to mourn, as mourning is yet afar off."

With that said, Gretchen saw Elizabeth breathe deeply and stand taller as she nodded her head. "Yer right! Now's the time for us to be the steady rock for Lord Harry."

"Yes." And Gretchen left in search of the Master of Martingale.

## CHAPTER 20

# DELIBERATION

"LORD HARRY, SIR. Mistress Gretchen desires to speak with you if you'll allow her."

"Heavens, Calvin, bring her in."

Opening the door to the library, Calvin bade Gretchen enter. The room was dark but for two candles set in the window niches. The drapes had been pulled wide apart and the under-curtains had been swept off by cords. "I see you've the proverbial 'light in the window,' Lord Harry."

"Won't hurt. Now, what have you found?"

"Are your detectives here yet?"

"You knew I'd sent for them so soon?"

She smiled, and he nodded. "I have a bit of information they may be able to use to aid in the location of our daughter," she started.

"Tell me now, Gretchen. Say what you know."

"I'd rather not, sir. The time is not yet ripe for anyone to play around with this information in the hopes of circumventing the plan being laid out for her rescue."

"You speak in riddles, woman. If you know where she is, you must divulge it immediately."

"But, you see, I do not know where she is. Thus, any information forthcoming from my lips would be utterly useless. We must hold our enthusiasm for the future." She turned to go, "Please, apprise me of the arrival of the detectives. They will need my input before they begin the search."

"Where will you be?"

"Here in the Manor with your other downstairs servants."

"I was under the impression that Teresa had moved you into upstairs apartments."

Smiling, Gretchen said, "She tried. But I much prefer, since I was coerced into moving here, that I keep to the lower halls and so claimed a small cell for my room. I'm infinitely more comfortable there."

"Very well, you go. I shall continue to castigate myself... as I am the one in whom fault for this fiasco must ultimately be placed."

"Suit yourself, Lord Harry, but I fear you place too much credence in yourself for this occurrence when in actuality none of us had anything whatsoever to do with this turn of events."

"What are you alluding to?"

"Lord Harry, we mortals are simply vessels whereby the Creator plays out His plans for the unfolding of His universe. Our daughter has been and presently is in His capable hands and I can rest assured that they who have taken her will pay dearly for their nefarious behavior. In short... thank God we stand not in their shoes. We simply are not privy to the how nor the when of her rescue but are assured that she shall be brought home to us unharmed."

"Would to God you are correct."

She smiled as she left the room and headed toward the lower reaches of the manse.

Some few hours later, toward three or four o'clock in the morning, Gretchen was awakened by being shaken by her shoulders. Sitting up, she reached for the candle stub to light. "Who's here?" Upon the flaming of the wick, she easily saw that no one was with her, so she knelt by her cot and praised her Father for His angel's attendance. Slipping her linen skirt, shirt, and apron upon her frame and donning the cotton hose, she slipped her feet into the leather clogs. Going out into the black hall, she spied someone coming down the stairs toward her. "Calvin. They've arrived?"

"How did you know? I was on my way." Almost immediately, he answered himself. "Never mind. Come on, I will light our way. Earl and Paul arrived not five minutes ago and are waiting in the library with Lord Harry."

"Good morning, gentlemen. Has Lord Harry apprised you that I might have information to aid in the whereabouts of our Teresa?"

The men stood and both Paul and Earl nodded seriously.

Calvin had four chairs circled in front of the fireplace with a table centered that contained glistening stems of golden drink.

"Let us be seated," said Gretchen. "I've much to relate."

As she gave the men everything she had been provided, from having seen Teresa and her filthy state at the inn Daniel had her brought to, she then gave the most important information: that Daniel had secured passage to India for himself and Teresa and the red-haired woman, for an upcoming date. Gretchen then suggested the men split ways and one locate the place where they were presently housed, and the other hie to London for the sailing docket exposing exactly when the trio was to leave port. Between the Inn and the port, the men would be able to rescue Teresa.

Ever the unsung hero, Lord Harry spoke up and said, "Might I be allowed to aide in this? I am very astute at reading signs and following directions. Please, I need to be able to do something."

"Well, my part is mostly cut and dried as I'll be headin' to London. Mayhap Paul can use your help in finding the place." Earl glanced toward his partner.

"That'll be to my benefit sir. Four eyes are better anytime than two."

"When will we begin?" asked Lord Harry.

They all stood, and Paul said to Calvin, "Get your master into hunting clothes... I don't mean no high- class fox hunting outfit! No. Find him forest-colored clothes and sturdy old boots and a short cape to sleep in." Then glancing at Harry's head he added "He'll need something of a head cap, low and fitted and earth-colored. Don't get him up in anything that'll stand out. He needs to blend into the places we'll be goin'."

Calvin grinned. "Leave him to me. I'll see him camouflaged."

"Won't I need to pack a bag?"

Paul laughed. "No, sir. No extra clothes. We'll be ripe by the time this is over, but extra clothes will only slow us down, and time is precious." Looking over to Calvin, Paul continued, "Send word to the stables to have his sturdiest horse fed and ready as soon as possible. We hope to leave before first light."

Heading toward the door, Paul turned to Lord Harry. "Sleep if you can but be ready well before daybreak. Alert the cooks to have a small breakfast prepared that we can eat from the saddle."

`Calvin said, "Consider it done, sir."

## CHAPTER 21
# WORKING THE PLAN

THERE WAS NO sleeping committed by any of the men. Earl left immediately after they departed the library. Since he was to be taking the roads to London, it would be easy to keep on track. However, Paul and Lord Harry had stashed their victuals in the saddle bags and led the horses from the stable to the distant back gate. Tethering their steeds there where the miscreants had entered the grounds, the two men stepped through the gate. But instead of taking a straight shot toward the secreted, vine-covered trellis where Harry was led to think Teresa had been seated when she was taken, the two walked a circuitous path. "Why don't we go directly to the bench?" asked Harry.

"I must assume the kidnappers took the most direct path from and back to the gate. If we walk directly toward it, then there's an excellent chance we'd obliterate any tracks that could possibly have been made by them. And, I must assume too, that there was more than one man who took her. But we shall see as soon as there's light enough."

Upon reaching the benches beneath the trellis, Harry bent down and lifted a few stems of dried lavender. "She was certainly in this spot, Paul. Look."

"Great. But stay put until we can see the area better. Just sit where you are and relax a bit. It won't be long before ole' Sol'll be up.

Within ten minutes the adjustment of their eyes had given them nearly perfect sight. Standing Paul said, "Come here. Look 's like a pretty good struggle took place. There are bits of lavender scattered all along here." He began to walk and point. "There were three devils that took her."

"Why didn't she scream?"

"She may have tried. Clearly, they silenced her somehow. You can see she was dragged along here." He stopped. "Here as they came through the gate, she must have been carried because there are now only three sets of tracks. These look like men's boots and look here! If that's not a woman's boot I'm not Paul Clancy! So, they had a woman with 'em. That gives us another clue. She's being taken care of by some woman." He stopped and told Lord Harry to bring their horses. "We need to stay on the trail as long as we can."

The sun was up now to where they could see well enough, even as they entered the heavy forest. They kept on until suddenly they came upon a rutted farm road. "Ah! Here they all got into some ox cart. See there's no doubt about it. They tethered three horses to it to give them a rest. And look here, another small fragment of lavender blossom." He smiled. "It's as if she's trying to give us help in locating her."

"Can you tell which way the ox-cart went?"

"Easily. Time for us to mount up and save our strength. We'll just follow this path until we see where it leads."

"How about we eat our biscuits now. I find I'm starving."

"Sure. And that's sure a blessin' to know your innards are healed enough to want a greasy biscuit and cheese." He grinned at his companion.

"Listen, Paul. How about just call me Harry. It will make me humble and keep me from wanting to circumvent anything you order me to do. I do not want to be the cause of us not finding my girl. And, without doubt, you know what you're doing. I'll just follow your lead."

Paul grinned in the early light, totally aware of the slip of the tongue in speaking of Teresa as "his girl". "Sure, Harry."

By early afternoon, with the sun just beyond overhead, they entered a small farming village and there found a house with a swinging hand-painted sign that touted *Food Ready All Day* and *Room to Let.* "Harry, you stay out here and look busy while I go in and look around."

Harry began to check the reigns and cinches and whatever else he could do to appear very occupied. In a few moments, Paul returned. "They had her here last night and lit out early this morning. The maid said they headed out up the road toward the next village. There were three men and two women-one was very young and blond. Must have been your ward. But she also told me they left an oxcart out back, and she said the young girl who arrived with them was lying in the cart and seemed to be injured and unable to walk or ride. It's my guess they're making it for London. We've no idea when his ship sails, but Earl will intercept them as they board, or maybe before."

"Oh my God! There is no telling how badly they injured Teresa. Knowing this makes our venture more imperative than I considered before. We must catch them and rescue her before any more damage is done to her. I need to get her back to Gretchen as quickly as possible."

"Don't worry. We shall continue."

"Forgive my lapse in faith... So, we're headed onward?"

"You bet your boots we are." He took both horses to the rear to have them fed and tended to. "Go on in and order our repast. I'll be back in a minute."

"Yes, sir. I'll just get whatever the cook has prepared."

Paul smiled at Harry. "Yep, that's about how it's done. I will be right on in."

Once both men were seated, Paul leaned over and spoke, "You remember Gretchen said she saw the girl in an area with stagnant water?"

Harry nodded.

"Yes. Well, when I took the horses out to the stable there was a good size stand of pooled water out beyond the fence." He grinned and went on, "Stinks like hell."

As dusk encroached upon the pair, they began slowing the speed of their horses. Finally, Paul suggested they dismount and walk a bit to ease both man and beast. Harry was past ready to call it a day but bound and determined to not hold the advancement of Paul's plans hostage to his physical disability. He kept quiet. Soon, Paul stopped and bent over as if in pain.

"What's the trouble, Paul?"

"Oh, it's just an old injury acting up. It'll ease up in a few minutes and we can get on about our tracking." He began walking around a bit and swinging his arms and breathing deeply. "I need to take a quick break. How about you?"

"I can use a moment or two in those bushes over there. Be right back."

Within ten minutes or so they were cantering as quickly as they dared with the darkness ever-deepening. Both men were relieved to view a few shimmering lights ahead and silently prayed that there be an inn handy. As they rode into the village past a crudely constructed rock church, they surveyed several rickety buildings that were shut up tightly for the night but had evidence of the family residing above in candle-lit rooms. At the lower end of the main thoroughfare, they spied *The Red Rooster*. Stopping in the front of the inn, Harry took the horses to the rear of the where he gave them over into the care of a huge, burly, leather-aproned man who took them with a sleepy nod. "When you need 'em?"

"Before sunrise alright?"

"They'll be right fer ye. But ye'll pay me now." And he held out his huge hand. He did not quote a price, but Harry laid into his palm a coin of value that he thought sure was more than enough. The man pitched it up with a large smile and said, "They'll git an extra 'elpin'o' oats too."

Leaving out early ere the sun was actually seen, the two were rested and anxious to be on with this endeavor. "Do you suppose we may catch up to them sometime today?" asked Harry.

"Well, we've every advantage knowing there's now only Daniel and that redheaded woman with him. Glad we found out the two 'ne'er-do-wells' were sent off early on, so we won't have to concern ourselves with three men against two."

"Do you know if the innkeeper said they had the girl on a horse alone?"

"No. But sure we'll be able to determine that as soon as daylight comes on a little more and we'll be able to see how many horses we're tracking."

As the pair was passing a young maiden by the road, Paul signaled for Harry to stop. "G'mornin' miss. I wus wonderin' if ye might pass a bit of information to me... that is if ye have it."

She curtsied and asked, "Whut's yer have need to know, sir?"

"Me friend and I are searching for our daughter what was taken against her will by a man and a woman. We understand the lady might have red hair. That is if her head was uncovered enough to be seen. The man is right tall and might be dressed in dandy attire. They could be on two horses or perchance three. Have ye by any chance seen such a trio?"

The girl curtsied once more and brightened, "Why yes, sirs. Right at dusk yester-eve such a group came into my village." She turned to point back from where she had been and directly in the way the men were headed.

"Three horses or two?"

"Three, sir."

Harry leaned down and reached to hand her a coin. "Oh no, sir. That ain't necessary. Not for that little bit of information." She shook her head and backed up a couple of steps.

Harry felt in a pocket and brought forth another coin to add to the first. "Take it, child. You have no idea how dear is the relaying of your observance to us. You are instrumental in the saving of our daughter. May God bless you and your house."

Reaching to accept the money, she curtsied deeply and said, "And God go with you this day to lead you to your daughter, sirs."

She stood watching as they rode off toward Village Cullbert.

# CHAPTER 22
# THE EXTRAORDINARY MADAM

COMING UPON THE village, Paul said, "We need to dismount and leave the horses here in anticipation of them still being here. We need to enter the village as locals. Do you recall anything about Daniel?"

As they tethered the horses to a small bush situated near the first structure on the dusty street, Harry answered, "Gretchen relayed that he is tall and not too thin or plump, says he's really very handsome and stays well dressed. Hair a medium brown and curly. Too, she said his complexion is ruddy... probably from his stints in India."

"Well, let's not say anything about our mission. If you do talk keep it mundane, of no consequence. Understand?"

"Indeed. Count on me, Paul. Teresa has too much at stake for me to be forgetful and destroy our chances of rescuing her."

Strolling into the little settlement, they paused every so often to glance around. Paul motioned for them to take an alley and try to locate a stable. Back behind the main buildings the men stopped and grabbed each other. There, tethered to a post, were three horses. The post was near the back entrance of an establishment that might just be a boarding house.

Returning to the main street they saw that the building could be a saloon or dance hall with rooms on the top floor. Paul gently tried the front door and found it locked. Too early to open. Backtracking, they ambled to the back edge of the building to stand, in tandem. Their eyes were scanning the entire back area when Harry experienced excruciating pain and heard the deep thwack as something crashed into the back of his skull. He saw red, then black, falling forward into Paul. Paul was turning then to see the elevated cudgel coming down toward his pate. He quickly reached up, caught it, and jerked the man toward him across the prone body of Harry. Paul jerked the man with enough force to cause him to hit the ground where Paul heartily kicked him in the head. Watching the blood spurt, Paul slammed another kick to the groin. He then dragged the unconscious stranger over to a nearby pigsty which appeared to contain half a dozen goodly-sized hogs and threw him in.

He hurried back to check on Harry, who was deadly still, lying face down. Paul knelt and gently rolled him onto his back. He placed his ear onto his chest to gratefully hear a strong heartbeat. Then, struggling somewhat to lift the deadweight of Harry, he finally hefted him onto his shoulder and set off toward the stable.

Laying Harry onto a bale, he was relieved to see a burly young man walking toward him. "Friend, is there a physician nearby? My companion has been badly injured."

"Cut?"

"No sir. Hit in the back of his skull. I think a sawbones needs to take a look at him."

Scratching his head and shaking it all the while, the stabler admitted, "No sir. No one in these parts what can help much. But jus' mebbe' me ma could take a look-see. She raised me right well and I wuz forever gittin' into scrapes and broken bones too." He turned and motioned for Paul to bring the injured man and follow him.

Paul's eyes bugged out as the man opened the back door where the three horses were tied. *Gawd hep us!* But keeping his thoughts silent, he followed. They entered the large storage porch and went on into the kitchen where two women were busily preparing assorted foods. Paul scarcely glanced at them. On they went into a large room that housed a long bar and several tables. *Don't take us up those steps. Please.*

The young man walked directly by the stairs and through a door situated in the wall beneath the staircase. He turned, "Bring him on in here, mister. Lay him over on that couch. I'll go get my ma to come right on in."

Relieved, Paul laid Harry onto his back and into the deep cushions of a dark red velvet couch. Standing, he took in his surroundings. *Uhm... might be we done found ourselves in a nice brothel. The lady might just be the owner of this auspicious establishment. Maybe she'll have some information about Teresa.*

Hearing voices of the approaching son and mother, Paul prepared himself to greet the lady of the house. In strolled a beautiful, white-haired elderly woman, still in her bedgown. She came hurriedly toward Paul with hands outstretched. "Sir, my name is Sylvia Avondale. My son Elijah tells me your friend has suffered a severe blow to the back of his head. I shall take a look and determine if there is any help I might be able to offer." She leaned down and listened to his breathing. She gently fingered open his eyes, one at a time, to gaze deeply into them. Next, she called for Elijah to bring her scope. He swiftly bore a cone-shaped object, open at both ends, which she placed upon Harry's chest as she bent to place her ear near the narrow orifice. She moved it around several places. Motioning for Elijah to lift the man, she then placed herself at his back to listen around on either side of his spine. Finally, setting the cone aside, she gingerly parted Harry's hair and called for warm water and whiskey to be brought. Her son was swift in accommodating her demands. Sylvia mixed a goodly amount of whiskey into the warm water and bathed the wound until she could see that it need require nothing other than compresses of warm and cold until his recovery. Turning to Paul, she asked, "How long were you two expecting to be in our village?" She motioned for her son to help her get the injured man prone again and covered him with a large silk shawl.

"Might I be totally honest with you, ma'am? We are here in our attempt to find his ward, who was kidnapped by her nefarious father. The girl is around sixteen or seventeen."

"I see. Tell me more of your story, as I've already heard one version from, I believe, the man you spoke of as nefarious."

"Are they here?" Paul had suspected as much! Without waiting for her reply, he quickly continued. "This girl has blond hair, nearly the color of warm sunshine, and is very fair to gaze upon. But her life has not been one of ease. You see, she is the result of the rape of her mother by a Daniel Steadman Bordeaux. The child's mother died at her birth, and the child was taken in by the handmaid. The woman who raised her was herself set upon by the rapist and cut across her face when she attempted to rescue her charge. The girl we seek came into Lord Harry's life a number of years back, and he adopted her as his ward. I pray you understand the seriousness of our quest and will help us bring her back to safety."

"Your information explains a great deal, sir." She nodded. "And I believe you. After all, I had serious misgivings about the tale given to Elijah when the trio came tearing in here just before nightfall last eve. Since I was abed my son was up preparing the wood for cooking and was met by a man with two women shoving their way into the back entrance. I do believe the one you seek is upstairs and might be coming down shortly expecting an early meal before getting back on his journey." She stood as Harry began to moan and move about.

"Looks like our injured party might be rousing himself. Let us pray no permanent damage has been done. We shall soon know, as I'll ask him a few questions and you will be able to ascertain if the answers are lucid." She turned toward her son and reached toward him. "Here, Elijah, hand a cup of water."

As Harry roused and began glancing around Paul saw fear in his eyes, until he finally had Paul's face come into view. Then seeing the beautiful woman holding a china cup in her hand to offer him a sip, he smiled. She held it to his lips as Elijah helped to lift him upright. "What happened to me?"

Shaking her head, the lady said, "Take it slow, M'lord you've sustained a serious head injury." She held up her right hand. "Tell me how many fingers are up?"

"Three," said Harry.

"And why are you in my village, sir?"

He thought and looked around, once again looking at Paul. "Paul, are we searching for my ward?" He smiled and sat up a little bit. "Yes! We are on a mission of rescue. That is why we're here, isn't it?"

"Wonderful. From your awakening, you appear to be well enough to have your curiosity sated. And I do believe your man might have some excellent news for you." She looked up at Paul and smiled. Elijah stuffed pillows behind Harry's torso to brace him somewhat, then he and Sylvia headed toward the door.

Standing, Paul asked, "Ma'am! We need your help to trap Major Bordeaux. Ought we discuss how to go about it?"

Smiling wickedly, she said, "Trust me, sir. I have plenty of tricks up these sleeves, but you must first let me know where the woman with the red hair plays into this."

Shaking his head slightly, Paul said, "We must assume she's a cohort of the Major and not to be trusted."

"Excellent! Just leave your concerns in my hands. Make yourselves comfortable and stay out of sight." And the door was closed as she and Elijah left.

Paul turned to Harry. "How do you feel?"

"Like I've been run over by a herd of oxen! My head pounds like a sledgehammer being swung at the base of my skull."

"At least you seem to be lucid, and I must assume you shall fully recover."

"I do believe I can walk without too much trouble. Shall we try?"

Paul shook his head. "I think you need to rest here while you can. Besides, we need to keep low until we know Steadman and the redhead are taken care of. She said they are upstairs as we speak. Lady Sylvia has told us not to worry about them. I don't know what she'll do, but I firmly believe she has a plan to protect Teresa and take care of her kidnappers." Sitting on the sofa next to his boss, Paul said, "Wish I was a fly on the wall in her vicinity." And both men grinned at each other.

## CHAPTER 23

## RESCUE

IN THE KITCHEN stood a hefty red-faced man with a pristine apron snugged well beneath his armpits to protect his white shirt and trousers. "G'morning Mistress Sylvia."

"And to you too, Cousin." She poured steaming water into a china cup and dunked a tea-filled strainer into the water. Jiggling it several times she removed it and slipped in a scant spoon of sugar. "Bertrand! I'm going to require your most careful recipe this morning for two of our patrons, who undoubtedly will soon be seating themselves in the salon."

He grinned and perked up. "At your service, Sylvia! And what results will ye' be a'wantin' fer the two?"

"Oh... maybe just completely incapacitated for several hours... until the law can pick them up."

Rubbing his hands together, he said, "Leave it to me. But be sure to indicate exactly who those two are."

"Oh, never fear. You just have the recipe ready for their breakfast. I'll see that they receive it." Taking a sip, she asked, "Do you know which way Elijah went?"

"Yes, mum. I saw him out chopping wood a few minutes ago. Want me to bid him in?"

"Please."

"What have you need of Mother?"

"Ride as swiftly as possible over to Beltown and summon the Constable to come at his earliest convenience and be prepared to pick up two lawbreakers."

He turned and went directly back out and across the way to the stable where his mount was housed.

"Hurry, Lisle. Time's moving and we must be away. Get her ready to go." And he slammed the door and took the stairs two at a time down to the salon. Seeing their table already spread, and large china cups ready for their tea, he swiftly sat down and prepared to get as much down as possible so as not to be needing to stop until they were well within shouting distance of London.

As a young maid brought in platters of foods, he began filling his plate with enough for three men. He'd nearly finished before Lisle came down bearing a disheveled Teresa. Her eyes were puffy, and her clothes were wrinkled. "What's wrong with her?" he asked Lisle.

"Nothing that a bath and some clean clothes wouldn't cure. She ain't used to this sort of treatment, Dan. You dun kidnapped a real lady!"

"Shut up and fix your food and make sure she eats something too. We cannot tarry." He spoke with a mouth full, spoon stirring the air. "Gotta make London before this nightfall!"

As Lisle was seeing to her tea, slipping in a heaping spoonful of sugar, she noticed Daniel was slowing down. He appeared somewhat sleepy. "Did you not get your sufficient sleep?"

He moved a bit and sat up. "Oh yeah, I'm fine. I just need to get this done and on my way to India."

Lisle was hungrily downing her tea and shoveling in the victuals. She watched as Teresa picked at the potatoes and eggs. "Drink your tea, girl! We gotta get out of here."

"I'm just not hungry. I feel too tired to eat. I'll just drink my tea."

"Fine. I'm ready for another cup." She turned and motioned for the maid to bring a refill as she felt her hand loosen and watched as the cup fell in slow motion to the floor. She turned slowly back to see Daniel slumped over with his head in the half-empty plate, arms hanging limply down by his sides. She tried to reach for him and then felt herself unable to prevent her own decent toward the heap of warm potatoes. She closed her eyes.

As Sylvia came into the room, leading Harry and Paul, Teresa began weeping. "I knew you'd come! I knew you'd come find me." She ran to throw herself into the open arms of Lord Harry. They held each other as the smiling Sylvia and Paul witnessed their reunion. Harry put the child away from himself and held her at arm's length, "Are you alright? Have you been harmed in any way at all?"

With tears and snot running, she smiled and shook her head. "They kept me asleep most of the time."

Paul came to her rescue by shoving a white handkerchief into Harry's hand, which he used to gently wipe away the salty fluids from her face. "Thank you, Paul." Turning with Teresa still in his embrace, he continued, "And thank you, Madam Sylvia. You shall be rewarded for your trust in us, and for expeditiously handling a very dangerous matter. Have you alerted the authorities?"

"Indeed. They should be here within an hour or so. Until then, my cousin Bertrand will house the pair in safety, if not in comfort, until they can be escorted to jail to await their trials."

Harry, with his attention focused back upon his ward, said, "We need to see to your comfort, child." And then to Madam Sylvia, he asked, "Will you be so kind as to see to the toilette and comfort of Mistress Teresa? You shall be well paid."

Pitching her hands into the air and waving them around a bit, she said, "Why, by all means! We can easily abide by your wishes. I'll have her ready in traveling attire within an hour. You two gents, seat yourselves and enjoy a filling repast until then. The constable should be arriving soon, and your daughter shall be better prepared to eat after she's bathed and comfortably dressed." Reaching for Teresa, she said, "Come, child. Let us see to your ablutions." And reaching to gently touch the bruise at her temple, she added, "And I'll take care of this too." Then she loudly called out as they strode toward the broad stairs, "Bring bath water to my suite, now!"

The entourage accompanying Constable Frappington was quite taken with the surroundings in which they found themselves and became indulgent to a point of fawning when they listened to the story of the abduction from the lips of the beautiful blond Mistress of Gravelstone, Ward of Martinsgale. Once every embellishment was given and understood, Constable Frappington departed the village of Cullbert with much flourish, and the pair of criminals shackled and shamed, staring through the black bars of the coach. Frappington shouted his stern assurances that they would be awaiting their trials in Newgate as the several onlookers cheered.

## CHAPTER 24
## REUNITED

A FULL WEEK had transpired since the abduction. Virginia screamed as she saw the trio trotting toward the back gate. "They've got her! They've got her! Come quick! Mistress Teresa is home!" She began running toward them, closing the distance in a few seconds. "Oh, Mistress Teresa, praise be to Jesus you're home safe!" She fell to her knees and squalled mightily, causing Gretchen to stop to see about her even before she ran to grab her beloved child tightly to her bosom. The pair were allowed the time needed to assuage the emotions that had played havoc in their hearts for the past long hours and days.

Jimmy had secured the reigns from the hands of Lord Harry and Detective Paul, as well as the strands, left hanging from the steed upon which Teresa had been sitting when she unceremoniously leapt from her saddle.

Sydney was standing, hat in hand, watching with tear-filled eyes as the lost daughter of the house of Martingale was welcomed home.

The kitchen crew were all holding each other with hugs and smiles. Elizabeth and Calvin were arm in arm with hearts full of joy at the scene before them.

Lord Harry stepped forward and said, "You, of this house, are held in grateful appreciation for everything accomplished in seeing that our

Teresa was found in time. We shall never forget this day nor this date. Mistress Constance, please record this date on our calendar to be celebrated henceforth every year as Teresa's Day!" He grinned; then, ever the pragmatist, he shouted, "And now let us all get about and back to our routines." Turning to Gretchen, he said, "My dearest lady, see that your daughter is reinstated to excellent health and help her to re-establish herself into her rightful place here. She's suffered quite a traumatic episode and shall more than likely need to vent her adventures to your sympathetic ear."

"Indeed, Lord Harry." She led her beloved girl toward the open kitchen door.

Within just a few short hours, Martingale Manor was humming along as if nothing of import had taken over and interrupted the flow of matters.

Three days later, as everyone gathered for the evening meal, Lord Harry spoke to the group to assure them that Major Steadman was, indeed, incarcerated awaiting his trial in London. Word had been received from Earl, who was on his way back to Martingale and ought to arrive shortly. Gretchen quickly spoke up, "And what of his accomplice? The red-haired woman?"

"Well, I do not know, Mistress Gretchen. I simply did not ask. Why do you concern yourself about her?"

"I'd advise us all to be on the alert for trouble which could arise from her if she is freed. I continue to receive warnings of one ilk or another that contain images of a hank of red hair. From whose head it comes, I am not privy to—yet! But I suggest we all be on guard, and I suggest you, Lord Harry, advise Paul and Earl, once he arrives, to act with due diligence in this regard."

"Rest assured, Mistress Gretchen. We shall!"

## CHAPTER 25

## BACK TO NORMAL?

"OH, THERE YOU are, mistress! Madame Alexandra is searching for you everywhere. Do you have a moment to attend her?"

"Why yes, Missus Williston. Is she in her workrooms?"

"I do believe so. That's where she was not ten minutes past."

"Thank you. I shall hurry up."

Halfway up the center staircase, Teresa met Harry. "Oh, Teresa, my dear. Alexandra is searching for you. She needs your attendance desperately, or so she said."

"Headed there now, Lord Harry. And thank you."

Entering a beehive of activity, Teresa paused for a moment to observe the evident chaos within the well-lit room. Several girls were busy in the window's light, stitching diligently at assorted fabrics. Another two were cutting cloth and appeared as though they were randomly aiming the shears in every direction. Madame Alexandra stood, in deep thought, before a tall, headless form of muslin-covered wire, adjusting the draped lace, first one way and then another.

Teresa cleared her throat, and Alexandra spun around and wagged a long finger in the girl's face. "Thank God you're finally here. I sent word for your presence at least half an hour ago. Time is of the essence, my dear young lady. If I am to see to the completion of everything that must be done, then I am obliged to have cooperation from everyone, including your highness."

Properly stung, Teresa's eyes filled with unshed tears. "Truly, I am deeply sorry to be the one to have brought about the unsettling of your contentment. I apologize as profusely as possible, and beg your forgiveness, madam."

Suddenly a look of contrition came rushing over the face of Alexandra, and she bowed deeply. "No, child. You forgive me, please." Standing up to face her very important client, she continued, "I fear I allowed my mouth to overtake my good manners. You are in no way to blame for my uncouth actions. In defense, I simply say that the orders from your mentor, Lord Harry, have stretched to the limit my ability to cope. I took my roiling frustration out on the only person who truly does not deserve it. I beg your forgiveness."

Taking the hand of Alexandra, Teresa said, "Dear lady, if there's anyone who can understand the penchant we humans possess to cause us to make fools of ourselves by the overrunning of our words, then you are looking at her. Without further ado... you are forgiven."

"Thank you, dear." She breathed deeply and exhaled with some little force. "Now come and tell me what you think of this design." She lifted a slip of paper to display the sketch of a proposed gown.

With a small gasp, Teresa spouted, "Why, it's the most beautiful gown I've ever seen. Could this possibly be for me?"

"Yes, dear. I thought your coloring would be complimented greatly with the pale ivory of the fabric. I want to use heavy satin, since the weather will be colder, and I will be able to line it well to help maintain body heat."

"You think of everything, madam."

"That is my job. I'm not known as the Haute couturier of England for nothing!" She smiled in triumph.

She led Teresa over to a corner, where there sat a youngster of no more than ten years, busily forming open blossoms and buds as well as stems and leaves, all out of that same ivory satin. "This young lady is my sister's daughter and my protégé. Amanda, meet the lady of this manor, Mademoiselle Teresa Jane Lyons-Constantine."

The child leapt from the high stool and curtseyed before the beautiful lady. "I'm very pleased to make your acquaintance, my lady."

"Oh, darling. Thank you for that. It is indeed my great pleasure to make your acquaintance also. We must find special things to do together when you find a moment's solitude."

Smiling shyly, young Amanda climbed back onto the stool and picked up where she'd left off. Teresa lifted one of the blossoms to examine it. Perfect! The satin flower appeared as though it had fallen from its tether, ready to nestle upon the gown. Teresa could envision it, among many more, adrift down the side-front of the dress she was to wear for her debut. The sketch had shown a wreath of smaller blossoms and buds encircling the low neckline of the gown, as well as snugged within the gathers at the puffed sleeves, and scattered over the belled skirt. For the first time in her life, she realized she had become excited about a dress. It was the grandest dress ever seen, and she was looking forward to the wearing of it.

Teresa, dismissed by her dressmaker, left the busy area to see if she could locate her mother. She felt a huge need to be comforted by the rock of her existence. Hearing a voice behind her, she stopped as Madame Alexandra called, "Mistress Teresa! When you see your mother, could you please send her to me as quickly as she can come?"

"Yes. By all means, I shall."

Lord Harry had Teresa at the desk in his library. He was busy making the list of invitees, while Teresa was writing them out to be inserted into their envelopes. Each one would be delivered by the end of the month. It was now September, and the ball was slated for November 22. The moon would be full during those evenings and would lend an especial aura to the celebration.

Young Gordy Hammet took every available opportunity to find his way out to Covington Court to port the stacks of mail for Lord Harry—and to hopefully catch a glimpse of "Her Loveliness," Virginia Haviland. Gordy had been privileged to catch glimpses of her nearly every time he delivered the post. She was ever in the presence of Mistress Teresa. He figured her to be the personal lady's maid since her clothes indicated such rank. Gordy thought her the most beautiful girl he had ever laid eyes upon.

After work each day, at home with Da and Ma, he might be caught daydreaming when he was supposed to be seeing to the wood box, or hauling water, or some such thing. How could he help it if a vision of her kept sneaking in? She was beautiful. Da and Ma would understand one day when he was older and had made enough, or had enough put back, to be asking for her hand. At night, his dreams were filled with her soft body lying next to his.

"Morning Master Martingale, here's the mail for this morning. I'll more likely be back later on today, as the post is due in again from London before dark. I can bring whatever might be coming in when I'm making my way home. Won't be no trouble to swing by sir."

Taking the stack from the young man, Harry was amused to watch as Gordy craned his head this way and that, knowing the boy was hoping to view the lovely maid Virginia. Teresa and her maid were in the library, so he said to the young man, "I'm wondering if you'd be so kind as to come on in to the library to retrieve a stack of invitations to take them back with you for distribution. I'd be most grateful."

Brightening, he chirped, "I'd be more than happy to, sir. That's my job, now ain't it?"

Gordy was whistling all the way back into the village if anyone cared to listen.

## CHAPTER 26

# PHOENIX RISING

(THE GRAND CASTLE of Gravelstone Abbey had been practically vacant for the past decade. The only resident, besides the skeleton crew which maintained its viability for her, was the recluse Lady Sarah Hashbrooke Constantine. She was mad as a hatter, thin to the point of death. Those few surrounding her lamented the fact that she refused to even allow any doctor to come near. She ate with her claw-like fingers and smelled awful. She would not allow herself to be bathed or otherwise tended to.

The solicitors for the property had been informed that everything was in their hands and must be held until her death. Then, since the dynasty would have died out, it could become the property of the solicitors. Whatever they desired to do with it, the Lady really did not care.

Ever since her precious daughter's death had been accepted, both parents had declined. Lord Leopold had died, they said, of a broken heart not even a year after the passing of his beloved child. But for some reason as yet unknown to mankind, Lady Sarah lived, even though life held no meaning for her. She simply existed day by day, and now was simply wasting away. She did not have sense enough to understand the precarious state of her heath—not that she would have much cared.)

Harry came into the library with the stack of mail just delivered by Gordy. "My dear, do you suppose you might like to visit your new property soon? A letter from your solicitors has recommended you accompany young Skylar for a grand tour as quickly as you can find the time. He has graciously offered to escort you and allow you to become acquainted with the caretakers and to see what repairs, if any, or alterations you desire. The work could commence and might be completed before the time you will assume claim by your very presence."

"That might be a very good step for me to take." Looking up at her mentor, she said, "Yes. Please let Mister Preston know that I shall allow him to accompany me—at his convenience. Since he must come all the way from London for this venture."

"Very well, Teresa. I'll send word to that effect by return post."

Some days later, when Teresa was preparing to visit her property with Skylar, Missus Helen advised her young mistress that perhaps she might consider taking a crew of servants with her to see to making the common area clean since no one had been about the place for ages. Surely she would need to tour as much as possible before returning to Martingale Manor. Consequently, Teresa gave the job of assembling the crew to Helen who within a few frantic moments had gathered quite an efficient group to follow along, prepared to do whatever was necessary for the comfort of Mistress Teresa.

The carriages topped the rise and stopped. Teresa rose from her seat, opened the door, and was helped down to view the vast grassland where sheep were grazing. She stared in awe at the magnificent towers of her property, Gravelstone Abbey. She shook her head, disbelieving this estate was hers. Her inheritance. Her mother's home and her ancestors' for hundreds of years back.

Teresa thought for sure that she would experience a sense of fear upon seeing this home for the first time. Just the opposite was true. There came over her a feeling of pure peace and joy, a "coming home" feeling. Excitement permeated her thoughts as she climbed back inside the confines of the carriage. Skylar tapped the roof with his cane, the driver clicked to the horses, and the group moved forward.

The feeling of peace wavered as they rode on. The nearer they came to the walls the more disturbed she became. There were broken windows in too many places. The gardens were no longer productive, except for weeds and overgrowth.

Coming through the massive and scrolled iron gates, which were leaning drunkenly from rusted hinges, she began to cry. *Dear God, let there be someone here to greet me. A caretaker. Anyone. How could the solicitors of this property allow such dereliction?* she wondered.

"Have us taken to the back, please, Skylar. I need to see if there is anyone around."

He spoke directions to the boy and had them conveyed to the driver. The rest of the carriages—two others—followed suit.

Coming up through waist-high weeds, the driver made way to a small clearing near a massive wooden door set into the side of the discolored gray stone edifice.

"Stop!" called Teresa. "Someone is here. I see a cat and I hear the cackle of a hen. And see, yonder, a boy running toward the trees." She pointed. Virginia stared, wide-eyed.

The attendees began to dismount. Teresa was surrounded by Lord Harry, Skylar, Virginia, Gretchen, Sydney, and several maids, with assorted cleaning supplies—in case Mistress Teresa might want a particular area prepared.

Everyone jumped when the door was flung open with viciousness and out came a crumpled old man. "Who ye be? Ye ain't got no business 'round here! Th' Lady says so! Ye best be gittin' on yer way, 'acause ye bound to be lost! Now git!"

Skylar bravely stepped forward as the old man reached back inside to bring out a pitchfork.

Raising his hands in submission, Skylar said, "My good man, we have come bearing the owner of this manse, the Mistress Teresa Jane Lyons-Constantine."

Everyone drew back as an ear-splitting scream came from above!

The screaming faded, then began to swell louder. One could easily surmise that the screamer was coming forward, although travelling away down halls, or steps, and flailing through the massive innards of the castle. Every stone quivered from the feral screeching.

The old man turned and ran back inside and slammed the door. Soon, the screaming ceased. The company stood still and silent, waiting to see what would happen next. No one spoke, nor even whispered. No one moved as if to depart this mad place, least of all Teresa and Gretchen. They had a premonition that this just may be some kinsman.

They waited.

The big door creaked open enough for a small girl to exit out into the weak sunlight. She squinted toward the strangers and asked, "What you want here? We be all alone and fearful of strangers. Our lady is very sick and can't see anyone. She needs you to leave. Please."

Gretchen stepped forward and knelt in front of the little girl. "Don't be afraid, child. I am simply a scarred old woman with not a harmful bone in my body. My name is Gretchen, and I lived here when I was a girl. If you will allow me, I can heal your lady. Now, go ask her if she would like to feel better."

The child turned and ran back into the dark interior and closed the door.

After about three minutes, it opened again, and a horribly disheveled woman came outside and stepped quietly toward Teresa. She reached out to touch her long golden hair. "My Melanie! You've come home!" She turned and screamed, "My Melanie's back from the dead! My Melanie's alive!" And she ran out into the high weeds screaming at the top of her lungs, scattering chickens, pigs, and goats. Gretchen ran after her and caught her around the waist. As thin and emaciated as the woman was, Gretchen was easily able to lead the old crone and brought her back to the rear clearing, near to the house. Holding the scrawny woman close to her side, Gretchen was whispering into her ear, and everyone watched as the woman began to smile.

By that time, the crew was inside the filthy kitchen and had begun self-relegating the scullery crew to set up their jobs in the order most efficiently performed.

Teresa stood, immobile, tears of fear and trepidation streaking her cheeks, and somewhat in shock at finding the woman she now knew to be her grandmother still alive. The mother of her mother. Coming forward as Gretchen brought the old woman into the house, Teresa asked the young girl where the rooms of the lady were. "Please lead us there immediately. And bring fresh linens."

"Ma'am, we ain't got nothin' like that. We barely got food to eat. Me ma lets me come home ever so often to bathe up and change me clothes, but we ain't got no linens to speak of. Lady Sarah don't allow nobody to do nothin' for her at all. She's rotting as far as I can tell. We all expects her to be dead ever morning, but she just don't die. Clarence keeps giving her what food we can come up with, and she picks over what she wants and leaves the rest."

"How many people are here beside Lady Sarah?" asked Gretchen.

"Just the two of us mostly. Me and Andrew James. He's the gardener and caretaker. I just keep the place clean and try to make sure the Lady ain't dead yet." She smiled.

"No one else ever comes?" Teresa asked.

"Me ma ever now and again. She usually comes to take stuff off to our place 'cause she says none of it'll ever be used again, and she sells what she can to feed Pa and my older brother. You may have seen him, but he left soon's he could get away. He heard you coming first... probably gone to tell Ma."

As they were attempting to settle Lady Sarah, Teresa and Gretchen were taking turns in the kitchen to get water heated so they could bathe the lady. The rest of the crew had flung windows open to the cold air and were sweeping out bucketsful of dirt, ashes, and greasy dust.

Even Lord Harry and Skylar were doing their part outside with Andrew James to find eggs for food. Then Andrew said, "If'n ye can stay, I'll kill a hen and'll cook 'er fer yer supper." To which both men shook their heads.

Harry said, "Thank you, Andrew, but we cannot stay much longer. We must return to Covington Court. But we will come back soon to do what we can to help prepare this place for the Lady Teresa."

From the looks of things, it appeared as though the few people that lived at the estate occupied only three of the massive rooms and the kitchen area. Harry was sure the rest of the building was in dire need of care since he and Skylar had strolled through only a minuscule area of the entire structure. There was a tremendous amount of cleaning and refurbishing and corrective construction to be accomplished before Teresa could take residence. This would require months of concerted effort to get a decent portion of the huge Abbey in readiness for the comfort of its new mistress. Harry needed to inquire as to the best construction engineer to oversee the project as soon as possible.

The kettles were heating, and Teresa searched for a washbasin and a slab of lye soap. Gretchen had already removed her own petticoats and torn them into strips to use for bathing and toweling. The cot upon which Sarah had spent most of her days had been stripped and the feather mattress and bolster were thrown over a thorn bush, outside in the back, to air as much as possible.

All the while Lady Sarah lay on a low divan singing softly and smiling as she drooled. Her teeth had long ago fallen out, and Gretchen knew she was dying from the poison invading her heart from the filth within her mouth. However, she was deeply determined to do all in her power to reinstate this woman to the point of being able to truly recognize that Teresa was indeed the child of Melanie and the inheritor of Gravelstone Abbey. With Skylar in attendance, nothing but surety would be forthcoming as to the legitimacy of Teresa's claim.

Bringing several eggs, Lord Harry and Skylar entered the kitchen. The maids had done a tremendous job of getting the place much cleaner. They placed the basket of eggs on a table, and Harry said to the young girl, "If you can locate a pan, please cook the eggs for the lady. Make them soft so they can be fed to her more easily."

Then speaking to his companion, he said, "Skylar, we'd better take Teresa back to Covington Court. Knowing Gretchen, she will want to stay, but she will have a coach at hand for when she desires to return. I'll leave the maids here as well."

"Good! I am ready. Let me get Mistress Teresa. I'll be right back."

"No! Skylar! No! I am not leaving. I shall remain here with Gretchen and my grandmother. She is in desperate condition, and I will not leave her now. Particularly since I have just found her! I cannot leave." Shaking a dirty rag at him, she said, "You and Lord Harry go on back. But I want you to bring linens, soaps, pails, feather mattresses, and food. Lots of food. And bring red wine. She needs red wine."

"But...."

"No buts! Now go and come back with everything we need. I'll see you tomorrow."

"Yes, ma'am." Then she heard him mutter under his breath, "I can see you are plenty hard-headed! But I do love a determined woman!"

By the next morning Harry and Skylar, along with a full complement of willing laborers, arrived back at the service entrance of Gravelstone Abbey to find that a veritable miracle had occurred. The women had somehow transformed the kitchens into a clean and comfortable living area. It soon became evident that serviceable furniture had been gleaned from other areas of the mansion. There were even clean sheets upon the cots, and the feather mattresses had been replaced.

The greatest miracle was the sight of Lady Sarah, clean, brushed, and dressed in simple attire. The only two who were the worse for wear were Teresa and Gretchen. It appeared they had not taken one minute for themselves. Both were in dire need of baths and a good rest. Even the seven scullery maids appeared cleaner by comparison.

"I see you have been successful in your endeavors! What a difference you have made in here. And Andrew has even begun cutting away more of the overgrowth outside. I could actually see the chicken coops." Harry laughed.

"You'll be happy to know that I've brought along Missus Helen to relegate the help. My greatest difficulty lay in the fact that when I asked for help to come, there were so many I had to have Helen glean them out. I believe, under her capable guidance, we have brought more than enough hands to get this place on the initial road to recovery and, don't argue with me now, Teresa. You must return to Martingale to recuperate. Leave this for the time being in capable hands. You have other pressing duties to attend to."

"Alright, Lord Harry. I shall do that, but I must bring Grandmother with me. Gretchen tells me she truly does not have long left of this life. She sees death in her countenance. Even I can see it. So, I want her near me as much as possible. I am praying that she will be able to ken exactly who I am before she's gone from this earth."

"Very well. Get her and yourselves prepared and we'll return straight away."

CHAPTER 27

# TRANSFORMATION

SKYLAR RETURNED TO London just a few days after Lady Sarah was brought to Covington Court. He entirely missed the wondrous beginnings of her resurgence of mental cognizance.

Gretchen and Teresa spent every spare moment with Lady Sarah. Teresa saw Madame Alexandra reluctantly agree to fit the crone with simple proper clothing, beginning with underclothes and bed gowns. The seamstress was as thrilled as Mistress Teresa when the old lady finally understood that the beautiful new clothing was for her frail and dying body. "Why, I am not worthy of such extravagance, child. This old woman is beyond help, I'm afraid."

"But, Grandmother, if you desire, you may choose which of these garments you'd like to be wearing when that time of departure does ultimately arrive. What about that?" asked Teresa, smiling.

Laughing, tittering like a *jeune fille*, the old woman, now toothless and emaciated, was seen by Teresa, for a flickering instant, as the ravishing beauty of her youth.

"Daughter, if I had my desires laid out before me, I would choose you," laying her gnarled fingers over the smooth flesh of her granddaughter, "to be my progeny. I do believe we are something of kinswomen since you favor my darling Melanie."

THE MEDALLION

"Soon, Grandmother, your thoughts will begin to fill in those gaps of self-preservation by memory loss with the assurance that I, Teresa, am indeed the child of your child. Once you begin to ken this quavering sense of the past, then all will be explained in clarity for your complete understanding."

Lady Sarah smiled, gazing off toward the sunlit window, as Teresa watched a tear form and slip gently down the wrinkled cheek.

Cleaned, coiffed, and properly dressed, Teressa and Gretchen, followed by Virginia, were seen to be escorting the old lady into the large dining room for the evening repast. Lord Harry himself saw to her seating at his left hand, Teresa at his right. And, allowing no room for argument or glancing to attempt to "catch" any raised eyebrows from his staff, Harry insisted that Gretchen be seated at the "foot"—directly across from him.

Gretchen, not wanting to draw any more attention to herself than was already the case, allowed this honor. "Sir Harry, I thank you for this recognition, but beg, sir, in the future to be given the option of choice for the taking of my supper, sir."

Throwing his head back, he laughed quite hardily. "Ma'am! You! You, madam, are more fit to grace this table, or indeed this house, than anyone in present company. Without your unwavering commitment to us all, I'm assuredly convinced that quite a number of us would not be alive to enjoy this repast!" Slapping his hands upon the carved arms of the elaborate chair, he said, "Now, let us enjoy the wonder of this special evening and this well-presented table."

It had been seen to that the foods for the "old lady" were properly ground, mashed, or diced into dishes fit for babies. Being toothless did have some benefits, of sorts.

Seeing the woman ingesting her food, an idea came to Harry. "Gretchen! Please, allow me to interrupt your enjoyment of this meal for only a moment?"

"Why yes, Lord Harry. Of what do you care to speak?"

"Since I know, for a fact that you invented a number of items for the better functioning of varied tasks at this establishment, I have the bright idea that you just might be able to come up with some sort of external mandible that could be utilized for the mastication of viands, either at table or possibly prior to. What do you think?"

"Your suggestion is vastly appreciated; however, sir, I do think that your idea has already come to fruition."

"Really? When? How? Is it obtainable?"

"I do believe a number of advancements have been made rather recently, sir. With your permission, I shall take it upon myself to see Graham Blackman, a tinkerer, and blade-sharpener of my acquaintance who had an apparatus such as you speak of worn within his own oral cavity... and was rather adept at utilizing its potential. It is because of his extensive travels that he will be able to help us locate the ideal person to help in this endeavor."

Sitting back in his chair, Lord Harry was enthralled by Gretchen's exposé. "I swear, ma'am, you are a veritable artesian well of knowledge and information. Never have I met, nor had such pleasure in the acquaintance of, anyone with knowledge as extensive as yours." Looking around his table at the few gathered there, he said, "I've decided to place Gretchen over the governesses and tutors of Martingale Manor. They shall take instruction from her as to what shall be taught to our children."

Giggling gently, Teresa spoke up, "Dear Lord Harry, and exactly which children are to be instructed by our non-existent governesses and tutors?"

Grinning and appearing properly chastised, he laughed, "Well! The exact ones that shall, one day, scatter themselves throughout these halls!" He continued, "Never too soon to think of the future, my dear!"

Everyone laughed, even the toothless old lady.

## CHAPTER 28
## DEBUT DANGER

KNOWING THAT WITH each day's passing Teresa was becoming more excited over her upcoming debut—albeit a debut into the society of the outlying country estates—Lord Harry had also seen to it that a goodly number of very prominent and worthy young men from London had received invitations for this auspicious event. He had been thorough in his assessment of each gentleman. He was determined to protect her against any suitor he considered might have perversions—such as a propensity for fancy women, or gambling, or too handy with spirits—and might take this golden opportunity to ingratiate themselves to his ward, by lies or wily behavior.

But knowing that there was a certainty of failure, and against all odds for such a serpent would likely slither in beneath the floorboards, Harry had enlisted Earl and Paul to take up residence and to maintain themselves in "high alert" mode. The household was informed that the two men were to be spoken of as "cousins" to Lord Harry in the hopes that no one attending the ball might suspect their real positions.

They made themselves "at home," and might just be observed alone or in each other's company in unexpected areas of the mansion. Before long, everyone soon "lost sight of them" as they became such an integral part of the household—no longer taken as strangers but accepted as other members of the family. The men congratulated themselves for the ease which wove them into the fabric of life at Covington Court, thereby assuring Master Harry of their abilities to unobtrusively guard his beautiful ward.

Travelers could see the magnificent mansion of Covington Court ablaze with light from as far away as the last crest, about two miles from where they would enter the huge black iron gates.

As coachmen pulled their carriages in tandem up to the wide stone steps, the elegantly gowned women and nattily dressed gentlemen were handed up toward the massive open doors of Martingale Manor.

Young groomsmen guided the horses out, around the east of the house, and down toward the stables, where it would be determined if the horses would be stabled for some while, or if the owners would be expected to leave before morning to return to their homes. If their occupants were expecting to stay for some while, quarters had been prepared for the coachmen, runners, or baggage boys.

It appeared that Lord Harry had considered the comfort of everyone attending this auspicious gathering.

Coming in alone under the cover of darkness, amid a veritable pile-up of carriages, rode a lone man dressed in black, astride a black stallion. His top hat slanted low over his eyes. His heavy cape was wrapped over his chest. He jumped down and handed his steed over to a man who materialized from nowhere, and said, "Keep 'im close by. When I'm ready t'leave, I'll hold up a white glove... Dunna' fail me. Bring him immediately. Here..." And he tossed a coin to the man.

Bowing deeply without a spoken word, the "groomsman" nodded in understanding as he led the horse off toward the pair of huge fir trees that guarded the entrance to Gretchen and Sydney's formal gardens. *What blessed luck!* he thought. *I must alert my compatriot quickly. The man surely is out of his element; couldn't hide his brogue.*

Inside, the family stood at the ready in a formal reception line. As guests assembled, their names and ranks were heralded and they moved forward to bow or curtsey to the Lord and his attendant party. Upon taking their leave of the line, they headed toward the huge tables near the edges of the massive room, which held more food than could be considered to actually exist out here in the country. Where it all came from became a topic of conversation as guests gorged themselves and downed the assorted drinks and punches. All the while, an orchestra was performing gently from the wide, open hall far above the ballroom. As soon as the reception line was winding down, Harry thought he heard a muffled scream. After a moment's thought, he attributed the sound as coming from some high-pitched laughter. After all, the cacophony in the great hall was ear-splitting, to put it mildly.

Looking around he located his ward—the stunning Teresa. His heart skipped a beat as he made his way into her presence. Bowing before the girl, he reached for her gloved hand. She lifted herself toward him and had a sudden mad thought. *I love him. I shall not be deterred.* He smiled and led her out onto the center of the ballroom floor. Looking up at the orchestra, he nodded, and they began a slow, sedate number where Teresa would be shown off to every advantage.

He lifted her beautiful body into his arms and swept her around as the other couples soon began to join them. Expecting no less, Harry was interrupted soon—too soon—and he allowed Teresa to be taken from his arms. How quickly it happened! She was suddenly gone, but after all, that was the reason for this debut: To seek out the perfect man for his darling girl. He suddenly realized that he did not want to go through with this, but it was too late.

Standing with men who were nearly strangers to him, he listened to endless-mindless chatter about such mundane subjects as weather, unrest amongst their tenants, ever-increasing demands from the unwashed, and ill-fed underlings that were expected to go the extra mile to care for the needs of their overlords even before those of themselves. Harry thought, *My God, have they no compassion? Have these not hired good people that can be trusted to oversee the interests of everyone? Humph! Perhaps I must look to my own affairs more closely. I had better query Mister Poiler... sweep around my own doorstep before judging too closely.* And so, he joined their commiserations.

Soon, the conversation began to lag, and Sir Vincent Hadley looked at Harry and said, "Now, old man, do we or do we not have tables set up for a few games somewhere out of the way of this folderol?"

"Of course. Come, gentlemen, I'll lead the way."

Upon entering the smoke-filled room, Harry was nearly sick. *Good Lord, how can they stand this? Oh well, so much for fresh air. I suppose I ought sit for a while, to see how I do at gambling.*

Soon realizing every hand dealt was a dud, he stood, bowed slightly, and took his leave. Coming out of the room, he closed the door tightly behind him. Off to his right he, being out of the line of sight, watched as one of his hired men escorted a gentleman that sported a full beard out of the house. They exited through the windowed doors between the library and the day room across from where he was hidden in the shadows.

Quietly Lord Harry slipped through the dark room and quickly out the same doors Earl had exited with the bearded stranger. Keeping to the shadows, he listened.

"So, friend, confess. Tell me yer business here."

Twisting against his captor, the man spat upon the ground at Earl's feet and said, "Jes' a tad o' retribution! I wuz watchin' when ye devils cast me uncle in fer them hogs! Thank th' Virgin he was out cold and never knowed what 'is fate were."

"I see! So, you are one of the three men we were chasing. And, for what it's worth... your uncle nigh killed my friend with that cudgel. He had it comin'! Now, what'd you intend on accomplishing here, anyway?"

"Th' maiden was goin' to have th' same fate! Yes, indeed. I had her sty already picked out. Bein' as how I don't own one, I wuz gonna give her corpse over to the butcher's hogs this night, fancy dress an' all!"

"Speakin' of fancy dress... where'd you find these duds?" Earl asked and tweaked the lapel of the man's fine black coat.

"Lisle did it. She hollered as they wuz takin' 'er away for me to git 'em." He grinned.

"Don't think these fancy clothes will keep your rump out of prison, friend. You've just confessed that you intended to murder the girl and toss her to the hogs."

Shaking his head wildly, the man said, "Naw sir! Ye' ain't got no witness. This comes down to yer word against mine." He grinned in the face of his captor. Earl had to back up somewhat to remove himself from the fetid breath of the man.

Harry stepped into the light as Paul came off the end of the stone porch. Harry smiled. Paul spoke, "No, friend. There are three witnesses to your confession." Turning to Lord Harry, he asked, "Do you want both of us to port him to London?"

"No. I think we'll lock him in here for the remainder of the night. I want a good look at him tomorrow and to ask him a few questions about Major Steadman and the redhead."

Suddenly the man grabbed the holstered pistol at Earl's hip and swung it up to aim directly at the heart of Lord Harry.

A loud shot sounded, and Earl and Harry watched as the firearm swung down and the man's arm and body followed. They glanced to see Paul putting his revolver back into its holster. "Guess that takes care of that! Eh?"

All three men knelt upon the grass to see if the stranger was dead. His eyes were open, and they locked into Harry's. With difficulty and labored breaths, he said, "Me name is William Chambers. The man what hired me and me uncle left still owing us the money he promised. I think Lisle knew and wanted me to at least get some o' 'is duds."

Lord Harry leaned closer and asked, "How much did he owe you?"

"My share would'a been five pound. I wuz intendin' to do somethin' fer me ma. She lives in the village where y'all found th' maid."

"What name ought I search for to let her know?"

"MayBelle Chambers," he whispered. As the man drew in a wheezing breath, Harry noted blood streaming from his mouth, but the stranger continued. "She's old and alone. I was doin' this fer her. I swear." The man's eyes rolled up and his head lolled to the side.

Harry said, "Let's get him around the back to the kitchen and see if Gretchen can help us with him."

Harry had one leg, Paul the other, and Earl staggered backward holding the man by his armpits. It took nearly a quarter an hour before they got to the garden door. There, stood Gretchen. "Lord Harry! What has happened? I was sent back here but did not know exactly why… until now! Who is this dead man?"

"You already know he's dead?"

"I am led to come pronounce him thus. There is no doubt this man was shot in the back. The missile nicked an artery on its way, and is now lodged in the breastbone." Looking at the disbelieving men, she said, "Perhaps I ought to call one of the doctors out here to agree with my findings. Make it official, you know."

Gretchen grabbed a dirty tablecloth from the stack by the door and placed it across the divan. They laid him out on it where she got a good look at him. "I feel certain now about my premonition concerning the red hair. This man fits well into the vision I received about a hank of red hair. I am relieved of that stress at last."

"I agree, gentlemen. Gretchen, will you be so kind as to fetch Doctor Bristleman here? I trust him to make the pronouncement of this man's death and see to getting his body sent back to Village Cullbert." Turning to look at Earl and Paul, he added, "We'll need to inform the authorities as well as his mother. Will you two go with me to approach his mother and give her some plausible story as to his demise? I want to investigate his claim of the poverty of his mother, and possibly give her some sort of stipend." Lord Harry began to walk away toward the front entrance of his home, back to the soiree of his dear ward.

*Ever the cool and aloof lord,* thought Earl. *Takes everything in stride as if he knows the answers to life's problems. Must be nice.*

Harry's eyes met the eyes of Teresa as he entered the large hall from the ascent of the front stairs. His heart did a catch, and he was struck anew with the beauty and vulnerability of the girl. *My God, but she is unparalleled by any female ever seen. I must see that she is not taken advantage of by anyone! If only our circumstances were different. I fear living to regret giving her over to another.*

Once more Teresa was beset with "inward tremors", which invariably came on each time she was in his company. His studious aura... the unwavering knowledge that when he had her in his sight, she knew there was no interference into his world but the object of his scrutiny. She wondered at the surety that she had fallen in love with the man. From the time she first saw him, she'd sensed a deep desire to own him. "What is love anyway?" she spoke, surprised at the sound of her own voice which gave nothing away as to the deep emotions roiling within her frame. "Where have you been, Lord Harry? I've searched every face for at least half an hour expecting to find you at any moment, hoping you'd come dance with me again. Time is passing and I grow tired. I've danced with dozens of men but none as smooth as you." Teresa smiled into his eyes, and he smiled back.

"Of course, my dear. Come. Let us try this next set." He was beset with inward tremors from her touch and not unpleasantly so. Not entirely caught off guard as desire beyond simple caring flowed through his body and warmed his soul.

Harry had much on his mind and heart, but his greatest concern was for Teresa to be happy and carefree-at least this night, and then for as long as he could maintain that the events occurring this night had not transpired. How indebted he was to Gretchen. He was relieved to be able to place the responsibility for the ultimate disclosure to Teresa of the ultimate sentencing of her natural father upon that amazing woman. Gretchen would handle it with aplomb when given the proper time for the reveal. Harry relaxed and enjoyed this dance with his darling. *By Jove, I find it very difficult indeed to give this lady over to another for marriage. Quite a quandary I find myself in. This could get sticky!*

As the dance concluded, Skylar rushed up and took Teresa's hand. "My dear, please, just one more dance."

"Please, no, Skylar. Truly I hate to turn you down, but my feet are dead! I simply cannot do another turn. But, come, take me over near the windows. Let us seat ourselves and rest a little. Do you mind?"

"Of course. And I shall bring you refreshment." As Skylar walked away with her hand in the crook of his arm, Harry watched and felt a stab of genuine jealousy directly to his heart.

At the still-dark hour of six in the morning, the orchestra began to case their instruments, and yet a number of partiers still groaned. What did they expect? The musicians were worn out and sleepy. Pushing themselves to find their quarters for a few hours' rest before breakfast and leaving for their return trip to London, the musicians would snap their cases with gratefulness that another lucrative concert performance for them had come and gone.

The guests who had rooms in the house had long since left the ballroom and were even now sound asleep in their sumptuous beds. Mostly those who were still around were the bachelors hoping for one more opportunity to impress the beautiful heiress. She was the meal ticket they had been born for. If only they could be lucky enough to convince her or her guardian, Lord Harry Martingale.

Several young men and at least two widowers were still holding out for another day, pinning their hopes on doing some deep and meaningful courting of this ripe plum. Few had seen in the past anyone who could hold a candle to the beauty of this girl, let alone the wealth accompanying her. She was surely one of the richest prizes to be found in many a moon. They just needed the opportunity. Oh, the promise of possibilities to be found in a new day!

## CHAPTER 29

# JUST DUE FOR TWO

LORD-MAJOR DANIEL Steadman Bordeaux was sentenced to a life of penury upon the Island of Australia once the court was apprised and convinced of the rape/death of Melanie Jane Constantine and the kidnapping of her offspring. Lisle was awarded freedom once it was determined that she had been fed a line of lies by the Major in his attempt to woo her to his plans of wealth and status as owner of Covington Court as well as Gravelstone Abbey. Too Lisle was under the impression that as young Teresa was being held captive, her father's aim was that of rescue. She was to be the surrogate mother to the girl. Lisle never confessed that Teresa had apprised her of the fact that Daniel had kidnapped her. She plead to being duped and ignorant of the actual circumstances.

In retrospect Lisle considered she had been saved by the handsome officer, being taken off the streets of London and from the dead-end existence she'd been living since she'd been cast from her father's house. After being released by the Judge, she truly had nowhere to look for sustenance. Thus, she began to work her way back to Village Cullbert with the hope that the Madam there might still see some worth in her as one of the ladies of the establishment. Madame Sylvia had indeed hired her, but on a temporary basis until she could prove herself to be trustworthy to advance to become the companion to her gentlemen clientele. Presently she was working as a servant in the establishment when Lord Harry and his two detectives arrived to greet their hostess and healer of months past.

The weather had turned sour after the trio departed Martingale Manor, but the men were unconcerned with comfort. Harry was astride his favorite horse, while Earl was riding his sturdy mare, and Paul was on his dependable steed. But the three lead the horse borrowed from Elijah that Teresa had ridden back to Martingale Manor several weeks previously. Harry had initially informed his companions that since his and Earl's foray earlier he came to find himself relieved of the order and discipline his life had enfolded theretofore. His demeanor had become one of companion rather than that of lord and hired men. All three began a friendship that was open and agreeable. Harry often surprised himself as he literally could feel his body "letting go" of the stringent rules and regulations forcibly shoved onto his caste in the society of his age.

Travelling quickly, they found themselves at the edge of the sought village and Harry was not terribly surprised when they encountered the same young girl that had given them directions before. Stopping, he leaned over slightly toward her, "Do you remember me?"

She did a slight nod and curtsy. "Yes, sir. I do recall ye. But then it wuz only two of you."

Laughing lightly, Harry said, "You are correct, my child, and I have need of your knowledge once again."

"Whutchu want?"

"The house of a Mistress MayBelle Chambers, if you know of it."

"Oh. Law. Ain't no guessing about it, sir. Everybody here 'bouts knows Auntie MayBelle. She's the local witch thet we all go to, to get our fortunes done. She knows everything!"

"I see." The men glanced at each other. Harry asked, "Do you think she'd mind three strangers calling upon her this fine day?"

The girl swung her entire body as she shook her head, "No sir. You cain't catch Auntie MayBelle unawares. I'd venture to say even now she knows you three are here askin' about where she lives. Wouldn't surprise me none if'n she had a spot of tea ready for the three of you." She grinned up at the trio.

"Splendid. Then tell us how to get to her house, please."

She turned her back and pointed off to the right of the dirt road they were presently on. "Go across this field here, and you'll soon come to a rill. Cross it and turn to the right. Foller it. Keep the stream in your sight. Soon, you'll come upon her hovel. Call out before you hit the clearing even though she'll know you're there. She likes to hear her name called by whoever is a comin'."

Harry leaned over and laid a gold coin into the palm of the girl. "Gee, Mister. Me and Da is still livin' off the one you gave us when you wuz here last time. This'll do us through next year. Thank you, mister."

"What is your name, child?

"It's Peggy. Me name is Peggy Partridge and me Da is preacher Patrick Partridge. Me Ma's been gone for nigh my whole life, but between Auntie MayBelle, and t'other women of Cullbert, me da has had help in the raisin' of me and holdin' his job too."

"Well, child, we are grateful for your information and I now ask you for another favor."

"Ask away, mister."

"Would you be so kind as to take this horse into the village and turn him over to Elijah?"

Reaching for the reigns, she curtsied. "Surely I shall. I can put away my chore for that long wifout any worries. You can count on me."

"Thank you, Peggy. I pray you and your father farewell."

As young Peggy predicted, the men were greeted by the crone (who looked every bit a witch) as they dismounted and strode into the grassless yard. "Come in, my friends. I've tea on the table. Come in and tell me what I can do for you today."

Entering the cozy room, all three men had to stoop low to avoid cracking their heads; inside was not very much higher, but they were able to stand upright. "Have yer'selves seats." She poured four cups of strongly brewed tea and shoved a bowl of sugar toward the center of the table. They were somewhat surprised to see the cups were of the finest china and the spoons were sterling. Harry immediately began to wonder if MayBelle's son lied when he spoke of her poverty. "Now, speak. Tell me what it is I can do fer ye?"

"Thank you, ma'am." Harry began. He introduced himself and his companions. Then, drawing in a deep breath, he said, "But I have the idea you may already know the reason for our visit this day. Am I correct?"

"I don't inten' to hold ye' in suspense, sir. I know why ye're here. And I understand why ye're lookin' at this nice china and silver when my boy is dun tole you I'm livin' in poverty." She grinned a snag-toothed smile. "By way of comfortin' you gent'men as to my fancy wares, a highborn lady was bein' sent away by her lord husband to the nunnery just up from here a ways. She had brought only a few items she could pack and get away with. When her entourage arrived in Cullbert, she was sickened near to death, and they brought her to me. After three days she was cured of her imposed ailment and having very little in the way of money, she parted with these fine items you see here, with the instructions for me to sell them for my payment." She lifted one of the fine cups and gazed at it as she turned it round. "Just the havin' of such finery is payment enough for me. These fine treasures might appear as ribbons on a hog, but they bring some sort of sweetness into my old bones. I cannot sell something so dear to me. Thus... you men are participants in my joy at using them."

All three men leaned back into the crude chairs and sipped the tea with appreciation. Harry said, "Dear Lady MayBelle, as you surmised, we've arrived this day to attempt to right a wrong done to your son, even though he had joined a dastardly man to aid in the kidnapping of my ward..."

MayBelle was vigorously nodding her head as Harry was speaking. She held her hand up to interrupt his statement. "Sir! I am not unaware of the wrong turn taken by my son and his uncle. They came under the influence of stronger men who enlisted them both with ideas of easy money. Neither of them was any help to me in any way, and if you think to salve your conscience over the deaths of my kin, please do not allow it. I made my way alone by my talents and wits and will continue to do so. You may depart this house, this village, this segment of your life without any regrets. You owe me nothing."

"Mistress MayBelle, your words are indeed comforting to us, but if you'd allow it, I'd enjoy easing whatever burdens which are sure to come your way in the future."

"M'Lord. None know what burdens are ahead for us. I might be swept from this earth before you arrive back to where you came from."

"Be that as it may, will you accept a stipend from my hand to your heart?"

She looked down and nodded almost imperceptibly. "It would honor this old crone to accept the gift from your hand to my heart, sir."

The foursome stood, and the men all bowed before Mistress MayBelle, turned, and ducked low to exit the house. She watched as they rode off back toward Cullbert.

If one was listening, they might have heard MayBelle scream as she dumped the leather pouch of money onto the table: at first glance she was sure there were at least ten pounds of sterling in assorted coinage. Enough to care for her needs and to get her a nice burial. With trembling hands, she poured another cup of tea into a fine china cup.

Back in the village, the threesome went directly to Madame Sylvia's stable at the rear of her establishment. Her son was pounding out a shoe with sparks flying and hammer ringing. Paul got his attention first and said, "I see young Peggy has returned your steed. Is there possibly an unpaid amount due for the use of your horse?'

Shaking his head, Elijah smiled. "Lord Harry paid in advance enough for the purchase of the horse. I didn't expect for him to be returned."

"Well, don't concern yourself about it. I feel sure Lord Harry isn't expecting you to return any part of his payment to you. Your gelding was gentle but unwavering for the comfort of Mistress Teresa's ride back to Martingale Manor. We easily made it in two days." Turning back toward Harry and Earl, he asked, "Is the salon open?"

"Yes sirs. You can go in here at the back or mosey around to the front. Th' back'll be quicker, though."

"Thank you, Elijah."

Upon entering the large kitchen, they were surprised to see Lisle dressed as a serving maid with a large tray filled with wonderfully scented food, heading toward the swinging gate which led into the large salon. "Why, my goodness, sir..." glancing at Harry, "could ye be the man what came for the young lady what caused us to be nabbed here a while back?" Without much of a pause, she continued, "Yer girl described you to a tee! And 'andsome you be too!"

"Right-o, Mistress Lisle." Harry smiled. "You seem to have fared rather well from your connection with the Major. I understand the 'why' of the court's decision. I'm happy you were allowed your freedom. Just be careful from here on out. Don't heed every handsome man you come across as he may be lying to you."

She nodded and smiled. "Come, find a seat and I'll bring the food."

"First, could you tell me if Lady Sylvia is up?"

"No sir. It'll be well in the afternoon before she's ready to greet visitors."

Harry spoke to his companions. "Well gentlemen, how about we take a leisurely meal and hopefully see Madam Sylvia soon. What say?"

Both Paul and Earl agreed with the plan, already seating themselves at a large round table near the front window.

Sometime later they had leaned back into their chairs and were enjoying brandy and smoking cigars that had materialized from Lisle's hands. She was seeing to their comfort as they awaited Sylvia to enter the scene. Before long, Lisle came to nod toward the stairs. The men turned to watch the beautifully coiffed-and-gowned woman sweep down and into the salon. She immediately spied Harry and his companions and came gliding over to them with both hands outstretched. The three stood and bowed, and Harry took her hands in his. He leaned down and placed kisses upon the backs of each. She was delighted. "My dear friends... are you being served and treated well?"

Paul pulled out a chair for her to gracefully slide her frame into. She reached and took one of his hands, placing it within her own down upon her shoulder, and looked into his mesmerized eyes just long enough for him to feel a heat begin to etch itself within his groin. He quickly let go and sat, knowing his countenance was flushed.

"What might I do to make your stay unforgettable?" she asked.

"Lady Sylvia, we've brought ourselves back to this village to give our deepest thanks for everything that was done for us when last we were here, and we returned the borrowed horse from your stable."

"Ah, yes." She smiled at Harry. "You, sir, had a very nasty bruise... dangerous in fact. You could have been killed by your attacker. It was propitious that it happened here, and I was able to tend to your needs." She glanced toward Paul. "And you, sir, I heard you were able to overcome his attacker."

Paul blanched somewhat. "Why yes, ma'am. I got in a couple of good swings. Enough to stop him."

"Uhm hum. That is exactly what I heard. Seems Mistress Mulvaney's hogs were more than well-fed that morning. But not to worry. Everyone who knew the man is happier knowing he won't be around stirring up trouble. He and his nephew had become such that everyone was hoping they'd finally get caught and inherit prison to give us all some relief." She hesitated, then looked directly at Harry. "Do you have any idea what became of young Will Chambers?"

"Yes. He is the main reason we find ourselves here today. He was killed recently, and his body is being prepared to be brought home for his mother to bury wherever she desires. We came to see her and investigate her status. We left her with enough treasure to hold her for quite a while where she'll be able to live comfortably if she is careful."

"Mistress MayBelle is, I'm sure, deeply grateful for your intervention in such a manner. She lamented the loss of her boy to that devilish group he and his uncle had cast their lots with. I just hope that with the demise of these two that the others will crawl back into the pit they emerged from." Reaching for the brandy decanter, she motioned for Lisle to bring a small snifter. "Now, tell me how young Will came to die."

As Harry was reiterating the events surrounding the killing of William Chambers, she interrupted. "How on earth did Will manage to infiltrate the ball without getting cast out at first sight by someone?"

"He was dressed in a dandy outfit. Seems that Lisle had told him to confiscate the clothes left here by the Major. I suppose that's what he did."

She flushed, "Lisle!"

The young woman came hurrying over to the table. "Yes, ma'am?"

"Did you inform Will Chambers to take Major Steadman's clothes from this establishment?"

She immediately dropped her head and tears began to fall. "Yes, ma'am. I did do that, ma'am."

"Who gave you the authority to offer such?"

"Ma'am, I never thought. I figured the Major would never need 'em again and I saw Will outside when we wuz bein' taken. I whispered it to him since he was the same size and I hated to think they'd be cast out soon enough."

"So, you expected to see the Major in prison, did you?" She looked at the redheaded, flame-faced woman. "And what did you expect to become of yourself, Lisle?"

"Honest, ma'am, I figured I'd get the same."

Tempering her thoughts somewhat, she said, "I suppose you suffered enough thinking you'd be in prison too. The courts were truly benevolent in your case, as you conspired with a kidnapper and helped him in every aspect. Count yourself blessed, Lisle. But do not ever again take it upon yourself to assume any authority about anything as long as I can keep myself satisfied with your performance here. Know that you place yourself here by my good pleasure. See that you do my bidding and not your own." She turned to lift the little crystal snifter and took a sip.

All three men were duly impressed with the force of ownership held by Madame Sylvia. She brooked no interference of any kind from anyone. She smiled and said, "The young ladies who attend this establishment are local and stay in their own abodes until sent for. Elijah fetches them as they are needed, and he is very astute when it comes to surmising which maid will entertain each gent who needs certain companionship. Lisle is the only one who abides here, and I shall ultimately determine when or if she is ready to assume the highest position of pleasing any gentleman in private. Her presence works well for both of us. She's pretty enough to be found serving foods. Her beauty is such that those who come to dine are tempted to linger and order drinks and want conversation with her if she can spare the time."

All three men watched Lisle busily attending to three other tables. They were soon realizing what a jewel Madame Sylvia had in the hiring of her. She was seen laughing and stroking the shoulders of those she was serving. She was what one would speak of as "a natural." A few moments later Harry spoke up as all three men stood. "We must be heading back home. I'm sure Elijah has our horses ready. And the weather seems to be clearing up somewhat. We must make good time before nightfall."

She arose and said, "Wait here, Lord Harry. I have something for you to take back to your ward." She hurried away and up the stairs. In a few minutes, they watched as she descended the stairs porting a black velvet bag. She came and placed it into the hands of Harry. "This is why I was so terribly upset with Lisle; Her giving permission to Will. And no one here was ever aware of Will's thievery. This prize could so easily have been lost. I found this recently when I was gathering the belongings left by them that morning." Watching as Harry began removing the box from its' velvet bag, she continued, "My intention was to locate exactly where the Covington Court you spoke of was located when last you were here, and have Elijah deliver it. But your arrival today is most propitious."

Harry opened the box and nestled within the folds of black velvet was a star ruby as large as a robin's egg. Harry came close to dropping the thing. Paul and Earl came in close for a good look. "Good Gawd! Is that thing real?" Paul held it up and turned it over to note the back was rough and completely untouched. Returning the stone to the box he said, "I do believe it is."

Harry closed the box. "We'll soon find out." He looked to Sylvia and said, "My thanks to you lady for holding this for me. My lawyers will surely have knowledge of the best jeweler London has. I'll see that he's given the honor of valuing this fine ruby. He will know. I'm anxious to see to the worth of this for our Teresa." He smiled, stuffed the box into a jacket pocket, and reached out to take Sylvia's hand. She took his hand and placed it around her waist as she drew herself into a snug embrace. She kissed his cheek, and then turned to the grinning Earl and Paul and did likewise.

# CHAPTER 30
# DEEP FEELINGS EMERGING

HARRY WAS FINDING it difficult to appear disinterested in the suitors who came in constant hordes. He spoke of them when complaining to Gretchen: "I did not realize there were so many men around these parts who are seeking wives. I'm not surprised about Sir Geoffry or Squire Bellingham... after all, they seek a woman for their bed as well as caring for their children. I have no fear that Teresa would accept anyone of their ilk. Even if she did, I'd certainly not give my consent. Thank God, I am given the opportunity to deny anyone she may put forth as feeling worthy. At least I can protect her from terrible mistakes. Don't you agree?"

"Indeed, sir. I do agree. She must marry someone she feels she loves above everyone else in this world, especially her grandmother and myself. We must fade from her heart as she opens it to the man God has chosen for her."

"God? You mean you think God has a hand in finding her a husband, and not me?"

"We shall see, now won't we, Lord Harry? We shall see." Gretchen smiled, knowingly.

"Well, there are so many now... I had planned on hosting another ball for her in London in the spring. But I don't think I could stand it."

"Why, Lord Harry? Why could you not stand it?"

"I don't exactly mean I couldn't stand it. It's just that this has been upsetting for her, don't you think?"

"No sir. I think the ball was very good for Teresa. She was denied the childhood she ought to have enjoyed because of circumstances beyond her control. I felt it imperative to keep her out of sight, so to speak, for her safety. She has just now begun to live the life that was intended for her. Do give her every opportunity to seek out the perfect man to spend the remainder of her allotted days with. Let her have wings to fly, and then, when she lands, she will know without doubt that the man she chooses, and the one you shall approve, will be the one God was holding ready for her all the while."

"You pose a strong argument, Gretchen. I shall maintain my composure as she is allowed to gallivant. And I shall not falter. There will be a spring ball in London for her. Madame Alexandra will need to be apprised."

Teresa spent every spare moment in the company of her grandmother. Each day seemed to bring more memories forward and into her speech. Reaching over to lay her frail fingers upon her daily visitor, she said, "Teresa. I saw Melanie last evening as I was being prepared for bed. I had not seen her in such a long time, and thought she was dead. But my dear she's very much alive. Yes. She stood right there," indicating a place near the fireplace, "and told me that you are her child. She said that you were born in the forest and that she was unable to get home, but that I must know that you are truly my granddaughter."

"Oh, Grandmother! She was telling you the truth. I am your grandchild. Melanie did indeed give birth to me."

"But who is your father, my dear? Who is your father? I do not recall our Melanie wedding anyone! No one. Melanie never had the opportunity. How can this be?"

"Never fear, dearest. As you can well see... I am alive and here, and Melanie is my mother, but it's sad to say..." She decided to give the old woman a lie instead of the worrisome truth. "They told me my father died long ago while serving in India." She watched her grandmother as she continued, "I was told that he was intending to marry my mother, but was sent away... into service, while he waited for her to attain marriageable age."

And Gretchen watched the expressions altering the countenance of Lady Sarah. First, the glimmerings of old memories. Gretchen could envision the opening of inroads to the past surging forth onto the table of surety for the old lady, eyes mirroring her realizations as they began to flood forward to be lifted from that table, turned over, and examined. She opened her eyes wide and then spoke, looking directly at Teresa.

"Your father must have been that young man... oh, what was his name... I cannot seem to recall! He took my Melanie away..." Then, seeking out the eyes of Gretchen, she continued, "And you were there with her! I know you had to have been. You'd never have left my child!" She began to cry, sobbing deeply as both women gathered her into their arms in commiseration.

"I fear so, Grandmother. I fear so."

"Where is he now?"

"They say he died while in India." Teresa glanced at Gretchen and shook her head.

Gretchen spoke up. "Lady Sarah, I believe the time has finally arrived when you are ready to hear the story of your beloved Melanie. I shall give you the full details of her life and death as well as the days of our Teresa to this point in her history if you believe you are up to receiving the telling of it all?"

With fire and determination set within her frail frame, Sarah drew in a deep breath and said, "I am ready to know it all, please, Gretchen." And she sat back into the comfort of the chaise, as Teresa lifted the coverlet and snugged it around her for extra warmth.

And so began the exposé of the events from over eighteen years ago.

At the last word, Gretchen sat back and looked over at the window as a dove flew in to rest from its flight. Taking its sighting as a good omen, she nodded in agreement. She saw Teresa overcome, silently weeping as she held Lady Sarah tightly within her embrace.

Turning to Gretchen, Sarah reached for her hand. "I knew you would take care of my child the best you could. I thank you for your constancy in the care of my beautiful granddaughter. I thank you, Gretchen. And especially for the scars you carry from your valiant attempt to protect our Melanie." Looking at Teresa, she continued, "And I thank our God that He took the life of that terrible young man. He certainly deserved death."

# CHAPTER 31

# UNEXPECTED LOVERS

EVEN DURING THE wet, cold, fog-enshrouded times of winter, with spring well a ways yet to arrive the environs of Gravelstone Abbey were alive with activity. From a mile away, one could hear the sounds of excited business. Every man, woman, and child old enough to work could be found gainfully employed. There was the repairing, rebuilding, washing, scrubbing, polishing, boiling away mold and mildew, wiping out the wine cellars and turning the bottles, opening all windows that could be opened, determinedly murdering all vermin, clearing all chimneys of soot, cleaning the well, and beating away dust from the turkey carpets, tapestries, and heavy draperies. All the while singing could be heard even above the noisy activities.

There were crews coming in from London, and they stayed in the homes of many of the folks of Village Gravelstone. The reopening of the Abbey was a rich boon to everyone and was the talk of the surrounding countryside as well as being spoken of quite frequently in London, as the conversations abounded. Mention was made, time and time again, of the stunning young heiress of Gravelstone Abbey.

From the lips of someone—no one could say who—came the exciting news of a spring debut ball for this girl. (The rumor was easily traced to Madame Alexandra if one was interested enough to inquire.)

But the heiress had been busy with the quest to obtain the best goldsmith in London, adept in the formation of artificial teeth for Lady Sarah. Once she satisfied herself that Sir Edmund Bedford was indeed proficient beyond measure in the art of making artificial teeth, she hired him. He, at last, had arrived and was installed in the room opposite that of the Lady Sarah. They spent much time together as he fitted, filed, and refitted the gold plates that would eventually be imbedded with the ivory from his inventory purchased for such specific use. Taking the necessary days and weeks to accomplish his best work yet, one day he inserted both upper and lower plates into the oral cavity of the Lady and handed her a large hand mirror. "See what you think M'lady."

Smiling broadly into the mirror, she turned first this way and then that, and to the great consternation of the goldsmith, she was silent. Sir Edmund held his breath and prayed, *Lord, please! I need her to be happy.* He leaned over to see the reflection of her face in the mirror and was rewarded with observing streams of tears flowing, unchecked, down her cheeks. Seeing her nose was also dripping, he graciously placed his handkerchief into her free hand.

At that point, she looked up at him with joy evident. "Sir! I perceive you have wrought a veritable miracle upon this lady. I am alive once more. I thank you deeply. Money is not enough to settle my debt to you. Is there any additional way I may convey my appreciation of this gift you've given me?"

"Lady Sarah, your happiness and satisfaction with my work are all the extra I require. Truly. You have given me the greatest gift... that of your acceptance of my labors."

"Then allow me to kiss your cheek, sir. I suddenly feel compelled to do so. These lips have not felt the wondrous sensation of a man's cheek for far too long. I need this touch if you will suffer this unseemly request."

Blanching not in the least, he replied, "Your request is gratefully granted, ma'am. I shall enjoy the sensation more than you, most likely." He smiled and bent over as she leaned forward.

Teresa stepped into the room at that moment. "Grandmother! Sir Edmund! Are you two much too long in each other's company? Have you no constraints? What are we to think? Really!"

Sir Edmund stood quickly and said, "My dear child, we were simply trying out the newly placed artificial teeth to assure that all her kisses would be placed properly and would affect the recipient as heartily as they did upon my own cheek. It is something I require of any lady into whose mouth rest my creations." Smiling, he said, "That is *if* the lady is of a mind to adhere to my request." He never hesitated on the obvious lie!

Gretchen entered as the trio was gasping for breath from laughing. "I take it the apparatus fits perfectly?"

One evening not long after the jeweler had been installed in rooms near to Lady Sarah, Lord Harry sent word to him to please attend him as expeditiously as possible. He was to bring his loupe to the library. Within the hour, Lord Harry had the door opened by Calvin who seated the good jeweler, then took himself outside in the wide hall so the two men could converse undisturbed. "You've my curiosity soaring, Lord Harry, particularly about the order to bring the loupe. What do you have for me to assess?"

Reaching to unlock a drawer at his hip, Harry withdrew a small box. Sitting it out upon the desktop, and sliding it across the surface toward Sir Edmund, he said, "This was gleaned from the belongings of the man, the Lord Major Daniel Steadman Bordeaux, the natural father of Teresa. He is as good as dead to this child as he has been sentenced to the isle of Australia to a life of heavy labor until his natural death." He watched the man gently open the lid, and then he continued, "This piece was hidden inside the pocket of one of his capes that was abandoned when he was arrested for the kidnapping of Teresa. We were given the stone by the woman in whose establishment he was found. I have no doubt that this gem was ultimately intended for Teresa, but it must first be determined if this could possibly be stolen property. The man spent a goodly amount of time in India, where I feel assured he obtained this jewel."

As the stone was turned over and over beneath the magnified gaze of the jeweler, eliciting murmurs, Lord Harry was anxious to hear the ultimate findings. "What have you gleaned, Sir Edmund?"

Edmund sat back and laid the stone gently back into the black velvet nest. "One of the finest... no! Without doubt, this is *the* finest star ruby I myself have ever seen. One of the rarest and finest of stones. The star is as perfect as nature could have produced."

"Could you have information as to its previous owner? Could it have been pilfered? What is its worth?"

"From the information received periodically from my connection to the International Jewelers Guild, I've not seen any evidence forthcoming that such a rare specimen was stolen. At least not in the past decade. Before that, I cannot say. But because of its worth and rarity, I feel secure in stating that it was either purchased or was gifted to the Major while he was abroad."

"And could you estimate the value in today's market?"

Shaking his head, he said, "This piece is worthy of crown jewels. Few could afford it. I am convinced that the Major was gifted with this prize for some outstanding feat while in India, as even there the price would be exorbitant. Here at auction, it would bring a great deal above ten thousand pounds. Only Royalty might be able to afford it. Thus, it is nearly useless as an exchange for monetary gain. Your best use of it might be on display in a guarded environment."

"Could it be fashioned into a pendant? Or is it too large?"

"No, indeed. A pendant could easily be worn around the neck and descend toward the cleavage where it would be seen to perfect advantage by the admirer."

"Then that's settled. Design the perfect pendant for an extraordinary present for our Teresa. Bring me your idea as soon as you've decided upon the ideal setting for the ruby."

Sir Edmund rose as Lord Harry was locking the box back into the desk drawer. He pocketed the key.

While Sir Edmund was kept busy in the manufacture of many fine pieces of jewelry and worthy objects of art, Lord Harry had him presently in the throes of designing a small tiara for Teresa to be worn at the London debut and as yet the man had not presented his vision of a setting for the ruby pendant. He was also contemplating the making of a very large copy of the medallion she wore constantly somewhere upon her body. At her debut, the gown had hidden the talisman flat upon the small of her back where it was held in a pocket sewn within her fine underdress of sheer silk. Lord Harry realized that the golden medallion was the material connection to her past life with Gravelstone Abbey, hence his desire to have it remade into a large decoration to hold a conspicuous place in the grand hall there.

Lord Harry stayed busy with his devotion to his ward, his overseeing of the advancements at Gravelstone Abbey, his visits to London to confer with his solicitors, and his managing the arrangements for the spring debut. On one particular morning, he was seen at the large fir trees at the entrance of the formal gardens. Dew was heavy, yet there were Gretchen and Sydney at work seeing to the setting out of hundreds of bulbs into the cold earth. Striding forth, he spoke. "You two are ever at it. I see the results of your labors, and I must say this place has to be the envy of everyone who has had a look at it. It is beautiful out here. A place fit for a wedding if ever I saw one." *Now, where in the world did that come from?*

Both Gretchen and Sydney arose from their kneeling positions and spoke together, "How did you know, Lord Harry?"

"Know? Know what?"

Gretchen spoke. "Why sir, Sydney has asked me to wed him, and I've agreed to it."

Throwing his head back, he laughed and shouted, "Joy! What an answer to prayer! I've been praying for this to occur." Then he sobered somewhat. "What I mean to say is that I have long thought that you, Gretchen, need someone with whom to spend your days. Especially once our Teresa has been taken in marriage and she will be attending to the needs and desires of her own husband and children."

"A propitious event, then, eh, Lord Harry?" asked Sydney.

"Indeed! And with your permission, Teresa and I shall host a most glorious wedding event and then see you off to the destination of your choice for as long as you desire!" he said, magnanimously.

"That's quite wonderful, sir, but I do believe Missus Gretchen and I must agree upon such an arrangement." He looked at the love of his life, eyes shining with overwhelming tenderness, and finished, "Don't you agree?"

"Yes. We do sincerely appreciate your kindness toward us, but we must discuss this possibility in private. We shall let you know our decisions concerning all aspects of our wedding sir, if it's agreeable to you."

"Fine! Of course, you must satisfy yourselves, but I do need to impress upon you both that whatever you may ultimately desire, please know that Martingale Manor will see it through to your complete agreement. Understood?"

Both Gretchen and Sydney bowed and thanked their lord with profuse words.

Christmas came to Covington Court and was welcomed as most every other day, but with a tad more excitement permeating the atmosphere. The staff decorated their spaces downstairs with holly and other greenery. The men saw that a large tree stump was dragged in to burn in the massive fireplace in the big hall. Teresa saw to it that the sitting rooms were embellished with holly, mistletoe, and orange trees she had confiscated from the greenhouses. Then Lord Harry had the pleasure of passing envelopes of money to the entire staff as well, particularly to those outside laborers who spent their lives living as frugally as possible. This yearly stipend was often what allowed their families to have a bit extra at this season of the year when gardens were nonproductive. Few there were who did not count themselves very blessed to be a hire of Covington Court.

Teresa had diligently produced a beautiful silk ascot (with Madam Alexandria's instruction) for Lord Harry. For her grandmother a delicately embroidered handkerchief, and for Gretchen and Sydney a framed sampler. For Virginia, a specially chosen piece of jewelry she knew was admired by the girl.

For Teresa, all gifts received were deeply appreciated, but none held a candle to the simple strand of perfect pearls presented to her by "her love". That evening, by the light of the burning yule log, Lord Harry slipped up behind Teresa as she stood talking with Gretchen and reached over her head to lower the heavy strand down before her face. She reached to touch the cool white strand and turned within his arms to gaze up into the dark eyes of the handsome, smiling man.

"Here is my offering to you." He deliberately turned her back around. "Hold still while I fasten the clasp. Let me see what this does to set off your gown of red velvet." He continued, "I swear you look beyond beautiful by firelight." He squeezed her shoulder and she turned back to face him.

She reached to stroke the beautiful pearls, and then reached to place a hand against his chest, lifting up to kiss his cheek, and whispered, "I love them. Thank you."

The new year opened with a blast of cold. The air was frigid enough to kill any plans from forming about a garden wedding. Gretchen and Sydney had wanted their nuptials spoken in the garden, but since they decided to not postpone, they opted for the little chapel. The vows were spoken in the cold, damp chapel on the hill, but the attendees, all encased within furs and heavy woolens, would not be kept away by the inconvenience of a few snowflakes and the icy winds off the choppy channel. Everyone capable of making it to the small stone building did. They were privy to the marriage of two of the most loved and respected people in Martingale Manor as well as Covington Village.

Upon the pronouncement of Sydney and Gretchen being declared "husband and wife," they were followed down the slope and around to the side doors which opened into a large room that had been set up as a reception hall.

The cooks had done themselves proud, as Elizabeth had a spread fit for a king! There were large silver bowls sporting steaming wassail of several different varieties, along with breads of every ilk, to be eaten with strips of meat pulled from a whole roasted pig, as well as pheasant and a large beef rump. There were fruits and sweets and pastries piled all along the length of the white linen-covered tables. And there at the far

THE MEDALLION

end was a cake any couple would be proud of. Gretchen knew that Elizabeth Collier had been hard at work to not only envision such an achievement but also to actually produce it.

Even before the platters were depleted, one could see replacements being brought in.

Everyone in attendance was thrilled to be in on this great occasion. Lady Sarah was putting her new teeth to good use while Sir Edmund followed her like a lovesick hound. She was heard to whisper, "I cannot see where Lord Harry could come up with a more profound blessing than this outlay. Why he'll be hard-pressed to outdo this for our Teresa."

"Yes, my dear, I believe you may be correct," said Edmund. He smiled brightly as he drew his hand along the back of Lady Sarah's waist in a most protective manner.

There was a blazing yule log still burning brightly in the massive fireplace, left from being lit on Christmas Day. It was large enough to stay burning until well into spring, when, if the weather tempered, it may need to be carted outside to burn itself out in a safe spot, or else taken on into the kitchen if needed there.

After some time, the clatter and chatter began to subside, and Lord Harry rang a small bell to call everyone's attention. "May I please have your attention? Please, I want to join my voice in congratulations along with Teresa to propose a toast on this auspicious occasion. I want everyone to join with me in wishing our beloved couple the very best this world has to offer; to wish them excellent health, and a long life in which to enjoy it." He raised his cup of wassail and said, "Here, here!" All followed suit, and even the servants outside the room could be heard expounding the same salute.

Teresa stepped quickly over to the couple and slid herself into the strong arms of her mother. Kissing her cheek, she then turned to Sydney and said, "You are now my father. I pray you and mother will be happier than can ever be imagined that ultimate happiness truly could be. May Father God bless your union. I love you both!"

With grateful tears shining in his eyes, he replied, "Mistress, you have my solemn oath that I shall do everything in my power to care for your beloved mother until my death. I swear."

Reaching to embrace him, Teresa nodded. "I feel secure in your love for her, too. I thank you."

The assembly all shouted. "Hurrah!"

Instead of taking any time away from Martingale Manor, the newlyweds decided to firm up the plans for their new cottage nearby. With the plot situated approximately halfway between the back gate of the manor house and the stone hovel where Gretchen and Teresa had spent the bulk of their years together, a young architect was busy making sure the small cottage was exactly what his patrons desired. No more than four rooms on the lower floor, with attic space above the two front rooms, and one fireplace centrally located that handily provided heat to the entire house, the largest side of which faced the big, high-ceilinged kitchen.

The cottage, which thankfully had a water closet included, also featured a hand pump in the storeroom off the kitchen. Gretchen had been content with her life up to this point but was now ecstatic over the obvious love of and for her husband. She continued to glance around expecting this dream to evaporate... which, blessedly, it did not.

Gretchen had earlier taken Sydney to her former home, even though she continued to use it as a laboratory of sorts. There were a plethora of herbs and other critical items kept there, and so she wanted to have their cottage home closer to it than where they presently resided inside the manor house.

The couple kept themselves busy with Lord Harry's gardens, as well as working with a local builder seeing to the prerequisites of their cottage.

Presently, she and Sydney were comfortably ensconced in a larger room downstairs in the manor house, not far from where she had been. She knew Teresa was well cared for by Virginia, Sarah, and Lord Harry. She was grateful. Now she felt free to live a life separate from her child, a life now entwined with another. A new love.

## CHAPTER 32

## ANOTHER WEDDING

HARRY WAS EVER busy, looking into the backgrounds of young men who continually showed up on his doorstep with cards, flowers, and small gifts. Seldom did any one of them ever get a glimpse of Mistress Teresa. Recently he had begun to dread the London debut, knowing even more activities would be in her future. There would be parties, theatre, lunches, outings, picnics, etc., ad nauseam. He must needs keep his "Team of Two" bodyguards in constant attendance. The men had become so much a part of the household at Martingale Manor that they were accepted as kinsmen.

If Teresa ever suspected that her every half-hearted outing with any caller was clandestinely observed, she did not voice any concern. Of course, Virginia too was ever at her side.

Sarah knew all too well that having a frail girl as a bodyguard did not help much. And she was very comforted by the knowledge that one or the other of the young men were ever on the alert whenever Teresa was outside the house, as well as most all the time while inside, too. She was assured of the safety of her granddaughter.

Meantime, Harry dreaded it but had begun the wheels turning to secure a pavilion at Almacks in London for the spring debut of Teresa. The London Martingale household in St. George had been apprised of the increased activity soon to begin so they could be prepared well beforehand.

To Harry, it appeared that the young gentleman with the most to offer Teresa might just be Duke Julian LaFitte. His lineage went well back through James the First, and his soon-to-be inheritance was the famous Iron Lady, Black Stone Castle on the Cornwall Coast. He would stand to take ownership when his father, Archduke Willim Edmondson LaFitte, passed on. And from everything Harry could glean, Duke Willim did not have much time left. He was pushing seventy, was blind, and had to be spoon-fed. There were nurses full time to care for him. His wife had long since passed away and in fact, had been buried ten days after the birth of Julian, their only child. The lady Duchess had been just seventeen when the boy was born to Willim and herself.

Harry thought possibly young Julian might know of the hardships associated with such a large estate and may well make a good match for his ward. He was only ten years Teresa's senior, at twenty-eight. A perfect match. But then again, so was he—Lord Harry himself.

Still, he felt pushed about going ahead with the London debut. It would give an opportunity for those eligible bachelors who knew of Teresa but had not had the invitation to get to Martingale Manor for her small November debut.

Since Madame Alexandra and her troupe had departed for London, Harry thought to go ahead and send "his ladies" off to London as soon as the roads became passable once more. Their departure was set for a time in early February. It was now late January.

Even with the cold, inclement weather, there abounded activity. Gravelstone Abbey was looking more complete each time Harry visited. He and Sir Edmund saw the large gold emblem installed over the grand fireplace in the huge entrance hall. From the east, the sun shone through the tall ironed-grilled stained-glass windows to cast a rainbow of colors upon the golden emblem of Constantine. With each inch of the rising sun, it seemed to shimmer and move upon its base. Lord Harry was well pleased, as was Sir Edmund. "One more task accomplished, eh, Edmund."

"Yes, indeed, sir. I am proud that you felt me proficient enough to render such an important decoration for such an exceptional palace as this one. I am grateful."

Laying a restraining hand upon the arm of Sir Edmund, Lord Harry asked, "When will you present me with your best idea for the ruby pendant?"

"Never fear, sir. Presently, I am beset with too many ideas and must needs determine which is my best effort. Soon. Soon I'll have a decent rendering of the setting so you can tell me if it meets your approval."

As the men were headed back toward Covington, Edmund spoke up and said, "Lord Harry. Might I speak with you concerning something very personal, and very important to myself and another of your family?"

Intrigued, Harry nodded. "By all means sir, I'm anxious to hear your thoughts... and shall be of help in any way possible."

Moving some little bit upon the carriage seat, Edmund harrumphed lightly, then said, "I would like your permission to ask for the hand of Teresa's—"

"*No!* Sir Edmund." Harry turned to glare at his companion. "How can you feel you are able to request such a favor?"

"No! No, Lord Harry... Please, please... you did not allow me to complete my sentence. Lord Harry. Please... I was going to complete my request to ask for the hand of her grandmother, Sarah."

With a stunned look on his face, which slowly began to break into a grin, and then into loud laughter, Harry said, "Why! Old man, I swear you are full of surprises! But upon my word, sir, if you have the Lady's agreement, then go ahead. You have my blessing."

"Thank you, Lord Harry, but as yet Lady Sarah has no inkling as to my motives toward her. But, you see, I have fallen deeply in love with her ladyship. And she seems to be very amenable to my presence. Neither of us is young, but we might enjoy a few good years left in the company of each other. I would do my best to see to her comfort. She is truly a wonderful lady, and so kind and gentle."

Harry saw in his mind's eye pictures of the old toothless crone flying out of the kitchen doors of Gravelstone Abbey. Too, he learned

THE MEDALLION

from Gretchen how she had attacked the hapless William Chambers the night of the ball when he'd entered her rooms. Clearing his throat, Harry said, "I am sure she is all of that and more, Sir Edmund. And I pray she will accept your proposal. I shall pray for that."

The auspicious wedding of Sir Edmund Wallington Bedford to Lady Sarah Hashbrooke Constantine was a great cause for celebration at Martingale Manor. The special license was obtained, and Lady Sarah wore the lovely gown she wore the night of the debut of her granddaughter. She was lovely—nothing was left of the nearly dead crone they had seen the previous year. Sarah was as radiant as though she were sixteen again. Everyone was grateful that she and Sir Edmund had found each other, and that love was such a dominant force in their lives together.

They were married in the same room where the reception had been held just a few weeks back for Gretchen and Sydney. It was smaller but equally sumptuous.

The only change occurring after the wedding was that Lady Sarah's room now included the room next to hers. Harry had a newly installed door placed between. And since he was having bathing-toilet rooms installed in several places throughout the mansion, he had the architect figure one near their rooms.

The same was being accomplished at Gravelstone. Everything was being upgraded while the repairs were being done.

Noting the thousands of blossoms popping up all through the gardens, Harry knew spring was not far off. His spirits were already full of joy at the happiness envisioned about the two couples: Sydney and Gretchen, and Edmund and Sarah. His family was growing. Time was flying, and he must consider his own future. Who were the ladies that drew his attention? Who was it that he might consider spending the rest of his life with? Here he was twenty-eight, and he ought to already have a small army of children running through the manor.

During the recent debut of Teresa Harry had danced with a number of lovely young ladies who flirted shamelessly with him. Their ploys were lost on him. He did not care for any of the pretty young women. Too shallow. Too preening. Too over-seeking. Just *too*! He was looking for someone who did not know he was "in the world," so to speak. He had enough sense to realize his status and wealth were the reason for such open availability by the groom-seekers. He did not want that reason to be their reason. No. It must be someone who did not know him. Maybe he could find her in the crowds at the spring debut in London. He must keep his eyes open. But no amount of attempting to be real could wipe out the feeling that his future bride was as close as his breath.

Maybe he needed to speak with Sir Edmund about designing a special wedding ring to hold for the future Lady of Martingale. *Something blue. I wonder if there is a blue gem like the color of Teresa's eyes...*

That afternoon, while Harry was busy in his library, a knock came upon the door. "It is open." Sir Edmund entered and waved a sheaf of paper before him as he strode toward the desk. He laid it gently before Lord Harry and said, "See what you think of this."

Lifting the paper and studying the rendering of what could be the perfect setting of the star ruby pendant, Harry looked from paper to Edmund and back. "It's perfect! Absolutely more than I would have thought it could be. It's perfect!" Sitting back and holding the paper up to get a better look, he asked, "Would it be in gold?"

"I've considered the hue of the eighteen-karat gold, and my own taste dictates it would be too overpowering to encircle the color of the stone. I thought to possibly plate the gold in sterling to more closely match the brilliant white star that moves across the undersurface of the ruby... What do you think?"

"Oh, no." Harry shook his head gently. "I've no ideas at all of what would best be used. You are the expert and shall certainly earn your due with this one." He shoved his chair back and slapped his hands upon the arms as he rose. "Get started at your earliest convenience. And, by the way, be on the alert for the finest blue stone about the shade of Teresa's eyes. I want a ring made using something you design. Use whatever gold or silver you desire to best set it off."

"Thank you for your faith in my abilities. I'll try to do all to please you, sir."

# CHAPTER 33
# LONDON DEBUT?

SIX CARRIAGES ROLLED into the stable area of Martingale Manor at St. George in London. The passengers had dismounted at the side front and entered the manse. The extra hires were busy porting all the luggage and other belongings into the nearest hall where the house staff could be seen dragging the assorted baggage off to the upper floors.

Within three days Madame Alexandra was inundated with job orders. She was thrilled to be in the exclusive employ of Lord Harry Martingale once again. He was found to have full pockets and was not stingy when it came to outfitting his darling ward, as well as the other ladies in his circle. Madame Alexandra soon came to realize that her niece, Amanda, was very adept at cajoling the two women who were the most difficult patrons to dress in the latest fashions.

With Amanda's shy childlike speech and honest flattery, both Lady Sarah and Mistress Gretchen were finally becoming accepting of several gowns fit for the balls as well as the theatre.

Madame Alexandra was overjoyed. Just the knowledge that her creations were being worn by the women of Martingale Manor was in itself fraught with the promise of more ladies desirous of her expertise— a winning situation.

Lord Harry was kept on the go daily watching his ward being squired by a plethora of eligible bachelors. He had informed the family that his kinsmen, Paul and Earl, would no longer be available to guard Teresa. He told the family that he let them go, when, in fact he bade them delve into the personal lives of several prospects who were vying for the hand of Teresa. Harry wanted no stone left unturned

in an effort to expose anything untoward that may be hidden within the lives of those certain men. For the lie to be effective, Harry decided he must be extra diligent in following Teresa for them to believe the men were no longer in the hire of the lord. Everyone believed it except Gretchen. She knew better.

Ever on the paths, following at a discreet distance, he kept her in his sights. He tried to be very unobtrusive, and in fact was quite successful. Until one afternoon when she just had been brought back to the manse by her suitor, she spied Lord Harry hurrying from the stable at the back of the house. As he entered by the side door, she asked, "Did you enjoy your outing, Lord Harry?"

"Why, yes, my dear. Quite."

"Did you see the black swans upon the garden pond?"

He suddenly became defensive, and so lied, "No dear, I was not near the garden pond. I rode over to the paths outside the cathedral."

"Then how is it that I found your silk scarf caught on a short twig just off the path of the garden pond? Do you suppose it blew there from where you found yourself near the cathedral?"

"Oh! Good heavens! Foiled! I did not want you to feel that you could not take care of yourself. But I do know Virginia is a scatterbrain. I saw her sitting on a bench talking with some sailor or other while you and your friend sauntered off. I simply felt it my duty to protect your every step. Please, do forgive my evasive story."

Laughing, she said, "Oh, you mean your lie?"

Caught, he smiled and asked, "Am I forgiven?"

Teresa reached out to squeeze his fingers. "Of course. I could never be upset with you. You, Lord Harry, are my reason for being. You are everything to me and my beloved family." She quickly ceased her prattle, realizing she may have said more than she intended.

Harry blushed, cleared his throat, and said, "I must be about my business. If you need me, I shall be down as soon as I get changed and will be in the library. Call me if you desire."

Later in his library, Harry mulled over in his mind the exact words spoken by Teresa. *Did she have any hidden message within her speech? Am I everything to her? I truly need to understand if she has any feeling at all for me other than as her lord. Maybe I best speak with Gretchen in private at the first opportunity. To even make a pretense of wooing another is too ridiculous to contemplate. Might as well admit that Teresa would suit very well. In fact, I do believe she has come to mean more than I ever might have thought possible.* He pushed his hands against the chair with a pat, and nodding, he rose. Breathing a sigh, he smiled at the thoughts roiling through his brain.

At dinner that evening the group was all gathered at the table in the small dining room. *My family!* thought Harry. *I am blessed beyond all men. These ones are true-blue. The cream of the crop. What has God wrought that I above all men should be so blessed!* Sitting back, he simply listened to the loving chatter at his table. There was Gretchen leaning in toward her beloved Sydney. Who would have ever thought that those at his table would be so easily accepting of each other? *Why, here sits Sydney, my gardener! And there, Gretchen, whom everyone called 'the witch'! My darling Teresa, who began her life in the lowest of service to my house. The biggest surprise of all is how Sarah has blossomed into a most attractive matron. Amazing what love can do! Amazing.* Suddenly realizing he was hearing his name, he returned to the conversation at the table. "Yes?"

Laughter came from all quarters. "I do believe we've caught you daydreaming, Lord Harry," Edmund said.

"I fear so, sir. What did I miss?" asked Harry.

"Not a great deal, sir, but you were asked if you had seen to the theatre box for tomorrow evening."

"Indeed. It shall be readied and I, for one, am looking forward to enjoying the presentation, simply by watching the play of delight upon young Teresa's face. She does so enjoy the theatre!"

At that specific time, in the midst of their dinner, there came the sound of great consternation and loud voices from beyond the wide marbled hall. Everyone at the dinner table stopped as they were, while the sounds grew louder, coming toward them.

Standing, Harry moved toward the salon, along with everyone else behind him. "What seems to be the bother, Thomas? Do you need help?"

About that time a very disheveled Alice shoved herself past the flustered butler and screamed at her younger brother. "Harry! You are responsible for the very death of me and our children! It was your greed in having us thrown out into the street that has brought this about! I hate you! I hate you!"

She was slobbering, and in such anger and screaming with such vitriol that one could easily see she was out of her head.

Marching toward his sister, Harry put out his hand to try to appease her. She drew back and slapped him viciously, as she continued to prattle on with abject nonsense.

Turning, with hand to cheek, Harry spoke to Gretchen. "Can you do anything for her?"

Nodding, Gretchen drew back toward the table and lifted a glass of wine. Stepping into the line of battle, she held the crystal glass up before the sight of this interloper and asked, "Isn't the sparkle beautiful, madam? Can you see how the lights glint and waver? This is needful for your beauty and shall give your heart rest. Here. Take it and sip just a little, won't you?"

As if in a trance, Alice reached and took the glass from Gretchen. She lifted it to her trembling lips and drank fully. Then, handing the empty glass back to Gretchen, she looked around as though seeing where she was for the first time. "Why am I here, brother? Do you know?"

Reaching to take her arm, Harry led her off to the salon and seated her before the fire. He stroked her head as she watched the flames jump and weave through the logs. Looking back for his help, he called, "Gretchen, come see if you can find out what troubles my sister, please."

"Yes, sir." Gretchen pulled a low hassock near the knees of Alice and sat herself beneath the sight of the lady. She began slowly and softly. "We are so very delighted to have you here with us this evening, Lady Alice. As you know, we are gathered here for the debut ball at Almacks. Your timely presence has brought great honor to this house, and we are delighted that you and your wonderful husband will be joining us. Why Teresa is overjoyed by your unexpected presence this evening." She finally lifted her eyes and glanced into the face of the now-quiet woman. Noting a bare glimmer of sanity beneath her façade, Gretchen continued. "Now, Lady, how can we be of service to you this evening? All you need do is speak your desires, and they shall be met."

Sitting up somewhat and glancing around, Alice jerked as if rising from a trance and spoke. "Harry! Harry!"

"I'm here, dear. What can I do to help?"

The dam burst and the tears began to flow. Her body was wracked with waves of distress as she cried loudly and loosely. After a few minutes, she leaned up, drew in a quavering breath, and said, "Benjamin is in trouble. Bad trouble. You are the only one who can help us."

Harry stood. "Everyone leave us except for you, Gretchen. Please. I need for my sister to have some privacy."

The company softly vacated the salon and headed back toward the dining room.

"Now. Start at the beginning."

"Well, I hardly know where to begin. I fear I have waited too long, hoping he'd work out his problems, but they grow worse with each passing day, it seems. We have lost everything. We're soon to be out on the street."

"How can this be? I had our solicitors provide for your upkeep generously. At least I was led to believe the money would certainly be sufficient for all six of you."

"Oh. It would have been, but Benjamin was so put out with your recovery and the taking back of Martingale Manor, that I believe he went crazy. He began living as though we had more money than Croesus. He was out every night with the sort of men who knew how to use him, and he simply gambled away our very breath. The children and I are held captive in two rooms of the home you provided, trying to stay away from the windows so that anyone who comes to the door will believe we have left.

"It takes everything I have to keep our children quiet. We hardly have enough to eat now. We sleep on dirty linens, and it has been ages since our clothes were cleaned. We are living like rats, Harry! Like rats."

"Where are the children now?"

"Standing outside on your porch."

"I'll get them in, sir," spoke Gretchen as she vacated the room quickly.

By midnight, the children had been bathed, dressed in clean nightclothes, and tucked into pristine beds. Gretchen had initially taken the children into the dining room, where they were fed until they could eat no more.

Now, as Alice watched each of her children asleep, she cried softly. Harry took her arm and led her out, down the hall toward another prepared room. "Can you eat a little, sister?"

"Possibly a touch of fruit and cheese? If that's all right."

"Go on into your bedchamber. Your bath is even now ready. Afterward, there will be a hearty repast brought up. You rest, sister. Tomorrow we shall see to Benjamin."

Coming back down the staircase, Harry spied Gretchen at the bottom. "The children are all abed, and Alice is at bath. After she has a bite to eat, she'll be abed also."

Passing Gretchen, he motioned for her to follow him. They went into the library. "In the morning, I hope to be out early, but I do believe I'll have need of your sharp intelligence. I must quickly locate this group of piranhas that feed on those unfortunate souls out looking to be skinned."

"You are as perceptive as I expected you to be, sir. You recognized that Lord Benjamin was emasculated when he was found out trying to wrest the manor from your hand, and then to see him and his family held at your mercy might have proved too much for his ego to handle. He deliberately set out to lose it all in a feeble attempt to blame you for his downfall. He needs a good lesson in humbleness as well as in self-fortitude. I feel sure it must be there. We just need to bring it out and reinstate his self-worth."

"You are truly a wonder, Gretchen. How grateful this house is for you to have been assigned by God to raise our Teresa. I have no doubt that she will ultimately prove to be a queen among the women of this era." Standing he said, "Now, it's off to bed for us, dear lady. I hope Sydney won't be too upset with my taking you from him for such things."

"Never fear, Lord Harry. Sydney knows me well enough to realize that we are here for such purposes and must go where we're most needed."

Separating at the top of the stairs, they bade each other goodnight.

# CHAPTER 34
# CAMOUFLAGED COUPLE

AT FIRST LIGHT next morning found Harry and Gretchen in the offices of Harry's solicitors. Young Skylar Preston was thrilled to be chosen by his cohorts to handle this sticky problem. He was to see to the sale of the house, which ultimately would not produce nearly enough to make a dent in the debts of Lord Benjamin.

Harry had Skylar send word to locate exactly where "his men" were at present. They had been given the task of investigating every suitor that Teresa had accepted any contact with.

Now, the men must be given the extra duty of finding exactly the person or persons responsible for the evisceration of the hapless Benjamin. After all, he was ultimately the responsible one for the dereliction of his duty to Alice and his own progeny.

They had informed Lord Harry that the Whitechapel area was the cesspool which fed and succored many of the human vermin of the city. Consequently, a cab was called and was in the process of porting Harry and Gretchen to that smelly district of London. They were both stricken by the horror of the sights and sounds.

"Lord Harry, stop this cab. We must return to the manor forthwith!" Looking into his stricken face, she continued, "We must get back quickly."

"Right!" Pounding on the roof, he had the cabbie swing around and head back faster than they came.

"Do you fear ourselves to have been in danger, Gretchen?"

"Without doubt, sir. Yes. We must prepare ourselves for a foray into such conditions. We dare not enter this area with ourselves appearing as we are. No. We must alter our appearances, then we will make better use of our time once we become unnoticeable."

"And how are we to do that?"

Sitting back to smile at him, she said, "Leave it to me, sir. You won't recognize yourself... or me!" Laughing, she said, "This scarred face will be right at home in that setting!"

That evening Gretchen announced that everyone must not become overly curious as to what she and Lord Harry had to do to find and help Lord Benjamin. Paul and Earl had informed Lord Harry that he had been seen in the company of shabbily dressed men in Whitechapel. She felt it expedient to give everyone enough information to elicit their help yet remain dumb as to the danger of their proposed exposure to the underside of London—though it was dangerous mostly to those who "didn't belong there."

Next morning found every cast-off piece of clothing, every dirty ragged shirt, every pair of filthy shoes and hose and hats (one was removed from the head of Madge the cow) gathered so Gretchen could go through them all. The only decent items worn by the pair were their underclothing.

Gretchen laboriously dressed Lord Harry first. She was able to fit a pair of stable shoes upon his feet, sans socks. Before she barely completed his costume he'd begun to scratch.

After she had them both ready—at least by the way of thinking by Lord Harry—he was surprised to find her digging into the fireplace hod to smear soot upon his cheeks and especially in his hair and along his neck. She did not want to take any chances that he might be recognized by some sharp-witted tavern master. Those men could spy out an imposter in a heartbeat.

By late afternoon, Gretchen and Sydney had the pair ready to leave, and no one in the manor would ever have suspected who these two strangers could possibly be.

Dressed as they were, in order for them to begin to approach a cab in this present part of London, they were accompanied by Sydney, who instructed the cabbie that the two beneath the blankets were to be taken toward the Thames and then let off as near to Whitechapel as possible. The cabbie was given extra for his trouble.

"Don't ye have a worry about them two, sir. I'll git 'em outa here fer ye right quick like. Th' likes of 'em ought never be in this place to begin wif'!"

Smiling, Sydney reminded them to be careful.

Once they were dropped off, the pair gave their blankets to a couple living on the street with four little children.

"Which way ought we to head?" asked Lord Harry.

"From the stench, I would surmise this direction. Toward Whitechapel" Pointing, Gretchen stepped lively with Harry following. After a few blocks, she turned toward her companion, "I believe we need to come up with aliases and not use our correct names... just in case, you know."

"Alright. Give me an idea."

"You're Roy and I'm Marrie." She grinned. "How's that?"

"We'll give it a go, what?" Laughing. "Are we married?"

"I guess; we can try that and see how it goes." Pausing to glance around she said, "I swear I think someone is following us, Roy."

Leaning in to whisper he said, "Yes Marrie, Paul and Earl, I'm sure. I felt we could be in much trouble without help nearby. I had warned them we would be arriving soon and to be on guard to find us. This part of the world is not for us, 'goodwife.'" And he grinned again.

Smiling, she took his arm and stepped lively onward. "Think we need to amend 'goodwife' to 'mum,' seeing as how I'm old enough to be your mother. I don't think anyone would ever suspect that I'm your wife!" They both tittered somewhat quietly, so as not to draw attention to themselves.

"Do you know exactly where we're going?" Marrie asked.

"At last connection, Paul informed me that they traced Benjamin to the section of London that we're now headed to. I am simply following his directions as best as I can recall them. He was insistent on giving me landmarks instead of streets—said that would be infinitely more trustworthy. And, I must say, thus far I feel we are totally in accord with his excellent directions, and besides, they are following and will make sure of our path as well as our safety."

As they worked their way inland toward the northeast, the stench of the Thames began to diminish some little bit. It mattered not what time of year, except only in the dead of winter: The rottenness of that river was trouble to the rulers of London Towne.

Harry thought to himself that if he might ever become a part of that ruling body, he just may be able to come up with ideas to help in some way. For now, he would not allow himself to think of it. *I must keep my mind on what Gretchen—Marrie—and what we have ahead of us.*

They decided to enter a large establishment where they might find food and beds, and where Paul and Earl could find them easily. The *White-Cap Tavern & Inn* in Whitechapel was just up from the India docks a ways.

They found seats near the kitchen door. A young girl of about ten years came to the long table and said, "Whut's kin I gitchee frum d'kitchen?"

Trying to emulate her speech, Harry said, "Ow's abut ye brang a coupl'a small ales, huh?"

The child drew back somewhat and stared at the pair. "Y'aint frum aroun' 'ere, is ye?"

Smiling broadly, Harry replied, "Why no, miss. As a matter of fact, we ain't, but thet doan make us no less thirsty, now duzzit?"

The child laughed, and said, "I'll git it riteaway, sir." She headed off to the bar on the far side of the smoky room.

Gretchen spoke up and said, "Roy, you bes' let me do the talkin'. I mioght git by a tad better."

"Sure, mum. Go ahead. Have a hand at it."

The pair was at ease and laughing when the child returned with the two mugs. Before she even had a chance to set them down, Harry began to reach for a coin in his pocket. Suddenly a large, aproned man loomed over them and said, "Ye ain't from these in-vire-irons. Air ye lost, per chance?"

Standing, Harry reached out his hand and said, "Why, my good man, you find yourself to be correct in that assumption." Throwing caution to the winds, he continued, "I and my mother are here on a desperate quest to locate a kinsman, whom we believe may be hiding in this area, so as to not be found. We also believe he may have been aided by a group of nefarious gamblers, out to find such rich a pigeon as himself. Could it be possible that you may have heard of such a dastardly bunch?"

Drawing a large fist across the rich beard on his chin, the man mused a moment, then said, "Why, as a matter 'er fak, we has them kind ever around these parts. They's a reggeler pack o' them wolves sneakin' round to drag off the less than sensible to sum poppy den to wait 'fer to be shipped out to parts whut'll pay for slave labor. 'Pears it's a rite lukertiv undertakin'."

Harry dropped back onto the bench with a slump. "Gawd, I never thought of that!" Eyeing Gretchen, he said, "What do you think we need to do?"

"First off, Roy, we must be about finding a spot to stay the night and query this good man..." Turning toward the large man, she added, "If it is agreeable with you, good sir."

"Will ye' be needin' one or two beds?"

Smiling, Gretchen said, "My son and I will need two beds... but in the same room if you don't mind. We need to be sparing of our money." Then she said, "And we'll order our supper of whatever your cooks have in the kitchen. It smells very good sir."

"Aye! Lady, it be that. Me goodwife sees to all the cookin' and the serving up too. She willn't scant ye. I guarantee ye' won't leave yer table hungry." Drawing up with a large breath, he said, "An, ye'll sleep like babes! We don't have no critters in our rooms. Peg keeps the beds aired and the linens boiled—fresh as sunshine, they be."

"Excellent!" spoke Harry before he realized how that sounded in the ears of this man. "Sorry, sir, I suppose you must know that we're like fish out of water here."

"Don't ye take me fer no fool... Ye both got 'upper crust' writ all over ye... not by yer clothes, no. But by yer bearing. Ye jes' ain't downcast er downtrodden enough to be frum around here. But, not to worry. Yer secret's safe wif me..." He laughed out loud, as did both Roy and Marrie.

"Sir," asked Gretchen, "will you be available to help us with some of our many questions and concerns about our kinsman—later after we've eaten and only as you have time to spare?"

"By all means ma'am I'll count it a pleasure. Now, I'll send fer yer vittles and alert Peg to git our best room ready."

He left, and so large a presence was he that his departure caused a breeze of vacuum to swirl around the odd couple seated at the long table.

The serving girl that had brought their mugs of ale now placed a basket holding a pile of whelks upon the table. She said, "'Eere's yer sum whelks fer to 'old ye 'til yer supper is brung."

Laying a hand over Gretchen's, Harry said, "I will step out for a moment to see if my men are close at hand. I shall be right back."

Harry left the table and stepped outside to see if his men would show themselves—that is if they were still in the vicinity. Before long, Earl came and leaned against the side of the building, lit a cigarette, and asked Harry, "'Ow're ye doin, friend?"

"Fine. And you?"

"Couldn't be better. Like a smoke?"

"No. But thank you."

"Here." Reaching over to hand the cigarette to Harry, he said, "Take it so we can talk."

Harry reached for it. "I cannot smoke this thing, Earl. I'll cough! It'll kill me."

"Don't inhale it! Just hold it like we're enjoying a smoke together and listen to me. All right?"

Taking the cigarette and holding it off away so the smoke wouldn't get in his face, Harry asked, "What do you have for us?"

"I was just on my way here to tell you. Paul found your man over on Emmet in an opium den. They've got him so full he's layin' naked and sprawled out like he just come into the world. Stole ever piece of them fine clothes he was wearin'."

"Can we go get him tomorrow?"

"Sure, you can wait 'til the morrow... that is, if you're willing to risk him being taken tonight aboard some Asia-bound ship, but I'd suggest you get him now while you have a chance... while Paul is still there guarding him."

"Wait here." Harry handed the cigarette back to Earl and slipped back into the smoky inn. Seeing Gretchen talking with the owner, he strode over. "Forgive the interruption, but Earl knows where Benjamin is being kept. He says we'd better try getting him tonight, for later may be too late."

He turned toward the owner and put out his hand again. "Please allow me to introduce myself and my companion. I am Harry Martingale and this is Madam Milburn."

Taking his hand, the large man answered with a slight bow. "Right. I knew right off ye wuzzen who ye said ye wuz, and me name's Jakob Miesterberger at yer service. How can I hep ye?" Motioning for his guest to seat himself, Jassy, Jakob's wife, placed two steaming platters of viands upon the rough table.

As Harry and Gretchen plied themselves with the wonderful foods, Harry kept up his end of the conversation with Jakob. "We are on the trail of my brother-in-law, Lord Benjamin Truluck. I've just received word from a hired detective that he has located him in a nearby opium den. It seems they have stolen everything from him. In fact, he's without a stitch of clothing. I'm wondering if perchance you know of someplace where I may purchase a set of clothes of any sort, whereby we can haul him out and bring him here for safe-keeping?"

"Well, now. Let's see." And he again dragged a fist across his bearded chin in deep thought. "Whut size be he, sir?"

"Close to my size," answered Harry.

"Then that'll be easy. Me boy whut's gone to sea left a few things in his old room. I'll send li'l Molly up to git whut she deems needed."

Laughing, Harry said, as he motioned to Gretchen, "This wonderful lady is the mother of my ward, but she'll be best at going to get the few things we'll need and, Sir Jakob, will you have another room for us to hold Benjamin in until he can recuperate enough to travel?"

"Thet I will, sir. Thet I will. I'll tell Peg right away."

Finishing up her food as quickly as possible, Gretchen followed Molly upstairs to a back room and began to go through the few clothes. Several pieces were chosen to clothe the naked man to make him presentable enough for them to drag him through the streets back to the *White-Cap Tavern & Inn.*

## CHAPTER 35
## ANOTHER RESCUE

LEAVING TOGETHER IN the dimming light, Harry and Gretchen followed Earl through streets and alleyways for what seemed like miles. The longer they travelled, the seedier became their surroundings. Infants could be heard in never-ending cries. Dogs growled from shadows. Rats could be heard scrabbling with cats and other vermin in every alleyway. The stench was breathtaking, and periodically they passed some sailor in close contact with some poor girl making a penny in the only way available. Gretchen thought, *How terrible for these poor souls.*

Earl stopped ahead and motioned for them to hurry. "Paul is supposed to still be here. I'm going inside first to pay so I can find him if he's still here."

"You mean Benjamin is inside taking opium?"

"Of course not! I think they've drugged him with it. But we gotta make 'em think that's what we're here for. If they suspect us of anything other than that, they could kill us in a thrice."

"Now if I don't come out in five minutes, then you know that both me and Paul are in there. Y'all come in and just ask to pay for the night since it's late enough. They'll expect us to be here all night."

"Do we have to be here all night?"

"Naw. We can leave anytime after we find Paul and Lord Truluck. They won't worry about it since they'll know we've paid for an all-nighter."

A few minutes later, Harry and Gretchen entered the shoddy building. The first thing they encountered was an aged woman seated on a high stool behind a high desk. She looked down at the couple and said something that neither understood, but Harry reached for the money that Earl had told him to use, and he laid it upon the desk. She nodded deeply and pointed to a pretty girl holding a curtain open. Beyond in the semi-darkness, Harry and Gretchen saw what appeared to be the fires of hell. Only there were no literal fires, just the low lights gleaming upon blood-red silk wall draperies. There were low beds and large pillows scattered throughout the room. In many of the areas, there were men and women lying in obvious oblivion. Moving nearby were small boys tending to those who were actively inhaling the vapors from the heated bowls. The air was permeated with the sickening odor of opium.

As their eyes adjusted to the dimness of the room, Harry tugged on the sleeve of Gretchen and whispered, "They're over there." He indicated an area on the backside of the room, more-or-less hidden behind a black lacquered screen. Both Earl and Paul were lying on either side of Truluck. His naked body was covered with a silk kimono and appeared dead.

"Give the clothes to me," said Earl. "We'll get him dressed as quickly as we can. You two lie down here, on the other side of me."

A young boy came bringing a long bamboo pipe with a large bowl holding a ball of solid opium. Kneeling down, he lit a candle to begin the heating process. Gretchen reached out and took it from his hands. She indicated that he could go help someone else. She was going to help her friends instead. After a few hand signals and mouth signs, the lad left them.

As quickly and as unobtrusively as possible, Benjamin was soon dressed in clothes that at least covered his body. The buttoning of his shirt was skewed but it didn't matter, as long as they could get him out.

"Come this way," said Paul. "They leave out'a here by this curtain. I know there's a door back here 'cause I hear the port sounds every time it's opened. Follow me."

With Paul leading the way, and Benjamin being dragged between Earl and Harry, Gretchen bringing up the rear, the five made the hallway (with no help from their burden) beyond a heavily embroidered curtain. There at the end was the door to freedom. Four souls were each praying in their own way for this escape to be successful.

As they stepped out into the darkness of the alley, they saw a trio of sailors out in the street entering the den. They were loud enough to be easily heard by the escapees. "'E'll never know what 'appened, now will 'he? Boss says he's already got them slavering over this 'un, whut wid 'im bein' a lord 'n all." They laughed raucously as they entered at the front and let the door swing closed behind them.

"Hurry! We've no time to waste. They'll soon discover their pigeon is gone and all hell will break loose."

Frantically running the back alleys, keeping in the darkest places, they fled. Gretchen was now leading the way since she memorized exactly how they had come. Benjamin was carried piggyback upon Paul's broad shoulders. Earl kept his hands on Benjamin's rump and back to help ease the burden and to keep him from slipping off. It was as if he were a dead man. They received no help from him at all.

Finally, they reached the *White-Cap Tavern & Inn* and went to the rear door which led into the kitchen. Gretchen opened it and peered inside. There was Jakob stabbing at the ashes in the huge fireplace. He turned as they stumbled into the warmth of the room. Paul unceremoniously dumped Lord Benjamin upon a low bench, from which he immediately slithered off and piled into a noxious heap upon the floor.

Coming over to take a look at the man Jakob said, "Oi, he be a fine lor' a'right! Th' man needs plenny o' help. Ought I send fer a doctor for him?"

"No need for that, sir. I am a physician and will tend to him. Do you have a room ready?"

"Right! I'll take 'e on up. Foller me."

Gretchen was relieved that the room chosen by Jakob was the last one on the left—farthest from downstairs. "Do you have a key for this room?"

"Yes' mum. I'll send it up by Molly right away."

"I must warn you all that his recovery may take longer than you might expect. But don't fear. He shall recover and may be considered cured, provided he does not come in contact with opium again. He'll have every opportunity to live a decent and normal life." Gretchen told Harry, "You'll have our room to yourself for a while until he begins to come back. Once that begins, I will lock us in, and you must not worry about either of us. Inform Master Jakob that I will not require anything extra, as I shall sleep in the quilt upon the floor. I need to keep Lord Benjamin upon the mattress, if possible."

Molly soon came with the key for Gretchen. "Dear, would you be so kind as to see that I have plenty of clean rags and warm water brought up three times each day? Just knock on the door and I'll get it."

"Whut about yer meals, Mum?"

"Just take my food into the room of my son, down the hall, and I'll eat it in there. And thank you, Molly."

"Are you certain you will be all right in here all alone with Benjamin?" asked Harry.

Nodding, she said, "You take care of yourself. And be sure to thank Paul and Earl for their wonderful help with this, I don't think we could have done it without them."

Reaching out to hug Gretchen, Harry said, "You are a true wonder, and I'm blessed to count you my friend. Thank you, madam. Have a calm night."

She stood silently listening to Molly and the men retreating down the hall and down the steps. She then strode over to the bed and gazed at the man who'd been so arrogant and self-serving while under the roof of Martingale Manor. *I doubt he'll ever feel led to be so proud again. Oh well, he deserves to be helped as much as anyone does. Those who need it most, need it most!*

## CHAPTER 36

# CONTRITION

DAY THREE FOUND Benjamin wide awake but very ungrateful to be so. He suffered symptoms of having a terrible head cold, with attendant runny nose, which soon escalated to where his body was shaking and shivering. He drooled like a teething infant and sweated like a rock splitter at hard labor in the summer. Soon he took on painful cramps, and Gretchen tied a knot into a scrap of linen which she placed around his face where he could chew on the knot to keep from screaming. On day four he asked for water, but he could not hold the tumbler. She let it dribble into his mouth spoonful by spoonful until he seemed satisfied.

Neither of them was disturbed by his voiding and defecating without privacy. Each day the chamber pot was placed outside the door and a fresh one was brought in. Gretchen had been able to get to the other room to eat a bit twice each day while Benjamin seemed to be calm. Harry stayed with him during those hours and wiped his face and tried to keep him aware of what was transpiring with his recovery.

The morning of the fifth day, Gretchen told Harry, "We need to get him home as soon as possible. He will probably get better sooner if he can know his family forgives him. Can you get us home soon?"

"I'll connect with Paul and Earl and have them get us out of here today."

"Good. We must do all available to us. And, Lord Harry... please one minute more. I've noticed how lame your friend, Earl, is getting. I believe I know wherein lies his problem. If you do not think it is interfering of me, do you believe he'd allow me to tend to his malady?"

"I shall immediately query the man and then we shall know. Too, I'll remind him how grateful he should be to have your care and concern."

Downstairs, Harry spoke with Jakob and told him their plan to leave as soon as possible. He paid extra for all the help that had been provided to him and his family. By the time a hackney was pulling up in front of the *White-Cap Tavern & Inn*, they had Benjamin bundled up to be handily lifted into the coach by Jakob, where they could situate him in the middle between Paul and Earl, with Gretchen and Lord Harry in the opposite seat. Standing at the door bidding them farewell were Jakob, Peg, Molly, and Jassy, the goodwife. "If'n ye're ever out this way agin, sir, we'd count it a pleasure to serve ye. 'n' we 'opes yer kin be right as rain real soon, sir."

Reaching through the open door, Harry took the hand of Jakob and said, "We shall return first opportunity. You may count on it and thank you for all the help. We would never have been successful if not for you and your family."

As the coach pulled off, Harry was heard to say, "Soon, friends, soon."

As the five pitched and swayed inside the cab, no one found any need for conversation. Gretchen was silently thanking Almighty God for His intervention and guidance in the dangerous foray to rescue Lord Benjamin. She let Him know how much she was ever indebted to Him for her knowledge of helping him begin the withdrawal from the forced addiction. *I wonder exactly how much of that poison they forced into him. He certainly could not have inhaled it to the point at which we found him. They had to have poured it down his gullet. It is truly a wonder they didn't kill him.*

Harry was thinking of how much he owed Gretchen for her knowledge and expertise. *What can I possibly do to show my appreciation to her and to Sydney? After all I've robbed him of nearly a week with his new wife.*

Paul and Earl appeared to be sleeping as soundly and as soundlessly as was Benjamin.

Pulling into the side yard of Martingale Manor, they were met by everyone at home at the time. Only Teresa and Virginia were away. Someone explained, "They're over at the Milliner's."

Stepping down from the cab, Harry aided Gretchen. Then came Jason, the muscular handyman, to help draw Lord Benjamin forth from the arms of Paul and Earl. "Here, Jason, bring the wheelchair, and we'll have him in and settled quickly."

Followed by Alice and the children, all snubbing softly, they lifted and rolled the unconscious man into a large front room that Gretchen had prepared before they left on the rescue mission.

Once inside, she asked the children to be escorted out while she and Alice tended to the invalid. Gretchen leaned over to whisper to Alice, "Please, ma'am, do not speak out loud of any concern that you may have. I'll try to answer your queries as best I can, but he remains very tender even as of today. We are making some progress and have hopes for a full and complete recovery."

"All right, Gretchen. I will try to modulate my voice, but might I weep a little? It seems that is all I've been doing of late. I feel so lost and quite lightheaded, and a bit ashamed that I cannot seem to cope with this event in our lives. I find that I am now in more debt to my younger brother than I would ever have thought to be."

"Cast away those feelings, my dear. They are not worthy of your concern. Simply accept that everything possible shall be done to reinstate your security of life and limb and that of your children. Lord Harry is not one for retribution from someone who became so lost as did your Benjamin. We have spoken of his breakdown and have determined that everything possible to bring him back to a full and productive life shall be done.

"Now, here, help me get him undressed and into a comfortable position so he can rest."

The two women worked, heads and hearts together, as they stripped away the old clothes, bathed the gaunt man, and redressed him in diapers much as Teresa had done for Lord Harry during his terrible illness. The bed had been prepared with fresh sheets and warm quilts. Gretchen had the windows flung open to the brilliant sunshine which flooded into the room.

Turning to Lady Alice, Gretchen asked, "Can you sit for a while? I will head to see Cook for special meals to be prepared. I believe he might be able to begin a bland but nourishing diet. If he wakes, just murmur gently to him as you would a baby awakening from a nap. Touch him as often as he'll allow it. If he recognizes you, tell him that he has been sick and is now on the mend... that foods are being prepared and he must continue to rest." She then added, "I do not expect him to be filled with terror or a danger to you at this point... If he becomes unmanageable, simply come out quickly and lock the door. The key is outside in the lock. All right?"

"Yes. And thank you." Alice took a seat near the head of the bed facing her husband so she could watch his every breath.

All four children were seated just beyond the door, and Gretchen told them, "Go in now for just a moment. Then you must come right back out and leave your father in your mother's care. I'll wait here for you to come back. Hurry, now."

The silent children filed into the bright sun-filled room to view their father, pale and drawn upon the bed, and their mother crying softly. They all circled Alice and placed their arms around her to help her cry.

She stood and lifted the youngest over to Benjamin and allowed Kitson to kiss his father. In turn, each child leaned over to kiss their father: Maudie, Christina, and Matthew, the eldest.

"Now, children, go back and find something to keep yourselves busy. Your father shall soon be fine and will be up and about, but we must persevere until then."

Opening the door, she ushered them out, only to see Gretchen waiting outside in the hall. It was then that Gretchen pointed to the key nestled in the lock on the hall side.

The recovery of Lord Benjamin Truluck was slow and painful, but once he regained full consciousness of his situation, it appeared as though his strength of resolve also blossomed. Ever desirous of the company of Lord Harry, he heaped apology upon apology on his ever-patient benefactor.

"Harry, old man, I am never to be trusted again, at least that's how I feel at this point. Is there any way you can think of that I might redeem myself?"

"Ben, let us begin by dropping the self-flagellation. It serves no good purpose. But, in deference to your profound knowledge, I feel surely there is an opportunity awaiting, crying in need for your particular expertise. Let us discuss ideas that you have swirling within your brain... things that you have always had a penchant for, things that you'd like to see accomplished. Possibly things for the betterment of those less fortunate, perhaps."

As the two sat in contemplative silence, it was suddenly broken by voices heading in their general direction. Both men stood as Teresa swept into the room, followed closely by her grandmother, who spoke up quickly. "Please, Lord Harry, forgive this untimely intrusion, but I cannot countenance this travesty of injustice any longer!"

Eying both females, Harry settled upon his ward. "Heavens, child. What is this about?"

Trying to get a word in edgewise, Teresa was being outdone by Sarah. "Sir! Pay no attention to this child! She has no idea what she's wanting to capitulate! You simply must not allow her to have her way this time!"

"Well, someone must enlighten me as to exactly what it is that I must or must not preclude." Looking directly at the distraught Teresa, he said, "Let us sit. Now calm down and get your thoughts in order, then explain everything where both Lord Benjamin and I may be able to help you extricate yourself from this quandary."

As he spoke, he was also glancing to watch Lady Sarah wringing her hands, all apace.

"I want to go home!" cried Teresa.

"Home? Why, we are home, my dear."

"No! This is not where I desire to be and you well know it, sir! I dislike London more each day I arise... It stinks to high heaven... it's crowded... the people are insolent and pushy, and I hate it here!" With that she began to cry in earnest.

Trying to appear unruffled by this exposé of feelings, Benjamin asked, "And, dear child, exactly when did this change of heart begin?"

Without any forethought, she blurted out, "When I came to the conclusion that there is not a man alive in all of London that I want to spend the rest of my life with. They are all stiff and holier-than-thou, they feign affection, and their breath smells bad as well as their bodies. They stink worse than London does." She drew in a vast quantity of air and howled as though the moon were too full. "The one this morning was worse than all the rest together!"

"And exactly who was this monster, my dear?" queried the ever-patient Lord Harry.

Turning, wringing her hands, she cried, "The very one you were so sure would be *the* one... Duke Julian LaFitte! He is fawning and stupid, and he slobbered into the palm of my hand!" With that, she wiped her hand smartly upon the skirt of her gown.

Mincing forward to hold the girl, Sarah, smiling, said, "She truly doesn't know how important this debut is for her future. She has been raised to believe in fairy dust and honesty. Which are in short supply in this generation. Sir, I deeply beg you to insist upon this debut. Why the perfect gentleman may just be waiting in the wings as we speak."

Standing, Harry enfolded both Sarah and Teresa within his arms and kissed the heads of both. "Give us a while to mull this over, will you? I feel sure we can work something out for the benefit of everyone. All right?"

Snubbing, Teresa nodded as she was led out by Sarah. Closing the door softly, the men listened to their arguments fade down the hall.

"For what it's worth Harry, I agree wholeheartedly with the girl! Especially for me the experience of London has nigh proved my demise. Of course, I do understand that I, myself, am to blame for the mess I've made of things, but I reiterate, I'm ready to get out of here myself and back to the country."

"That's fine, Ben, but I do want to be frank with you about your situation." Harry sat up, wiggled his rump into the horsehair cushion, harrumphed a tad, and said, "Let me assure you that *if* I felt you could be utilized to your fullest potential at Martingale Manor Hampshire, then I would hold forth no objection... However, I cannot see where there's room for both of us there." Holding up the palm of his hand toward Ben, he continued, "Honestly, Ben, you have a fine education and an even better mind. I know you have always been interested in engineering and mechanics and I firmly believe that at this very propitious slice of time in which we find ourselves, there lie opportunities floundering, waiting for the right mind to grab hold, and solve the problems and horrible conditions in which thousands of Londoners now live.

"When we were in the east section it was blatantly evident that there is great suffering. Much, I believe, is brought on by the miasma of the stench. I swear I tried to not breathe when we found ourselves close to the Thames.

"Jakob of the *White-Cap Tavern & Inn* says folks are beginning to die off again with dysentery. I cannot figure why some die in the same areas when some do not; there has to be a common denominator. And that is the big elusive answer to all the cholera epidemics.

"I was told by Jakob that two of his nephews are working for a couple of men who are diligently on the trail of identifying exactly how the body is affected by the stench."

"Harry, I'd be very much interested in doing something like this to aid my fellow citizens, but where on earth would I begin?" asked Benjamin.

"If you feel up to it, old man, we can hop over to Whitechapel and talk to Jakob. He'll surely know how to make contact." As the two arose from their chairs, Harry continued, "And, to keep ourselves up to date, we need to discuss whether or not to proceed with the debut."

"Yes. I know the women would rather have it than not, but it is, after all, for Teresa, and she ought to be given the greatest consideration. Don't you think?"

"I agree, Ben. She has more sense about what she needs or wants than most of us. She's already lived a life of the most strenuous sort, and now to be forced into such a ridiculous display of flesh to choose a husband who'll spend only enough time with her to assure an heir to inherit everything that rightly belongs to her is grossly overrated."

CHAPTER 37

# LONDON'S SHAME

WITH THE HELP of Gretchen, the men donned well-worn but clean clothing for their foray into the Whitechapel area. This ruse was for their protection. No one would suspect the two, thusly dressed, of being lords.

Three hours later they entered the old, weathered door to the musty interior of the *White-Cap Tavern & Inn.* As soon as their eyes adjusted to the smoky room, they were greeted with unabashed hugs from none other than Jakob. "Me friens! Me friens is back. And lookin' mighty good now! Yessir, mighty good. 'Here, 'ev a sit down by 'th winder whir ye c'n see th' docks. I'll hie ye both me bes' ale and a few whelks ter munch on."

Quickly heading to their table came young Peg with two sloshing mugs. She was followed close on by Molly with a basket of the mollusks.

"Molly, would you be so kind as to ask your father to rejoin us? We need some dire information if you please."

"Why, sure, sir. I'll git 'im ri' away." Hesitating just a moment, she added, "But, sir, I sure liked yer better when ye were in the ole clothes and not so fancy cleaned up. I c'd unnerstan ye better." And she ran off to the kitchen.

The two visitors had just begun to dig into the whelks when Jakob came up. "Whut c'n I hep ye wid?"

"Can you sit with us a moment? I'd like to ask a few questions."

"Sure, I can. But if sommon needs service then I'll hev to tend to thar needs and then I c'n come on back. All right?"

"Fair enough." And Jakob sat heavily on the bench next to Benjamin, across the table from Harry.

"When we were last here, you and I were talking one evening after everyone else had retired for the night. It was after we came back with Ben here." He nodded toward his brother-in-law. "Do you recall telling me about some men coming to visit you and your family to inquire about your water supply, and if anyone in your family suffered with cholera?"

"'Deed I do, sir. Why, after they left then the boss man came by wid two other fellas to pick our brains about how we got our water and how we disposed of the house waste. I tole 'em all I knew and they left."

"Do you recall if they ever gave you their names?"

Nodding, he said, "'n' they give me their cards too if I needed to tell 'em more after I think it up after they left here. They tole me they'd be back too."

"Wonderful! Do you still have their cards?"

"I'll git 'em." And he rose and went behind the bar and opened the till. He brought them straight away to the table and laid them before Harry.

"Exactly the information we have need of. Thank you."

Sliding the cards over to Ben, Harry said, "Copy down the information. You'll need it."

Then, he sniffed the air and asked Jakob, "What do you have cooking back there, my good man?"

"Why, me Jassy is got a beef goulash from the old country. Might ye be a wantin' a wee bite?"

Nodding, Harry smiled, "I do believe I might enjoy a small bowl with a right good chunk of bread to sop with. What do you say, Ben? Are you up to some real food?"

"My mouth is set for it I can tell you that! I'm verily fed up with the bland diet of recent weeks. I believe it'll begin to put some meat back on my bones."

"Know what you mean, Ben. Why, after my illness it took months before my clothes began to come anywhere close to fitting again." He laughed. "Now I find that not only have I filled out, but I have also begun to realize that I must soon get a new wardrobe done. I've gained weight as well as muscle. Living a strenuous life has made me not only look better, but I also am gaining strength daily. Truth be told, I love the activity attendant upon the lifestyle that came by way of my open acceptance of all those who share their lives with me. I would never desire to return to the 'lord and master' days of the past. Being coddled isn't my cup of tea!"

"You know, brother, I do believe you are correct. This newfound life is rife with freedoms I'd never have considered before. And, I must say... I like it."

Leaving the establishment with the promise of a return visit very soon, the men ordered the driver of the hackney to get them to out to Soho as quickly as possible

Rapping the great brass knocker upon the black lacquered door, they found it soon opened by a sloppily dressed gentleman, still in his robe and slippers. "May I help you, gentlemen?"

"Yes. Good afternoon to you, sir. We are here to speak with a Doctor John Snow."

"And you are?" he asked.

"My name is Lord Harry Martingale and this," turning to indicate his companion, "is my brother-in-law, Lord Benjamin Truluck."

Stepping backward, the man swung the door inward and said, "Please come in, gentlemen." He closed the door behind them and then asked, "How may I help you?"

"Doctor Snow, we must be asking you that question. Can you find a way that Lord Benjamin here may be of service to you in your quest?"

"Here! Let us go into my library. This way." And he stepped toward a long, wide hall toward the left end of the sumptuous home, calling as he went. "Rebecca! Here, now, please."

The men entered a dark and dusty tomb of a room that smelled of old tobacco and wet books. As he turned on an overhead brass gas lamp, he bade his visitors find seats before an overloaded desk.

As they seated themselves, a very pretty young woman entered. She greatly reminded Harry of Teresa the first time he had laid eyes upon her. But Rebecca was "dark" whereas his Teresa was "light." *Where did 'that' come from?*

"Yes, sir, Father?"

"Bring a touch of tea for these kind gentlemen, darling."

Quickly standing and facing the young lady, Harry said, "Really, Mistress Rebecca, we care for nothing at all. We took advantage of our time at the *White-Cap Tavern* for a quick repast there."

She smiled and asked, "Are you sure? It will be no trouble."

Harry smiled back. "Truly, ma'am. But thank you." He seated himself once more.

"Now, good gentlemen... " settling back into the black leather chair, Doctor Snow tented the fingers of his hands and said, "tell me the reason for this visit."

Glancing toward Ben, Harry said, "I had reason to be in the Whitechapel area a fortnight ago and came across conditions I can only call 'deplorable' for any human to attempt to exist therein. I had the good fortune to be roomed at the *White-Cap Inn* and spoke at length with the owner. His name is Jakob Miesterberger. It is through him that we obtained your whereabouts and herewith present ourselves."

"Go on, sir. I perceive your story does not end there but is barely begun."

"You are correct. You see, we were on a mission to rescue Lord Benjamin. He had found himself in great debt from irresponsible gambling and ended up in the clutches of a group that regularly supplies slaves for foreign markets. He had been drugged and left for pickup in an opium den not far from the *White-Cap Tavern & Inn,* which is not far from the India docks.

"Right after we rescued Ben, I had the opportunity to listen to Jakob and his vast concerns about the next expected cholera outbreak. He said it was imminent, but that you and a Reverend Whitehead had been to query him as well as had a couple of other men in your employ." Pausing, he asked, "Am I correct?"

"Why, yes! I remember the man, I do believe, he's large, and round, and very likable... has a balding head. There are three females attending to his establishment."

"That's the one. Well, since Benjamin here has found himself to be penniless and, we believe, has come to his senses, we are seeking some way for him to contribute to the betterment of the citizens of London in any capacity. He has a degree in mechanical engineering and is quite astute in addressing problems head-on." Stopping momentarily to rise and walk, he said, "To put it bluntly... is there any way in your war against ignorance and the ultimate cleaning of the Thames that you might find a need for such a man?"

"Jakob told us that you believe the Thames to truly be the root of the trouble with London's water supply," added Benjamin.

Doctor Snow suddenly stood and reached forth his hand to Lord Benjamin, who also quickly stood. "My good man! How propitious is this arrival! Of course, you shall aid myself as well as other like-minded men that are ready to rid London of this evil sickness."

Reseating themselves, he continued, "My cohort is a Reverend Whitehead. He and I seem to differ on exactly how the disease is contracted and spread, but we shall leave no stone unturned to pinpoint the source of this killer.

"Now, to get you started. Exactly how soon can you make yourself available to us on a twenty-four-hour basis? We must be as aggressive as possible." Looking down at his attire, he explained, "I've not even taken time to attend to my toilet and dress decently. Which, I must say, is a constant thorn in the side of Rebecca. But I find that while I'm in the throes of exploration I dare not pause for such mundane things." He smiled.

Harry reached over to touch Ben's hand. "Can you abide staying in London for the benefit of not only your family but also the needy people residing in this dangerous environment? If you will acquiesce to this, then I shall move Alice and your children back to Martingale in

Hampshire where they can be well cared for and give you no cause for worry.

"We might locate a place for you near here to be at hand should the Doctor have need to see you at a moment's notice. What say you, Ben?"

Before Benjamin could even nod his agreement, Doctor Snow said, "Here, here! If a place is the only stipulation, then I shall count it a right blessing if you will stay here. Rebecca needs another man to care for. It's her 'cross to bear.' At least, she's always saying that to me."

They all laughed.

"Then, it is settled, Harry. Let us get back to St. George and inform the rest of the family. We shall return tomorrow as soon as we can gather the few belongings that I will have need of."

"Fine. If by some chance I happen to not be here, don't fear. Rebecca shall see you put up in a room upstairs near to mine. You'll be pleased to know there is a new water closet between our rooms." Shaking hands all around again, the two left the library.

As they headed toward the front door, they heard Doctor John bellowing at the top of his lungs for Rebecca to attend him quickly. They smiled.

"I'm very excited about this new beginning, Harry. At my age, I would never have considered such a vast change in my status, but this is much needed, old man! Much needed."

"Yes," said Harry. "I do believe you shall do everyone proud, as well as give your own ego quite a boost. You will be much better at this sort of thing, I think than anything else presently available."

CHAPTER 38

# NEW BEGINNING

ALICE AND THE children had gone with Harry and Benjamin the next day to see that her husband was installed comfortably in the stone mansion owned by Doctor John Snow who seemed to be overjoyed to receive them all and ordered the harried Rebecca to bring tea and scones as refreshments for them all, then magnanimously suggested that she herself join them.

Harry had assured Benjamin that whenever money was needed, he must immediately speak to young Skylar Preston of *Phillips, Preston, and Preston* law firm. Skylar was the one to whom all instructions had been given to deal with Ben and his quest for a cleaner London.

The decision having been made—not only to accommodate Alice and the children but also for Teresa as well—the company packed for three days to get everything of need ready for the trip back to Hampshire. It appeared that even Sarah had given in to the desire by Teresa to be shed of London.

By the time, the very neat and trim group that had departed London arrived at the rear gate of the mansion in Hampshire, they appeared as though a band of nomads had taken over. It seems that Teresa was so insistent upon them taking as little time as possible off road, that she pushed everyone to the limit of their endurance in attempting to placate her demands.

As the entourage drew into the sideyard, there came a flurry of activity in aiding everyone to dismount and to haul the baggage into the house. Much ado about everything was tended to, and within a couple of hours, the mansion once again settled down and appeared to breathe a sigh of relief.

The children all were ensconced in the upper reaches, where the newly hired nanny and governess would soon be in attendance. That bit of business had been placed within the capable hands of Alice, their mother, and the ever-reliable Gretchen. Too, she and Sydney were back in their little cottage, getting all settled in and preparing for the busy weeks of spring ahead.

Soon Earl sent word to Gretchen that he was free and could now come to meet with her as she had previously requested. She sent word back to him to come to her cottage as soon as he could. Within a few days, Gretchen saw him coming down the path toward the house, and she opened the door just as he arrived. "Come in, sir, I'm so happy to have you visit with us. Come. Sit here. I'll prepare you a cup of tea if you'd like."

"Thank you, ma'am, but I'm in a sort of hurry. Lord Martingale gave me leave for a few minutes, so I need to be gettin' back soon. Tell me why you wanted to see me. I've been at sixes and sevens ever since he told me of your interest in helping me, back when we were all in London."

"Indeed." Gretchen seated herself beside him and spoke. "During the times we have been in the company of each other, I have noticed a puffiness around your eyes, and the redness of your hands. And, too, I see where you seem to have some difficulty walking. Am I correct?"

"Why yes mum, but I never gave it much notice. My feet only bother me a little toward the evening. Sometimes I need to let the buckles loose to open me shoes a bit. Why? Is this something I need to worry about?"

"I perceive your body has difficulty in voiding enough fluids, thereby causing an over-abundance of liquid to be retained within the tissues of your body. This is dangerous in that if it continues too long, it can bring about heart problems.

"I suggest you allow me to provide you with several doses of different diuretics to see if one of them won't be best in helping your kidneys process and void the excess fluid out through your bladder." She stood and ambled over to a low table where there were assorted boxes and bottles which contained unidentifiable contents—at least from Earl's point of view.

He sat, dumbfounded, watching her busily at work. "Why, ma'am. Is such a thing possible? Me own mum died with her legs and feet so swollen 'til they nigh filled our small foot tub! None of us knew anything about any such thing as what you're speakin' of."

"Oh, yes. I do believe you'll fare much better when you can determine which of these combinations of herbs will work the best in ridding your body of the excess buildup of fluids." She began to put together several little packets of ground herbs for him. She numbered each packet from one to four. Handing them to him, she said, "I've put a different mark on each packet. You are to use one small spoonful each morning in a cup of water, or tea, if you prefer... from the first packet for three days, then stop for four days. Pay attention as to how each packet helps you to release the fluid. At the beginning of the next week, take the next packet and use it for three days, then stop.

"Do this for all four weeks and come back. Be prepared to tell me which one worked the best to rid your body of the fluids."

"Can I drink anything while I'm doin' this?"

"Oh yes. You may indeed drink whatever you usually drink. In fact, you must drink. Do not deny your body of the fluids. They are necessary for the body to live in the best state of health."

Standing, Earl slipped the packets into his coat and thanked her profusely. "Might I pay you for this, ma'am?"

"No sir." Reaching out, she touched his shoulder. "I only ask that you return to let me know how well they worked, and which one was best for you."

As Earl looked into the eyes of this wondrous woman, her scars faded, and he witnessed something he'd never considered before now.

*She's not of this world, but from another time and place.* He strode quickly toward the open door, then bowed and backed out. He said, "Thank you again. I'll be back after about four weeks. All right?"

Gretchen waved him out of the yard as he headed back up toward Martingale Manor.

Teresa and Virginia found their places on the third floor, next door to Sarah and Edmund. Alice kept her old space at the top of the stairs near the nurseries and playrooms of her children, at least until the new hires could arrive. Harry was quartered on the second floor facing south. He enjoyed the sight of the wild channel and loved to watch the gulls and other assorted sea birds coming inland over the high walls.

That afternoon Virginia was becoming more concerned about the aberrant behavior of Mistress Teresa. She watched as the young woman sat, fidgeting, standing suddenly, scurrying across the room, only to stand staring out the window. She noted her lips moving and her head nodding, only to be disappointed by not hearing one single sound. Finally, unable to maintain her silence, Virginia asked, "Is there anything I can do to help you, mistress? You seem to be in quite a quandary."

Turning toward her companion Teresa said, "Nothing you can do will alleviate the bind I fear I alone have placed upon myself, Virginia." She walked toward the trunk at the foot of her bed and opened it. She drew out first one shawl, discarding it across the counterpane, and reached for another. Throwing the light green mohair shawl around her shoulders, she asked, "How does this look?"

"Why, it's perfect. Matches your dress exactly. Will you allow me to select a piece of jewelry or two to complete the effect?"

Turning to peruse her image in the tall mirror, she nodded. "Yes. Find something to best set this off."

Virginia was rummaging through the box and pulled forth a pair of jade ear drops set in yellow gold. "Here. These will be beautiful. See? What do you think?"

Smiling, she nodded. "Yes, I've always liked these. Harry gave them to me on my last birthday. I love them with this dress."

Virginia caught the lack of protocol as her mistress omitted Lord Harry's rank.

Teresa handed the medallion to Virginia. "Fasten this around my neck. Place it where the medal is in the center of my cleavage."

Stopping momentarily, Virginia scrutinized the medallion, looked at her Mistress, and said, "I need to clean this. There's a dark spot here on the back."

Turning quickly, Teresa said, "No! Do not touch that. It's to always carry that stain; very precious. Imperative to me for it to always remain. Don't ever clean it away, you hear?"

Bowing slightly, Virginia assured her mistress that she would guard it with her life; causing Teresa to smile.

"If you don't mind my asking, exactly why is the stain so important?"

"Virginia. If you must have your curiosity satisfied, then I'll tell you what I was told about it." She sat on the dressing stool and reached beneath the dresser to draw forth a small drawer in which there lay a tattered green ribbon, more threads than ribbon, actually. Not touching the shreds but holding the container up for Virginia to see. "There are more of the same stains here upon this ribbon too." Sliding the drawer back beneath the dresser, she drew in a small breath and said, "The afternoon that I was born Gretchen was there and my mother's blood was washing over her hands and arms as she delivered me." Teresa lowered her head but cast her glance back to a time she could never recall but imagined. She continued. "Before Gretchen could stop to clean away the blood, my mother handed this talisman over to her with the name I was to be given and that Gretchen was to be my mother. That moment was when the stain was smeared upon the medallion and some parts of that ribbon."

Standing she said, "Now you know why it's so important to me to maintain the stain. It's the blood of my mother."

Virginia was awestruck. Nodding, with eyes wide and brimming with tears, she replied, "Mistress, you are one blessed child having two mothers that love you with all their hearts."

Smiling, Teresa drew up and said, "Now! Let me get on with my quest." She raised a fist upward and shouted, "Look out world! Here comes Teresa Jane Lyons-Constantine!" She turned quickly back to her mirror and Virginia watched as Teresa licked her lips and pinched her cheeks to cause them to redden. "Virginia, I'm simply fed up with all the folderol of society today. I think the time has come that I take matters into my own hands. After all, I'm no small fish in the pond." Turning away from the mirror and reaching to stroke the arm of her companion. "I've decided this day I shall marry my Lord Harry. I shall not be deterred!" And she sped off toward the door.

Harry was thus preparing to head to his library to get a letter off to Doctor Snow and Benjamin. *I'll drop by upstairs to see if Alice wants to add something to my letter.*

Coming out into the upper hall, he witnessed Virginia begging her charge: "Don't do it, miss! You must not do this thing! Too unseemly! Please."

About that time Teresa pushed her maid aside and stepped out into the hall. Dressed in a gown of light green silk, gathering a mohair shawl across her shoulders, the flashing gold medallion gleaming upon her breast, she glanced up to see Lord Harry staring at her. From where he stood, she appeared an apparition of sorts, or perhaps an angel. Harry's breath became suspended as though waiting for something wonderful to occur.

She came toward him as a warrior to battle hell itself! Virginia was mincing along behind her with head down, shaking sadly. Harry began to retreat, taking one step back from the determined look in the eyes of his ward. She did not slow down, but upon nearing the object of her destination, she reached out and, with a fierceness completely unexpected, she drew Harry into an embrace, pulled his head down toward hers, and kissed him soundly!

He stood as still as possible until he felt the kiss reverberate into his mind, his lungs, his heart, his kidneys, and other places, vibrating throughout his body. With determination set, he then grabbed her with his own strong arms and pulled her even closer. Bending her backward, he put his soul into the kiss and deepened the contact, pulling her snug against his body.

With eyes wide as saucers, Virginia smiled and looked around to see if she were the only one privy to this exchange of lovers! Yes, lovers! That's what it looked like to her!

Finally, Harry drew back and let go of his tight embrace, but only enough to allow Teresa to breathe. She drew back to look upward into his black gaze. Feeling the heat rise from them both, she whispered, "I love you, Harry." And she leaned in again for another kiss. He obliged.

Whispering deeply into her ear, Harry said, "Never let it be said that I turned down such a golden opportunity to bring to my bed the most beautiful and desirable woman in all of England. I shall have trouble with the proper waiting."

"We'll have such a marvelous marriage. I love you with all my heart, dearest Harry."

He drew her snugly against his body and reveled in the feel of her soft breasts against his chest, so close that he could feel the heavy gold medallion. He smiled and kissed his lover again and was rewarded to feel her lips opening to entice him further. He obliged—heartily.

Virginia turned and ran toward the rooms of grandmother Sarah and Sir Edmund. Not bothering to knock but one quick tap, she opened the door to beg, "Come quick! We're going to have another wedding, or my name isn't Virginia Haviland."

EPILOGUE:

Truly, a wedding of magnificent proportions was performed in the huge hall of Gravelstone Abbey the spring of the following year. Madam Alexandra had been enlisted to design the wedding gown for Teresa in pale pink silk.

Laying upon the fine cleavage between her breasts there shone forth the dazzling star ruby pendant surrounded by diamonds and pearls. Virginia had woven pink silk roses and pearls through the blond tresses of the bride.

As she came down the stairs, Harry swore he'd never seen a more beautiful sight in his entire life. *And to think she's truly mine. God am I thankful she had more sense than I did. She is everything I've ever dreamed of in a wife. God help me to be the husband she'll always love and trust.*

From the last step, Teresa turned and came toward the great hall where the gathering of her beloved family waited. There was her Harry-the man she'd fallen in love with when she'd first seen him in his terrible state. She had made up her mind then that if he lived, she'd find a way to make him love her, even though their stations had been worlds apart. She had never spoken of this desire to anyone other than to God in her nightly prayers. And not knowing how He would answer, yet she had her heart set for this event. And there he stood waiting for her! Tall, wonderfully handsome, his dark hair curling softly against the white ruffle of his shirt. The buff trousers, snug against his muscular thighs. She watched as his eyes swept over her in obvious desire and her heart sped and beat in desire returned.

As if in a dream, Teresa heard the priest drone on, until at last, she became aware of Harry reaching for her hand. She knew she'd spoken the required vows and listened as Harry had done likewise, but when she watched as the brilliant blue diamond was slipped upon her finger, she began to weep. Looking up to meet his gaze, she said, "I have loved you all of the days past and shall love you all the days of the future, husband."

He reached and gathered her body into his strong embrace and kissed her fully, not drawing away until they both began to hear the laughter and applause.

Since the threat of cholera had all but been beaten, Lord Benjamin had been reinstated in Martingale Manor at Covington Court as the man in charge until his son, Matthew, would come of age to take it over to hold for the first male issue of Harry and Teresa. At that time, Benjamin and Alice would be freed up to install themselves and the children in the London house. At that time Harry would see to it that the London property would be in young Matthew's name alone.

Harry saw to it that everyone was well taken care of, including the village of Covington, the ports, and the wharves where the fishermen plied their living.

Keeping the commoners hale, hearty, and healthy kept their overlords in the same vein. Harry had changed his abode to that of his wife. Gravelstone Abbey now housed not only themselves but also Grandmother and Sir Edmund, along with Virginia and her new husband, Gordy Hammet. The housekeeper, Helen Collier-Smyth, was confiscated from Martingale, much to the consternation of Elizabeth.

Within a year the huge mansion was running along like well-oiled gears. Under the direction of the "everywhere at once" Helen, no one could slouch off no matter where they thought they might be hidden to sneak a nap. She would find you!

In addition, she had brought in more than fourteen other capable folks from the village to attend to all the various and sundry jobs inside the home that must be done to provide for her charges. She was truly, at long last, the master of her ship, and she loved the responsibility. But Helen was astute enough to realize that she must mentor several of those coming along to be able to step into her large shoes, to keep Gravelstone running along smoothly.

Sydney and Gretchen kept their places on the Covington Court property, but when working at Gravelstone, they occupied four rooms in the servant's quarters. They saw to the establishment of pastures, gardens, and stables. The favored souls that found their way to Gravelstone were heard to comment with such explanatory phrases as, "magnificent beyond words" or "must cost a fortune to upkeep." Little did they realize that most of the "upkeep" was accomplished by the residents and family. All souls attendant upon the welfare of Lord and Lady Martingale were considered family and they knew this to be so. Teresa might just be found down in the village on market day with her basket searching for the desired turnip or pumpkin. She and Helen set the best of foods to be found upon their dining tables.

In the year 1879, little giggles could be heard coming from the upper floors of the mansion. Teresa had birthed twins at Christmas time, and one year later they were both running from their nurses.

Harry spent every spare minute in the arms of his beloved, striving to fill Gravelstone with as many children as they were capable of.

In the last decade before the turn of the century, Teresa gently informed her husband that the one she presently carried would be their final child. Gretchen had informed her that seven would be the number of their children. Seven-the perfect number. There would be no more. Harry accepted the news, knowing Gretchen knew what was best; after all, she had been the one to send Teresa to him, to begin with. Gretchen knows! And Harry smiled as his Teresa came to slide her arms around his body and offer her lips to be kissed. He obliged.

## FINIS

# HOMES AND CHARACTERS

**Gravelstone Abbey** - ancestral castle belonging to the Constantine Dynasty
**Martingale Manor London** - property of Josiah Martingale
**Covington Court Hampshire** - manor belonging initially to the Bordeaux family, renamed Martingale Manor at Covington Court, property of Josiah Martingale upon his marriage to widow Bordeaux

**Sarah Hashbrooke Constantine and Leopold Flanders Constantine** - owners of Gravelstone Abbey
**Melanie Jane Constantine** - only child of Sarah and Leopold
**Gretchen Benchley Lyons** - gypsy child aged seven when given into service at Gravelstone as maid and companion to three-year old Melanie Jane Constantine
**Teresa Jane Lyons** (Constantine) - illegitimate child of Melanie
**Josiah Martingale and Bessie Mae LeMons Martingale** - owner of Martingale Manor London
**Alice and Benjamin Truluck** - daughter and son-in-law of Josiah and Bessie
**Matthew, Christina, Maudie, Kitson** - four children of Alice and Benjamin
**Harry Martingale** - son and heir of Josiah and Bessie

**Peter Freedmon Bordeaux and Beatrix Steadman Bordeaux** - owner of Covington Court
**Daniel Steadman Bordeaux** - son of Peter and Beatrix

(Bessie Mae LeMons Martingale and Peter Freedmon Bordeaux died the same year - thus Josiah Martingale married Beatrix Bordeaux and took over Covington Court, renaming it Martingale Manor at Covington Court. The family Martingale was installed at this inherited Manor House at the opening of our story, although they still owned the Martingale House in London as well.)

**Constance Williston** - head housekeeper at Martingale Manor Hampshire
**Calvin Collier** - valet and right-hand man to Lord Harry
**Elizabeth Collier** - wife of Calvin and head cook
**Doctors Bogart Bristleman and Clifford DuBuque** - physicians to Martingale Manor Hampshire
**Helen Collier-Smyth** - aide to Constance Williston and general house manager
**Gladys and Edith** - upstairs maids
**Sydney Milburn** - head gardener
**Rodney and Jimmy** - sons of Sydney
**Gordy Hammet** - Postal carrier
**Virginia Haviland** - maid to Teresa
**Solicitors: Phillips, Preston, and Preston** (Edward, Doyle, and Skylar)
**Madame Alexandra** - dressmaker from London
**Earl and Paul** - pair of detectives
**Edmond Bedford** - goldsmith
**Sylvia Avondale & son, Elijah** - characters in Cullbert
**Lisle** - woman accomplice of kidnapper

Other characters come and go throughout the story, but the memorable ones are named above.

Made in the USA
Columbia, SC
31 July 2022